"You're always lashing out at everyone."

"Did you ever stop to think that maybe everyone needs to be lashed out at?" he suggested.

"And maybe you think you need to keep everyone back."

"Good answer," he congratulated her. "Except for the word *think*. I don't think. I need to keep everyone, with their humdrum problems, back. I *know* I need to keep them back."

"Why? Because you're afraid you'll let someone get too close?"

Munro took her completely by surprise when he said, "Yes." But then he returned to the colors he enjoyed displaying to the world. "Because when people get close, they suddenly feel compelled to share the most intimate, boring parts of their lives. I don't have time to get nauseous on a regular basis."

The man was a master at put-downs, but she wasn't buying it. There was a heart inside there—there *had* to be.

MARIE FERRARELLA

This *USA TODAY* bestselling and RITA® Award-winning author has written more than 150 books for Silhouette, some under the name Marie Nicole. Her romances are beloved by fans worldwide.

THE Next NOVEL™

DOCTOR
in the HOUSE

MARIE FERRARELLA

DOCTOR IN THE HOUSE

copyright © 2007 by Marie Rydzynski-Ferrarella

isbn-13:978-0-373-88141-3
isbn-10:   0-373-88141-X

This is a work of fiction. Names, characters, places and incidents are
either the product of the author's imagination or are used fictitiously,
and any resemblance to actual persons, living or dead, business
establishments, events or locales is entirely coincidental.

This edition published by arrangement with Harlequin Books S.A.

® and TM are trademarks of the publisher. Trademarks indicated with
® are registered in the United States Patent and Trademark Office, the
Canadian Trade Marks Office and in other countries.

TheNextNovel.com

 HARLEQUIN®

PRINTED IN U.S.A.

From the Author

Dearest Reader,

Every once in a while, writers feel the need to challenge themselves. It is perfectly easy to take a good-looking, witty man and turn him into the hero of a story, the reason the heroine's heart appreciatively skips a beat. But to take a man you would just as soon strangle as look at and make him into that same hero—more important, acceptable to you, dear reader—well, that's not the easiest thing to master. And there, in a nutshell, is the challenge.

Dr. Ivan Munro is referred to by the people who work with him as Ivan the Terrible—and he likes it. His only concern is saving lives. What patients do with those lives after he saves them is of no concern to him once he sheds his hospital scrubs. Until Bailey DelMonico is assigned to him as his resident, Ivan is perfectly satisfied with being completely self-contained. But Bailey, the product of missionary parents, sweet, selfless but not a wide-eyed innocent, slowly, by her sheer presence and relentless optimism, chips away at the good doctor's glacier exterior, until she finally uncovers the man within. Her journey produces more than ice chips for happy hour. Both she and her disgruntled mentor grow in directions they never anticipated. I hope you join them on this trip and find the journey enjoyable.

As always, I thank you for reading, and with all my heart I wish you love.

All the best,
Marie Ferrarella

To Dr. David Neubert,
who is everything a doctor should be.

CHAPTER 1

D_{r.} Ivan Munro liked saving lives, liked making a difference in those lives. It was people he didn't care for.

People with their endless complaining. People with endless details about their humdrum lives that he had absolutely no interest in. If he possessed so much as a thimbleful of mild curiosity regarding his patients, he would have gone into a medical discipline that required contact with those patients on a fairly regular basis.

But such contact would have necessitated feigning interest on his part and he had never been one to lie or even seen the need to lie. Ever. For any reason whatsoever. The truth, any truth, was what it was and needed to be faced. No sugarcoating, no beating around the proverbial bush. Just shooting straight from the hip.

He'd chosen neurosurgery as much as it had chosen him and he'd selected it for three reasons. The first was to heal, to pit himself against the power that delivered such a low blow to the individual on his operating table. The second was that it was the only way he could possibly make it up to Scott, even though Scott was no longer around to see the results.

The last reason was distance. Neurosurgery afforded him distance. Once he tackled a condition, he could distance himself from the recovering patient and thus move on, leaving the chore of hand-holding to the patient's friends, relatives and/or referring physician, all people who were far better suited to the tedious chore than he. They were the ones who either wanted or felt compelled to establish and maintain a rapport with the patient.

He'd been told, more than once, that he had the bedside manner of an anaconda. He took it as a compliment. Ivan could not, *would* not, allow emotions to get in the way of his making a judgment call.

Unfortunately, emotions or some sort of cursory display of them, was what most patients thought they both needed and were entitled to. His chief of staff, Harold Bennett, a man he grudgingly admired and respected, told him that was the way patients knew that they were in capable hands. They measured capability by the physician's capacity to act as if he or she cared.

Ivan cared, all right, cared that he successfully eliminated the tumor, or reconnected the nerve endings, cared that he did no harm and only accomplished what he'd set out to accomplish: to make the patient better than he or she had been when they'd first laid down on his operating table.

But as for verbally talking the patient through the steps of the surgery before it transpired to set to rest any fears that patient might have, well, that just was not why he got up each morning to come to Blair Memorial Hospital.

Being "patient with patients" wasn't something he was any good at and he saw no reason to pretend that he was. He wasn't in medicine to forge friendships, only to save lives.

"They call you Ivan the Terrible, you know," Harold told him over the lunch he'd insisted that his chief neurosurgeon share with him in his office.

There was an ulterior motive for the invitation. It was that most painful time of year again. January. Time for the annual review where budgets were wrestled with and unpleasant decisions had to be made. It was a time to lightly sprinkle praise and to make a sincere call for improvement. This meant even from a man who clearly *did* have the ability to walk on water, but did not, to any and all who took note, possess so much as a single drop of humility.

"I know," Ivan replied, his attention appearing to focus on his sandwich. "It's my name. Good sandwich," he commented in the next breath, infusing as much interest and feeling in the last sentence as he had in the first two he'd uttered.

After almost a dozen years, Harold was skilled at tiptoeing into conversations with his chief neurosurgeon. "Funny, I don't remember seeing 'the Terrible' on your application form."

"I didn't want to brag," Ivan replied in the semi-raspy voice that was his trademark. As far as anyone knew, it had been awarded him courtesy of a near-crushed larynx he's sustained from an incident in his late teens. An incident that he never talked about. Rumor had it he'd offended someone and they'd tried to hang him. The rumor tickled Ivan and he never bothered correcting it.

Harold tried again. "Ivan, I know that you're good at your job—"

Dark eyebrows rose on a relatively unlined forty-six-year-old forehead as Ivan looked up at the man across the desk. He stopped eating.

"'Good' is a very mediocre word, reserved for things like pudding or foodstuffs chosen for breakfast and touted in mindless television commercials. It also can be used to praise a child for mastering accomplishments society requires, like potty training. 'Good boy, good job,'" Ivan added for emphasis and as examples. "It also blandly shows up in greetings. 'Good morning. Good afternoon.' Or in partings. Such as good night or goodbye. Equally as bland and in no way descriptive of what I do when someone comes to your illustrious hospital holding a severed hand and expecting to be reunited with it so that it's of some use to them."

The chief of staff closed his eyes for a moment, searching for strength. He and Ivan had known one another for twelve years now. He had been the one to hire him and he was as close to a friend as he imagined Ivan Munro had. But there were times when the man's personality was a little hard to take. Specifically the hours between dawn and midnight.

To get to his point, Harold acquiesced. "All right, you're magnificent at your job—"

"Better," Ivan allowed charitably, nodding his head and once again focusing on his pastrami on rye.

It was getting late. He had a meeting scheduled at one, Harold thought. At this rate, he was never going to get to his point. "Look, I didn't call you here to praise you—"

There was a hint of a smile as Ivan looked at him. "Good— see how I worked in your word?—because you're doing not that excellent a job of it."

Abandoning finesse, Harold blurted, "Ivan, you need to learn humility."

Ivan cocked his head, as if he were deliberating over the request. He obviously found it wanting. "Why, Harold? Will it make me a better neurosurgeon?"

Harold blew out a breath. "It'll make you easier to get along with."

Ivan laughed shortly. He paused to take a sip of the iced coffee—he required and consumed all forms of caffeine whenever possible—before commenting on what he felt was the absurdity of the last statement.

"I'm not here to get along with people, I'm here to put together people's pieces, remember? You want someone easy to get along with, hire some clown in big, floppy shoes and a red rubber nose. I don't do floppy shoes or red rubber noses, Harold."

Harold looked at him over the half glasses that were perched on the tip of his nose. He wasn't about to be dissuaded or diverted from the path he was determined to take. "We have classes now."

Wide, rangy shoulders that could have belonged to a one-time football guard rose and fell carelessly at Harold's words. "You've always had classes, Harold. This is a teaching hospital." Holding his sandwich with both hands now, the pastrami overflowing at the nether end, he fixed Harold with a penetrating look. "The question is, do you have hot mustard?"

Harold sighed. Reaching for a packet of the requested condiment that was on his side of the tray, he pushed it across the desk toward his irritating neurosurgeon. "Classes that teach interns bedside manner," he doggedly continued.

To his surprise, Ivan nodded his approval. "Excellent."

Harold squelched the urge to pinch himself. His association with Ivan had taught him never to jump to an obvious conclusion even if it was shimmying before him. "You mean that?"

"Of course," Ivan attested with feeling. "The more of those

little buggers who come out knowing how to coo and make it 'all better' for Sally or Bobby or whoever, the less likely we'll be having this annoying conversation again."

Harold sighed. "How is it your parents never drowned you?"

"I was too fast for them," Ivan deadpanned, then nodded toward the chief of staff's plate. "You going to eat that pickle?"

"Why?" Harold asked. "You're not sour enough?"

"Touché." Not standing on ceremony and aware that the older man didn't really care for pickles, Ivan commandeered it and dropped it on his own paper plate. A tiny yellow-green pool of pickle juice formed. Ivan played along with the chief's quip. "Let's just say I don't need any input in that category."

"No, by God, you don't." It was more of a lament than an evaluation. "All right, I can't force you to take that class."

"Glad you see that."

Harold wasn't finished. "But I can assign you a resident."

Ivan's expression was deceptively bland, but his eyes locked on the other man. "Not if you know what's 'good' for you—see, there's that word again—or for the resident."

And then Harold said the unthinkable to him as he shook his head. "This is not negotiable, Ivan. You refuse and you're gone."

CHAPTER 2

Silence hung in the book-lined office, mingling with the smell of pastrami and the faint odor of lemon-scented furniture polish. Outside, the sky was appropriately gray, nursing a Southern California January that had been fraught with rain for most of the month. The fluorescent lighting seemed somber and dim.

"You're not serious," Ivan finally said.

Harold was relieved. He'd half expected Ivan to continue his silence—by leaving the room. Dialogue gave him hope. "Very."

Ivan frowned. "I don't respond well to threats, Harold."

"This isn't a threat, Ivan, it's reality." It wearied him to have to go over this, but the alternative—to lose Munro—was unthinkable. "As you probably already know, the board is not exactly crazy about you. You've alienated over half of them."

Ivan pretended to look both aghast and saddened. "And here I was, getting ready to ask them to go to the prom with me." He shook his head. "You just never know, do you?"

Like a full-on game of doubles played across an extra-wide tennis court, meetings with Ivan always exhausted him. Didn't the man understand that he was on his side? That he was one of the very few who actually were? "Ivan, this isn't a joke."

"Isn't it?" Ivan scowled at the very thought of having to

nurture a fledgling surgeon. "How am I supposed to do my work with some wet-behind-the-ears lower life-form following my every move, sucking up to me and trying to absorb everything like a nondiscriminate sponge?"

Maybe the man wasn't aware of the way he sounded. Maybe he should have brought in a video camera so that he could play this all back for Munro and let the neurosurgeon witness first-hand just how abrasive he came across. "Now that's what I'm talking about. You've *got* to change your attitude."

Unblinking, cold brown eyes fixed on him. Ivan's face remained expressionless as he asked, "Why?"

The answer, Harold thought, was very simple. He smoothed out the edges of his bow tie with his thumb and index finger. A sign to those who knew him that he was nervous. "Because people hate working with you."

Ivan shrugged again. "Easy enough solution. Get new people."

The man just didn't get it, did he? For the sake of a tenuous friendship and because Munro was the best neurosurgeon he had ever known in his thirty-year career, Harold persisted. "Ivan, if you don't change, you can't operate."

Something resembling a smirk crossed Ivan's lips. But when he spoke, he was deadly serious. No quips, no sarcasm. "I don't operate with my attitude. I operate with my skill. Everything else is secondary and unimportant."

Some people preferred to be nonconfrontational. Sadly for him, Harold thought, the chief neurosurgeon of Blair Memorial did not number among them. Arguing appeared to be something Ivan both enjoyed and keenly relished, sharpening his wit as if it were a sword in need of constant honing. So rather than continue on a field of battle where he was hopelessly out-matched, Harold moved aside what was left of his ham-and-Swiss sandwich and pushed forward a dark blue eight-by-eleven folder.

Ivan perused the cover with a smattering of interest, but made no effort to open the folder. "If that contains a bribe, Harold, I'm afraid you're out of luck. I only take bribes on Fridays. Today is Monday." With a nod of his head, he indicated the calendar on the chief's desk. "Try me again at the end of the week."

Harold pressed his thin lips together. He could almost hear his wife's voice in his head. Rachel had been after him for years to retire. If he'd listened five years ago, his hair might still be black instead of completely gray. Ivan, he noted, still didn't have so much as a single gray hair.

"I'm perfectly aware what day it is, Ivan," he replied tersely. "And no, it's not a bribe in the folder. It's your career."

Ivan glanced down at it, then back at the chief. "The folder should be bigger, then."

"Open it," Harold instructed.

To his surprise, Ivan smiled. Patiently. As if he were humoring someone not entirely in possession of his faculties. A few more sessions like this, Harold thought, and Munro might be right.

"Is it me," Ivan asked, "or are you getting testier in your old age?"

"Oh, it's definitely you," Harold told him with feeling, his meaning clear. "All you. Now open the damn folder, Ivan."

"Well, since you asked so nicely." Ivan set aside the last of his sandwich and carefully wiped his fingers on the stiff napkins that had been provided along with lunch. Crumpling the napkin, he tossed it on the tray and then opened the folder.

Inside was an application for residency at Blair Memorial. The obligatory two-by-two photograph was glued in the space provided in the application's upper left-hand corner. Ivan glanced at the photograph, ignored the application and allowed the cover to fall back into place.

Raising his chin, he looked the chief of staff in the eyes. "Turn her down."

About to take a drink of his bottled water, Harold nearly choked. He stared at Munro in openmouthed disbelief. "Excuse me?"

"Turn her down," Ivan repeated, enunciating every word as if the man had suddenly been struck deaf and born slow.

It took Harold less than a heartbeat to find his voice. "On what basis?"

"She's too pretty," Ivan told him matter-of-factly. He turned his attention back to the last of his sandwich and his iced coffee.

"What?" The single word fairly vibrated with incredulity.

"Pretty," Ivan repeated. "Attractive, comely. I believe the term 'handsome woman' would have been applied to her a century ago." His eyes narrowed as he looked across the desk at the chief. "That might be more your style, anyway."

He *had* to know Ivan's reasoning here. "And since when do looks even remotely figure into the selection process?"

"A woman who looks like that—" Ivan pushed the closed folder even farther away from him "—is not going to keep her mind on her work. She'll be too busy flirting with all the eligible doctors and would-be doctors." He rolled his shoulders, mimicking the exaggerated movements of a femme fatale. "And they'll all be buzzing around her like so many bees who've lost their way to the hive." Wrists pointed down, he wiggled his fingers in the air to illustrate. "Want my advice." It really wasn't a question, merely a declaration. "Nip this in the bud before it even starts. Tell her 'thank you but no thank you.' Better yet—" his eyes glinted as a thought came to him "—refer her to Sloan Memorial," he said, referring to another teaching hospital in the area. "Let them deal with her and the chaos that she'll leave in her wake."

Harold had leaned back in his chair, waiting the neurosurgeon out. When the silence finally came, he seized it. "Are you through?"

Ivan looked down at the paper that had held his sandwich. A dollop of the spicy mustard was all that bore witness to the pastrami extravaganza that had been his lunch. He smiled as he crumpled the paper and placed it and the paper plate onto the tray. "I guess I am." He pushed back his chair, ready to leave.

"I didn't mean lunch," Harold informed him. "I meant with your tirade."

The choice of words amused Ivan. There were obviously holes in Harold's education. "That wasn't a tirade, Harold. When I have a tirade, there's much rising of hair at the back of the neck. Usually involving the necks of the people I'm tirading against. Believe me, you'll know when I deliver a tirade."

"I'm not considering hiring her at Blair Memorial," Harold said evenly.

"That's good to know." Ivan began to rise to his feet. "Now, I'm afraid that I have to—"

His next words had Ivan sitting down again. "I've already hired her."

The surprise on Ivan's face melted away a moment after it appeared. He shook his head sadly. "Big mistake."

Harold wasn't through. "*She* is your surgical resident."

"Bigger mistake," Ivan declared. When Harold made no attempt to rescind his words, Ivan grew serious. And annoyed. "Haven't you been listening to a word I've said?"

"I've listened," Harold informed him succinctly. "And like you've done so many times before, I've chosen to ignore what I've heard." He leaned forward, trying to appeal to Ivan's charitable nature—if such a thing existed. "There's no leeway here, Ivan. She has an excellent grade point average—"

Biting back a choice expletive, Ivan waved a hand in disgust at the words. "Oh well, an excellent grade point average, that'll save lives."

"And she comes highly recommended."

"By who?" he demanded, getting to his feet again. He shoved his hands deep into his lab coat as he began to pace the length of the overcrowded office. A stack of folders piled up in one corner toppled, sliding down like gleeful children on a sled sampled the first snows of winter in the mountains. "Some online dating service?"

"By professors at John Hopkins University," Harold countered, turning in his chair to watch Ivan stride around the room on legs that had always struck him as being too long. "Professors for whom I have the utmost respect. She's impressed every one of them."

Ivan's expression was nothing short of sour. He snorted as if he'd expected nothing less. "I won't ask how."

"Don't be insulting, Ivan."

"Insulting?" Ivan echoed. "You call this insulting? I haven't even *begun* to be insulting."

One of the reasons Harold Bennett had risen to his present position of chief of staff of one of the best hospitals in the Southwest was that he kept both his head and his temper during times of crisis. To see him angry was as rare as viewing the tail end of Halley's comet. It was visible, but not very often.

But at the moment his expression was serious, closely bordering on angry. "If you do anything to make her leave, *anything* that will make her time here at Blair anything but informative and well-spent, I promise you, Ivan, there will be consequences. Consequences that you won't like."

Ivan looked at him, utterly unaffected by the prediction. "In other words, there'll be no change from now."

CHAPTER 3

"Do your worst, Harold." Ivan drew himself up to his full six-three height, which was quite a bit taller than his chief of staff. His imposing personality made him seem even taller. "I can't be expected to do my job while babysitting your latest project. And why is she your latest project?" he asked suddenly, skillfully turning the tables as he mounted his offensive. The best defense was a strong offense did not just apply to football, but to life, as well. Ivan continued to fire questions at him, just quickly enough so that Harold couldn't answer. "Did you lose a bet? Is she your goddaughter? Or perhaps Rachel's grandniece?"

Harold pursed his lips. When it came to Ivan, he hated admitting anything. The neurosurgeon always managed to turn the information into a rapier that he skillfully wielded.

"Not that it has any bearing on this," the chief of staff began grudgingly.

Ivan's well-shaped eyebrows rose as if to coax the rest from him. "Yes?"

Harold knew that somehow, some way, Ivan would discover this on his own. It blunted the edge if he admitted it first. "I know the young woman's uncle."

Crossing his arms before his chest, Ivan leaned a shoulder against the doorjamb. "Aha."

"No 'aha,'" Harold replied tersely. "That just happens to be an extraneous fact, one I know you with your unrelenting capacity to dig and burrow would unearth on your own in short order. I just want you to know that it doesn't mean anything." He saw the smirk on Ivan's lips and felt compelled to defend his decision further. "I want only the best people working here at Blair." He did his best to sound formidable and knew in his heart he fell short of the mark. "Which is why I've gone to bat for you so many times. If I hadn't, you and I both know that your head would have been on a pike somewhere near the entrance of the hospital years ago."

"Very medieval imagery, Harold. I had no idea you had it in you," Ivan congratulated him, then paused at the threshold, the integrity that was his foundation keeping him from his exit. "So, in other words, I owe you."

Harold snorted. "In any words you owe me."

Ivan blew out a breath, a condemned man resigning himself to his firing squad. "And there's no other way to repay the debt? Shine your shoes, take you to Disneyland? Wear a hair shirt for a week?"

Harold smiled, anticipating a truce. "The hair shirt has possibilities, but we can explore that at another time. I told the board that you were taking an active part in training our residents—"

Ivan allowed himself a smug moment. "In other words, you, Dr. Harold Bennett, chief of staff, our standard bearer of the truth, lied."

Harold's faded gray eyebrows drew together in one tufted, ragged line. "I don't lie, Ivan. And in order for you to remain in the board's good graces, you are going to have to at least appear to be involved with the residents."

A fate, Ivan thought, only slightly less worse than death. Or maybe it was a tie. "Couldn't I just drink hemlock?"

Harold spread his hands out. They were wide hands, capable hands, but not the hands of a skilled surgeon. He'd always envied Ivan that. But then, he was not at the top of people's hate list, either. People liked him. In the long run, that balanced things out.

"Fresh out, Ivan. Now—" sitting up, he straightened the files on his desk and moved the tray aside "—you have the rest of the day to bemoan your fate. Report to my office tomorrow morning at eight."

The dour look on Ivan's face, the one that sent residents and attendings scrambling for high ground, returned. "I always thought I'd be shot at sunrise, not eight."

Harold laughed. "Don't put ideas in my head, Ivan. Tomorrow, eight."

"Eight." Ivan sighed mightily and then nodded, his slightly unruly mop of deep chestnut hair underscoring the motion almost independently. "Well, not that this hasn't been fun, but I have a surgery to scrub in for." He paused one last time to level a steely gaze at Harold. It was obvious that his seas were choppy. "If Mr. Dombrowski never dances again, it's on your head."

It was hard to tell whether or not Ivan meant it. The man did not possess what passed for a typical sense of humor. Maybe it *was* time to start thinking about retiring, Harold thought as the door to his office closed, with Ivan on the other side.

To reassure himself that he had done the right thing, Harold pulled over the dark blue folder and reviewed the pages in it again. He looked down at the picture in the file. The young blonde was smiling.

"I'm sorry," he said to the image. "But he really is as good as he thinks he is. And you'll learn a great deal. Once you get over hating me."

THE FOLLOWING MORNING, Ivan briefly entertained the thought of picking up the phone and calling in sick. The idea died. Not out of some misplaced nobility on his part, nor did he revisit his resistance and find it suddenly appalling. What he found appalling was the idea of a resident living in his shadow and calling it hers. He didn't call in to postpone the inevitable because he didn't know how. Didn't know who to call because in the twelve years he'd been with Blair Memorial, he had never done it.

Sick or well, he had always shown up at the hospital. Even on the worst of days, he mustered on. Day in, day out. Ivan took no note of the months or even the seasons. Had Blair's chief administrative assistant, a young woman aptly named Debi by her intuitive parents and afflicted with a case of terminal perkiness, not felt compelled to decorate the hospital halls, he wouldn't have known what month it was. The woman felt some sort of obligation to celebrate every holiday known to God, man and the eternally vigilant greeting card people.

If the woman had left well enough alone, he wouldn't have even known when holidays like Thanksgiving and Christmas came around. Except for his older brother John, who he hadn't heard from in years, he had no family. No one to drag him off for the purpose of spending the holidays with them. Because of that, each day seemed identical to the one that had come before. Some days necessitated short-sleeved shirts, others generated a need for sweaters, but by and large, the days Ivan experienced were all the same except for the weather.

Ivan switched on the TV just before he prepared to leave the apartment he'd been living in for the last twelve years. Living in Southern California, he was accustomed to periodically hearing the dire predictions of "the big one" coming, the earthquake of the magnitude that would destroy life and civilization as they all knew it.

He should only be so lucky today, he mused.

Buttoning his shirt and tucking it into his slacks, Ivan paused to listen as a very blond woman with flawless skin, what looked to be surgically enhanced lips and hypnotically blue eyes, summarized the day's current local news.

Same old, same old, he thought.

"C'mon," he murmured under his breath, talking to her as if she could hear. "If the big one's coming, now would be a good day for it to get here."

But the woman seemed entirely oblivious to the idea of earthquakes or any disturbances that might be called upon to rescue him. Contrarily, she appeared quite content to pour her heart into a story about how the department stores were bearing up to the after-Christmas slump in sales.

Ivan gave it a few minutes, waited to hear something promising, then shook his head as the story dragged on forever.

If more people were like him, he thought, the department stores would find themselves in a permanent slump. As a rule, shopping had never tempted him. He bought only what he needed and he needed very little. A few serviceable shirts and slacks with an equal number of socks and underwear to go with them were practically all he ever required.

His one weakness, his only hobby, was Philharmonic concerts. He attended them religiously, going all over the western map, arranging his schedule and people's operations, whenever possible, around concert dates. Music was the very core of his existence, the only time he ever felt mellow, although he would have opted to be burned at the stake rather than admit that to a living soul.

He preferred to be viewed as a godless, soulless, unrelenting holy terror who inspired admiration, respect and fear in his fellow surgeons, not necessarily in that order. As for the hospital's fresh crop of residents, in Ivan's view, they hardly existed, ranking only slightly higher than the rodents that could be found on the food chain.

And, though the thought really bothered him, he was going to have to put up with one for the sake of continuing to do that which gave his life purpose and meaning.

Grunting, he switched off the television set and then tossed aside the remote. It bounced off his sofa, falling on the floor beneath the glass-topped coffee table. He left it there.

"No earthquakes," he muttered, disgruntled. That meant that he was going to have to find a way to get this resident to request a transfer. And quickly.

He smiled as he left the house. No problem. By the time he was finished with this resident, she would think pairing up with Satan was an improvement.

CHAPTER 4

She sternly told herself that she wasn't going to be nervous.

In all honesty, she hadn't thought she would be because ordinarily, she wasn't. Life, which had tossed its curveballs and its change-ups at her when she least expected them, had trained her to be prepared for anything. An ordinary case of first-day nerves did not figure into it.

Having gone through all that she had in her thirty-four years, Bailey DelMonico liked to think of herself as fearless.

For the most part, especially in the eyes of her family, she was.

And she should be now, she told herself. With a stifled sigh, she discarded the plaid garment she'd just tried on and returned to her first choice, a subdued pencil skirt. Black to match the chief of neurosurgery's heart. Or so she'd been led to believe. Her two housemates, Jennifer and Adam, first-year residents at Blair Memorial, same as her, had sworn to it more than once.

Could be all talk, she reasoned, zipping up the skirt. Besides, no matter what this neurosurgeon's reputation was—justified or not—she was fairly certain that he wouldn't consume her for breakfast.

Bailey smiled to herself. She had already faced someone like that. Several "someones" like that, actually, if she were keeping count. Reformed cannibals. Those were part of the "perks" of having missionary parents who were famous for being the first to tread where angels feared to go.

Those angels, her father was fond of scoffing, were an overly cautious breed. And then he'd follow his comment up with his booming laugh. A laugh that somehow always made everything seem so much better. A laugh that was full of warmth and hope. And love.

Bailey pulled her honey-blond hair back and stuck in a few strategic pins to hold it up. It made her look older. Constantly mistaken for someone in her early twenties, she had a feeling she needed all the help she could get to be taken seriously.

God, but she wished she could hear her father's laugh now. But she had left all that behind her. Her parents, their mission and her other life.

Her second other life, as well, she thought cryptically. Technically, she was about to embark on her third life. The first had involved being the daughter of two prominent, dedicated missionaries. She'd been halfway toward fulfilling her parents' fondest dream and becoming a missionary herself before she realized that was *not* what she wanted. Her "second life" began when she'd decided, after a visit back to the States to check out colleges, to rebel against "all that goodness" that surrounded her. In her third year at Stanford, during spring break, she ran off and got married to the son of a professor. At the time, she'd thought that was what she wanted.

And it was. For about two months.

Slowly, she discovered, much to her surprise, that "all that goodness" she was fleeing was actually packaged inside of her. Not in such a way that she felt compelled, as her parents, Grace and Miles, were to spread the word of God and medicines in the darkest parts of the world. Her take on "goodness" was to help the sick and make them well. She wanted to become a doctor, a surgeon. The best surgeon she could be.

That was where she and her husband, Jeff, differed. She wanted to be a surgeon, he wanted her to be his wife and nothing else. He'd laughed and told her that taking care of him and his needs would always be more than a full-time job for her.

It took very little for her to realize that he was serious, that "carefree" was perilously close to "irresponsible" and that "drop-dead gorgeous" only went so far in the scheme of things and was a very poor trade-off for respect. There was nothing about Jeff she could respect and he in turn seemed to have none for no one, least of all her.

What she'd foolishly believed was the greatest love of all time was merely a case of intense infatuation. She was more in love with the idea of love than she was with Jeff. She just hadn't been smart enough at the time to know the difference. Jeff had been a feast for the eyes, beautiful in every sense of the word, but only outwardly. Inwardly, he lacked even the simplest of attributes that went into comprising her parents and her older brother, Simon.

Accustomed to selfless people, selfishness, especially of the magnitude that Jeff eventually displayed, was something Bailey found she just couldn't get used to or accept. So, eighteen months after she said "I do," she said "I don't" and the marriage she'd thought would last forever was terminated.

Her parents waited for her return with open arms. And for a while, it was all right. But from the very beginning, she was restless. Restless because she'd discovered that there was another road she wanted to follow. One she was certain she was capable of traveling to the very end. One she swore to herself she wasn't choosing just on a whim. She was a different person than she'd been six years earlier.

In their work, her parents were predominantly concerned with healing the soul, but not exclusively. They also fed the belly and brought medicines to the body. It was that part that interested her, that captured her imagination and fed her passion.

She applied to twelve medical schools, was interviewed by nine and was eventually accepted by six. She chose Johns Hopkins and threw herself into her studies. Being away from home the first time around, the taste of freedom in abundance had made her almost giddy. But the second time she was away, it was with a clear purpose. Bailey settled down and settled in, focusing on her goals and the career that she wanted with all her heart.

She had something to prove to everyone, most importantly, to herself.

The course work was hard, she was harder, determined to make up for what she considered lost time. With single-minded purpose, even though she worked to put herself through school, Bailey managed to graduate in less time than the average medical student. She fed on her own energy and enthusiasm, sometimes going for thirty-six hours at a time. Her letters of recommendation were glowing and well deserved.

She came to believe there was nothing she couldn't do.

"I have the strength of ten because my heart is pure," she murmured to the image in the mirror as she inspected herself one last time, reciting something her father had once read to her. Right now, she'd settled for the strength of two and a half.

Her pulse was beating fast. She closed her eyes and told herself to calm down.

Breathe, Bailey, breathe. He's just a man, like everyone else. He has to put his pants on one leg at a time, same as you.

God, but she wished they were here right now, just for a few minutes. Her father and her mother. Or Simon. Or her uncle and aunt with whom she'd lived as an undergraduate. Someone she could turn to for an encouraging word. She liked her housemates, but right now, they were just contributing to the problem, telling her every single frightening encounter anyone had ever had with the great and terrible Ivan Munro.

Bailey pressed her hand against her abdomen. There was one hell of a huge butterfly inside, insisting on spreading his wings and flapping so that she felt utterly nauseous.

She hadn't felt this nervous since that time she'd looked into Jeff's eyes and knew that he was going to make love to her. Knew and worried that he would be disappointed because she was a virgin. So she did what she always did when she felt the slightest bit uncertain. She forged straight ahead. That time, she'd pulled out all the stops and made love to Jeff first, completely overwhelming him. She'd been so eager, so gung-ho, he hadn't even noticed the momentary resistance he encountered when he'd entered her. He'd been too busy just trying to keep up.

Jeff never even suspected that she hadn't been acting on instincts but on something she had witnessed as a young girl. Unknown to her parents, she'd snuck out to watch an elaborate mating ritual between two young people in one of the tiny African countries whose names kept changing nearly as often as the seasons.

Emulating it, she'd knocked Jeff's socks off and kept him enamored of her for months.

Before the bloom finally came off the rose and the sexiest guy on the planet became someone she found she really didn't like. Definitely not someone she wanted to spend the rest of her life with. Not unless she was firmly committed to doing what the Catholics had once referred to as penance. Because being with Jeff had turned into penance.

She laughed softly to herself, shaking her head. One of the pins in her hair began to slip. Bailey shoved it back, tucking her hair back around the pin.

All that seemed like more than a lifetime ago. And very small potatoes now that she looked back at it. It was not nearly in the same league as what she'd accomplished in the last few years.

And definitely not in the same league as what she was about to undertake today. She squared her shoulders and turned away from the reflection. Today, she was about to face the biggest challenge she'd ever gone up against.

Surviving Ivan the Terrible.

CHAPTER 5

He didn't look like an unholy terror.

Those had been Adam's parting words to her, to take care because Ivan the Terrible lived up to his name and ate residents for breakfast. Adam had issued the warning a minute before she, Jennifer and he had gone their separate ways just inside the entrance of the hospital. Adam was heading for the pediatric ward while Jennifer's residency was in cardiology.

Apparently, it didn't matter that Adam and Jennifer were assigned to different disciplines that had, in essence, nothing to do with neurosurgery. All paths at the hospital seemed to cross Dr. Ivan Munro's in some manner, shape or form. Everyone who worked at Blair Memorial knew about the man. His reputation preceded him, both as a surgeon and as a devourer of residents. Which was why, legend had it, he hadn't been given any residents to mentor in the last few years.

But maybe that reputation was exaggerated, Bailey thought now as she turned in her chair to look toward the doorway.

The man didn't seem scary at all.

As instructed, she had entered Dr. Bennett's office at exactly eight o'clock sharp. She'd arrived nearly half an hour earlier and had spent the time circling the floor. Punctuality counted, but sometimes, she'd learned, showing up early acted against you if people weren't prepared for you. So she had moved around on the first floor, never far from where she was ultimately supposed to be, all the while practicing every known remedy for stress she could think of. The last thing she wanted was to appear like some wild-eyed, overeager idiot who didn't know her left hand from her right, much less a suture from a scalpel.

Trying not to look as if she were drawing in a sustaining lungful of air, Bailey took measure of the man who walked in, or rather, sauntered in as if he owned the office and the hospital that went with it.

Bailey desperately tried to be impartial. Nerves would bring cold hands, a dead giveaway. She didn't want to seem too inferior on their first meeting.

Ivan the Terrible was tall, with an athletic build and wide shoulders. The cheekbones beneath what she estimated to be a day-old stubble were prominent. His hair was light brown and just this side of unruly. Munro's hair looked as if he used his fingers for a comb and didn't care who knew it.

The eyes were brown, almost black as they aimed at her. There was no other word for it. Aimed. As if he was debating whether or not to fire at point-blank range.

Somewhere in the back of her mind, a line from a grade-B movie, "Be afraid. Be very afraid," whispered along the perimeter of her brain. Warning her. Almost against her will, it caused her to brace her shoulders. Bailey had to remind herself to breathe in and out like a normal person.

Dr. Bennett had tried his level best to put her at ease and had almost succeeded. But an air of tension had entered with Munro. She wondered if the chief of staff was bracing himself, as well, bracing for some kind of disaster or explosion. Forewarned by everyone she encountered, she still didn't really know what to expect.

"Ah, here he is now," Harold Bennett announced needlessly. The smile on his lips was slightly forced, the look in his gray, kindly eyes held a warning as he looked at his chief neurosurgeon. "We were just talking about you, Dr. Munro."

"Can't imagine why," Ivan replied dryly.

Harold cleared his throat, as if that would cover the less than friendly tone of voice Ivan had just displayed. "Dr. Munro, this is the young woman I was telling you about yesterday."

Now his eyes dissected her. Bailey felt as if she were undergoing a scalpel-less autopsy right then and there. "Ah yes, the Stanford Special."

He made her sound like something that was listed at the top of a third-rate diner menu. There was enough contempt in his voice to offend an entire delegation from the UN.

Summoning the bravado that her parents always claimed had been infused in her since the moment she first drew breath, Bailey put out her hand. "Hello. I'm Dr. Bailey DelMonico."

Ivan made no effort to take the hand offered to him. Instead, he slid his long, lanky form bonelessly into the chair beside her. He proceeded to move the chair ever so slightly so that there was even more space between them. Ivan faced the chief of staff, but the words he spoke were addressed to her.

"You're a doctor, DelMonico, when I say you're a doctor," he informed her coldly, sparing her only one steely glance to punctuate the end of his statement.

"I have a certificate from Johns Hopkins University that says differently." Her tone was nonconfrontational and matter-of-fact. She was determined not to let Ivan the Terrible see that her insides felt like jelly. And she was just as determined not to be crushed into the ground like an insignificant bug at their first meeting.

Ivan didn't bother sparing her a second glance. "Shall I tell her where she can put that certificate, or do you want that pleasure?"

Harold stifled a sigh. He knew this was all for show, to frighten off the young woman. He couldn't very well discipline his chief neurosurgeon in front of a new resident, but neither did he want her madly running for the hills.

So instead, he smiled warmly at Bailey and shook his head like a weary father settling yet another squabble between his children. "I'm afraid that Dr. Munro is a little unorthodox," he told her, then tried to sound as positive as he could as he added, "But I promise you that you'll learn a great deal from him."

It wasn't hard to see that the man's eyes were requesting her understanding. She appreciated that. Bailey smiled as she nodded. "Probably a lot of words I never heard before," she allowed.

She thought she saw amusement flit across Dr. Bennett's face and it heartened her. She'd gained an ally.

"Now, until I say differently, Dr. Munro is going to take over your education. Dr. Munro—" he fixed Ivan with a steely gaze that had been known to send lesser doctors running for their antacids but, as always, seemed to have *no* effect on the chief neurosurgeon "—I want you to award her every consideration. From now on, Dr. DelMonico is to be your shadow, your sponge and your assistant." He emphasized the last word as his eyes locked with Ivan's. "Do I make myself clear?"

For his part, Ivan seemed completely unfazed. He merely nodded, his eyes and expression unreadable. "Perfectly."

"And if there's any problem," Harold continued, looking from the young woman to his chief sore spot, "I want to be informed of it immediately." The sentence was no sooner out of his mouth than he saw Ivan raising his hand. It didn't take a brain surgeon to guess exactly what the man was going to say. "*After* you give this arrangement at least several weeks to begin to work itself out." Harold pushed his chair back from his desk and rose, signaling that the meeting was at an end. "Now, if you have the time, Dr. Munro, I would appreciate it if you showed our newest resident around Blair Memorial."

To his credit, the chief of staff didn't even flinch when Ivan shot a dagger in his direction.

"It'll have to be another time," Ivan replied. "My schedule's full today."

"That's fine," Bailey cut in quickly, refusing to be the source of a clash of wills between the two men. "I've already familiarized myself with the hospital layout, Dr. Bennett."

"Oh?"

"My two roommates are residents here. I had them take me around during their off hours."

Ivan smirked. "Enterprising little thing, isn't she?" The words were only marginally addressed to the chief of staff.

His hand was on the doorknob. Bailey sprang to her feet, her chair making a scraping noise as she moved it back, then quickly joined the neurosurgeon before he could leave the office.

For his part, Ivan waited for her, nodded at the chief of staff and looked for all the world as if he had every intention of going along with the assignment that had been given him.

Optimist though he was, Harold Bennett knew better than to believe his eyes. A leopard did not change its spots and Ivan the Terrible was not about to become Ivan the Good because it was asked of him.

But he had seen something in the young woman's eyes, something that gave him hope that Ivan had met, if not his match, at least someone who was not about to topple over like a loosely packed sandcastle the moment the first disgruntled words erupted out of Ivan's mouth.

Ivan held the door open for her, allowing the young woman to leave first. He was male enough to notice that she was even better looking than her tiny photograph indicated and arrogant enough to feel that it had no bearing on anything as far as he was concerned.

Closing the door behind him, Ivan leaned over and whispered into her ear, "Just so you know, I'm going to be your worst nightmare."

She gave him only the merest of looks as she appeared to consider the statement. "Funny, you don't look like a burning cross on the front lawn." And then she glanced up overhead at the ceiling. "I guess it must be the lighting."

CHAPTER 6

Any hope that the man might possess a sense of humor and strike a truce died quickly. Munro looked angrier than Zeus upon learning of a rebellion spearheaded by the lesser gods. "First thing you're going to have to do is lose the attitude, Del-Monico."

His eyes seemed to shoot thunderbolts. She refused to look away, although it wasn't easy meeting his stormy gaze.

"Are you?" she asked innocently.

Abruptly he began walking again. "My attitude is a fixture around here." He slanted a glance at her as if she were an annoying fly that insisted on buzzing around his head. "A smart mouth is not going to get you anything at Blair except thrown out."

Bailey bit back the desire to point out that having a "smart mouth" certainly hadn't hurt him. One retort to show him that she wasn't afraid of him was all she was allowed. Anything more would not only be overkill, it just might also kill her chance to work at Blair Memorial before she started. Or at least, work at Blair under Munro. And from what she'd heard, Ivan Munro was capable of performing miracles in the operating room. She wanted to witness those miracles firsthand, to learn from them and eventually to become just as good a neurosurgeon as Munro. Because if you couldn't be the best, why bother?

So, even as hot words burned on her tongue, Bailey forced herself to stay sober and replied, "Yes, Doctor."

He thought he heard something in her voice, something he took exception to. "And mocking me isn't going to get you anywhere, either."

Her head shot up, surprised. "I wasn't mocking you, Dr. Munro, I was replying."

He resumed walking, his legs stretching out before him as he snorted his contempt. "I am a student of body language, Del-Monico. Yours is telling me to go to hell."

"I don't think so, Doctor," she replied, her voice as innocent as she could manage it. "I don't allow my body to use that kind of language."

He snorted again. "Right, no doubt that's the missionary in you coming out." The look he slanted her this time was positively wicked. "Ever hear the joke about the anthropologist who lost his way and the missionary's daughter?"

A little less than a foot shorter than the chief neurosurgeon, Bailey found herself fairly trotting to keep up now. She hadn't a clue where he was going and she was not about to be left behind. She'd told Dr. Bennett the truth, she had taken a tour of the hospital, but she hadn't exactly committed the entire layout to memory. Yet.

"The anthropologist and the missionary's daughter?" she repeated. "A thousand times, Doctor."

About to turn a corner, Ivan halted. He debated whether she was just about the best stone-faced liar he'd ever encountered or if his new albatross had actually heard the obscure joke he was referring to. In any event, the joke was only intended as a test to see how easily the woman blushed and, more importantly, how quickly he could take her down.

This, he decided, was going to be more of a challenge than he'd first imagined. For all he knew, it might even turn out to be a bit on the entertaining side.

"Then I won't bore you with it," he finally replied.

Her eyes met his. She made sure to keep her relief under wraps as she said, "Thank you, Dr. Munro."

For the first time since he'd been told about the ordeal he was expected to endure, Ivan allowed himself just the slightest hint of a smile. The corners of his mouth moved in a vague upward pattern before returning to their customary downward arc.

"I do believe you mean that, DelMonico." He glanced at his watch and lengthened his considerable stride. "I'm due in surgery in a few minutes," he informed her, although part of him bristled at making any sort of an excuse to this resident.

But if he meant his words to be taken as any sort of a dismissal, he was sorely disappointed. Rather than dropping behind and allowing him to continue on alone, she all but ran to keep up pace with him.

He frowned at her. "We don't allow skipping in the halls, DelMonico."

"I'm not skipping, Doctor," she informed him, hurrying. "I'm running."

Given that she was a lot shorter and in high heels, the woman kept up remarkably well. It occurred to him that she wasn't wearing traditional scrubs. Was that for his benefit? Did she think she could "get to him" by looking soft, supple and feminine?

He almost laughed out loud at the notion.

But instead he informed her, "We don't allow that, either."

She had always been extremely physical. Life as a missionary's daughter did not allow for hours spent on a sofa, in front of a computer or a television set. She'd learned to amuse herself the way children had before electronic devices had taken over the task. If need be, she could run like a gazelle fleeing a hungry predator. "Then you're going to have to slow down, sir."

She didn't even sound winded, he noticed. "And why is that?"

"Because I can't keep up using your pace."

Rather than shorten his stride, he increased it. "That, Del-Monico, is a given."

Bailey took in a deep breath. Gritting her teeth, she lengthened her stride as far as she could and quickened her pace to make up for the difference. They turned heads as they snaked their way through the halls.

She was right behind him when they reached the entrance to Operation Room One.

Only then did Ivan stop. He felt a little winded himself. He needed to make time for morning jogs again, he thought. Somehow that had managed to slip by the wayside. These days, he lived and breathed his work and little else. He couldn't remember the last time he'd been to a concert.

His eyes washed over her. Bailey did her best not to shiver. "Stubborn, aren't you?"

Bailey smiled at him in response. "My father said it's one of my best attributes."

"Fathers lie," he said flatly.

He wanted to get under her skin, to get her angry, so she struggled to remain clam. "If I may ask, what kind of operation is it?"

He gave her a look that easily would have left others quaking in their shoes. It annoyed him that he had no effect on her. "A complicated one."

"Good," she replied without missing a beat. "May I scrub in? I can—" She was about to tell him that she had her scrubs in her locker and could change into them faster than she could explain it, but she never got the chance.

She could see him shutting down right in front of her eyes. "You can scrub all you want, DelMonico," he said, putting his hand on the swinging door, "but you're not getting into my operating room."

She covered his hand with her own. The action stopped him in his tracks. Ivan eyed her over his shoulder.

"What are you afraid of, Dr. Munro?"

She had done what few people ever did. She'd caught him by surprise. "I beg your pardon?"

His voice was cold, brittle. Bailey felt like someone who had just walked out onto the plank and now tottered on the edge of the wood. But if she backed off, Munro would have nothing but contempt for her. More contempt for her, she amended.

"What are you afraid of?" she repeated. "That you might be wrong?"

His eyes narrowed into slits. "I'm never wrong."

Okay, maybe she should have been more specific. "About me, Dr. Munro. Wrong about me. You think I can't cut it."

"I *know* you can't cut it," he informed her mildly. "I'm not letting you cut anything."

She lifted her chin pugnaciously. "What are you going to tell Dr. Bennett?"

Rangy shoulders rose and fell. "That I tried but it didn't work out."

She pushed back his lab coat from the hand she was covering and looked at his wrist. "After only ten minutes?"

He inclined his head. "We both lasted longer than I estimated."

She drew herself up to her full five-foot-five height. "I'm not going anywhere, Dr. Munro."

He nodded, as if she'd finally caught on. "My words exactly."

Too late, Bailey realized her error. "Away," she corrected. "I'm not going away." As she spoke, her voice increased in strength and depth, even as she struggled to keep it low. She didn't want to be accused of screaming or creating a scene. "I've come a long way to be standing right here in this hallway, arguing with you, and if you think that your reputation as the devil incarnate is going to scare me off, it won't. I've seen the devil, Dr. Munro, and it's not you."

He stood there for a long moment, then drew his hand from beneath hers. Turning away from her, he pushed open the door to the operating room and walked through.

"Scrub in."

CHAPTER 7

Ivan was vaguely aware of the indistinct squeal behind him and then the sound of eager footsteps growing fainter.

He assumed it was the little-resident-that-could's way of showing her enthusiasm as well as her joy before she ran off to change into her scrubs and prepare for the operating room. Crossing the perimeter of the operating room, as much to show his presence as to get to the area where the sinks were, Ivan carefully took in every square inch.

Casting an aura of disquiet as he went.

As it should be. Complacent people were lax. Lax led to mistakes.

He wondered if he'd just made a mistake, being too soft. Telling DelMonico to scrub in.

It wasn't as if he would allow her to touch one of the instruments. His only intention was to let her just breathe the same air as his surgical staff. He and only he would tackle Mark Spader's brain tumor.

Brain tumor.

Alone by the sinks, Ivan took in a long breath and then released it. Like a magnet set on a table with metal fillings, the surgery before him drew away all thoughts of the resident and how he hated being harnessed with petty responsibilities that took away from the focus of his purpose here at Blair.

To mend as many patients as he could. To try, in some small, futile measure, to make it up to Scott for what he'd done. As if that were possible.

A dry, humorless laugh echoed within the small area as he shed his lab coat. He was already dressed in his surgical livery. Prepared, always prepared.

Except for that one night.

Against his will, thoughts came back to him. Scott Kiplinger was the reason he was here. Scott was the reason for everything, most of all why he had become a neurosurgeon. Because if there had been a neurosurgeon on duty that night, if one had been called to the ER in time instead of hours later, Scott might still be among the living. Walking, talking and being the best friend he'd ever had.

The best friend he'd killed as surely as if he had aimed that gun and pulled the trigger himself.

But he hadn't physically pulled the trigger. Scott's despair had pulled it that awful, beautiful afternoon in the meadow. That fateful afternoon when he had finally persuaded Scott to leave the confines of his house, where all the curtains were always drawn, shutting out life. Shutting in the darkness.

Scott had lived that way, never leaving his house, for almost two years. Ever since the accident.

The accident, Ivan thought darkly, remembering every vivid detail, that had been all his fault. If he hadn't been speeding, if he hadn't taken that curve so fast, if there hadn't been ice on the ground, if Scott hadn't been in the car.

If, if, if, IF.

Ivan sighed, scrubbing his damp hand over his face. Wiping it dry as he uttered a curse through clenched teeth, he then washed his hands a second time.

If.

Battling with the word didn't change anything. Didn't make him stay home instead of going out for a ride. Didn't make him sober instead of buzzed on three beers.

Neither did it change how very naive he'd been, thinking he'd scored a coup, getting Scott to leave his house. At the outset, it had seemed like the perfect plan, driving Scott to the meadow where he had loved to hike and run. Scott, the all-around athlete, getting in touch with his past. It had seemed so right at the time.

He'd thought, *believed*, that the sight of something familiar, something once so beloved, would finally, magically, bring Scott around. Would suddenly rally him to grasp on to the fragments of life that he still had and make him want to build on them.

Make him want to be among the living again instead of among the wheelchair-bound wounded.

Stupid, stupid, stupid, Ivan upbraided himself for the thousandth time.

He'd had no idea that the pouch Scott had brought with him, the one attached to his wheelchair arm, didn't contain the water bottle he'd said it did but the weapon he'd used to finally terminate all his pain.

Ivan closed his eyes as the hot water dissolved the heavy film of soap from his hands.

He could see it all so clearly. His sitting on the grass, to the left of Scott's wheelchair, foolishly talking about what strides physical therapy had taken in the last couple of years and how he would do anything, *anything*, to help Scott start living again. He'd talked about Scott's mother, about how he had to get on with his life, if only for her.

It was a topic he'd all but worn a hole in, but this time, this time, because Scott didn't argue with him, he had thought he was getting through to Scott. This time, he'd been hopeful that he could begin making amends.

And then all hope vanished forever.

Because while he went on talking, making plans, gluing together a future, Scott had quietly taken the gun out of the pouch, placed it to his temple and ended the discussion.

Permanently.

The sound of the gun being discharged was deafening. The horror of having his best friend's blood rain down on him never left him.

The feeling of hopeless futility imprinted its indelible mark on him that afternoon and changed him. The young, wild, carefree youth he'd been died along with Scott that day. The numbed man who eventually rose out of those ashes dedicated himself exclusively to becoming a neurosurgeon. It was the only thing that made sense to him. Becoming a neurosurgeon so that Scott's death wasn't entirely meaningless, that he hadn't died without changing anything.

And now, twenty-five years later, all that mattered was the same thing that mattered twenty-five years ago: saving lives. Reconstructing broken shells so that they could continue in Scott's name, even though none of them were ever aware of it.

Because no one else knew about Scott, except for Scott's mother. Telling her about Scott's suicide had been the hardest thing he had ever done in his life. Standing in the same room with the woman's overwhelming grief had been worse than hell.

"It's your fault, you know," she'd shouted at him, her eyes red-rimmed. "You're the reason he's dead. He should have never hung around with you."

He'd tried to apologize, but Scott's mother had just started screaming. Screaming like a woman whose heart had been ripped out of her breast. There wasn't anything he could say.

He shut down that day, purging every drop of emotion from himself. Barring its return as he focused on what he needed to do. What he swore at Scott's grave site to do.

But every successful operation he performed didn't bring a feeling of triumph that lived beyond one moment. Most of all, none of the successes tendered, in some small form, a feeling of absolution.

It truly was as if everything had shut down inside of him the day Scott died. Because Scott had been his only friend in a world that, for him, had been largely dysfunctional due to abusive, self-destructive parents, and when Scott had given in to despair and killed himself, the light simply went out of everything, leaving him standing in perpetual darkness.

A darkness he had, since that day, resisted leaving, despite the efforts of various people who came and went in his life.

He made no attachments to anyone. Instead, he coexisted, which was far easier. To become involved, even in the slightest way, was risking far too much and the only risks Ivan was willing to take, the only ones he actually ever took, were in the operating room. There he performed daring surgeries that other neurosurgeons would never even contemplate.

He did them because neurosurgery was the terrain that the

gods traversed whenever they took their constitutionals. And it was the terrain that he, Ivan, habitually crossed with long, confident steps. And no one ever knew about the insecurity that still resided inside.

Finished, his clean hands raised in the air, ready to have gloves drawn over them, Ivan pushed the swinging door that separated him from the operating room with his shoulder. The little-resident-that-could was already there, Ivan noted. He recognized her eager eyes above the blue surgical mask she, like the others in the chilled room, had donned.

Maybe she could keep up, after all. And then again, maybe she couldn't. Either way, that wasn't any of his concern. There was only one thing he cared about and it was lying, prepped and draped, on his operating table.

"All right, people," Ivan announced to the staff that closed in around him. "Time to make a miracle."

CHAPTER 8

"Oh my God, that was incredible," Bailey cried.

It was difficult to keep from shouting out the words as she walked from the operating room to the back area where the sinks were. Trying to steady her racing pulse, she took in a deep, measured breath. It didn't help. Everything inside her had kicked into high gear. It was the closest to high she had ever felt.

Bailey looked at the man she had been assigned to with genuine awe. "You were incredible."

Ivan spared her a glance that could only be described as "disinterested." The other members of the staff walked by, oblivious to the scene, trying to put distance between themselves and Ivan the Terrible.

"Yes, I know."

The sound of his voice, utterly devoid of any sort of emotion, penetrated the wild rush she was experiencing. Bailey could only stare at the neurosurgeon incredulously. He'd performed nothing short of a miracle. "How can you be so calm?"

One shoulder moved in a vague shrug. "Low blood sugar."

"I'm serious." She tugged her mask down lower until she could undo the ties at the back of her neck. "Don't you feel a rush, a surge?" She searched his face for a hint of what she was describing. "Isn't your heart just pounding?"

The disinterested glance only deepened. Flattery, even sincere flattery, which he presumed this was, was neither accepted nor rejected. It was allowed to float free through time and space, like an untethered balloon until it faded away. "I performed surgery, DelMonico. I didn't make love to the man."

The words threw her completely off. Bailey looked at the man whose fingers had performed nothing short of magic in the room behind her. Mild surprise gave way to amusement. "I didn't know you made love."

He threw his gloves away and removed the bland surgical cap he'd worn during the six-hour operation. Other surgeons, once they had endured and surmounted all the various trials and obstacles to get there, selected a cap in colors that had some sort of significance to them. Ivan's was the same color as it had always been. Blue. He didn't believe in donning peacock finery. He believed in surgery.

One tug separated the mask's ties at the back of his neck and he threw the mask into a bin. "There are many things about me, DelMonico, that you don't know."

Interest sparked in those deep blue eyes of hers. "I'm willing to listen."

"I'm not willing to talk." He figured that was enough of a put-down. Instead, her mouth curved even more. Ivan flashed one of his more deflating looks. "Careful, DelMonico, or someone's going to have to tie a rope around your ankle to keep you earth-bound. Why are you so exhilarated, anyway?" he asked, unable to understand her reaction. "You were just on the sidelines."

Sidelines or not, she was right *there*, where everything was happening. "But I got to see—" she cried, then abruptly switched sentences, so pumped she was unable to finish one thought before leaping to another. "You had half his skull off—His brain was exposed!"

"They call it 'brain surgery' for a reason, DelMonico." He shook his head, as if not knowing what to make of her, sincerely doubting that she was for real. "Maybe you should review your notes from Neurosurgery 101."

It was her turn to shake her head, but unlike him, her smile was wide. "You're not going to do it."

Despite the fact that he wanted to change out of his scrubs, he paused a moment to ask, "Do what?"

"You're not going to deflate me." She was far too excited about what she had witnessed, far too enthused about the work that lay ahead of her, to become just like him. She'd never believed in aiming low.

Ivan clucked his tongue. "Pity. There goes my fun for the afternoon."

Turning away from her, Ivan was surprised when he felt her hand on his forearm. He glanced over his shoulder and waited for an explanation for the detainment.

Self-consciously, she dropped her hand to her side. "How long?" she asked.

His patience was pretty well stretched to the limit with her. "How long what?"

She pressed her lips together. "How long before I can do something like that?" She nodded her head back toward the O.R.

"Oh, I don't know." He paused, pretending to think. And then his expression was dismissive as he raised his eyes to hers. "If you study very hard—maybe a century or two. Maybe longer."

A slam like that might have sent her reeling—or spoiling for a fight. But she was beginning to read between the lines and get a handle on him. The insults were a smokescreen. No one was that nasty for no reason. "You don't want me to like you, do you?"

His eyes narrowed, telling her how insignificant she was in the scheme of his life. "I really don't care how you feel about anything, DelMonico."

He believed that, she thought. But she didn't. She'd been taught never to focus on the bad, only the good. And if an animal swiped at you, it was only because he was wounded. The challenge here was to discover what Ivan the Terrible's wound was.

She folded her arms before her. "Well, you won't get me to dislike you."

Ordinarily, he would have turned and walked away without bothering to reply. But for once, curiosity got the better of him. "Not that, again, I care in the slightest, but why is that, Del-Monico?"

The answer was simple. Because she wanted to be the best and in order to do that, she had to learn from the best. She had to learn from him. Everything was always better when conducted in an air of congeniality rather than hospitality.

"Because you did exactly what you said back there," she told him. "You performed a miracle. That tumor looked like it was a miniaturized octopus with its tiny tentacles woven all in and out of gray matter, and yet you got it all."

He'd leaned against the wall to listen to her and straightened now. "Very poetic, DelMonico. Maybe you should think about becoming a poet instead of wasting your time here."

She wasn't going to let him bait her. She felt too good, too psyched, to let him burst her balloons and make her plummet. "I'm not wasting my time."

He leveled a penetrating gaze at her. "You're sure of that?"

There wasn't even a half second of hesitation on her part. "Yes."

"Ballsy," Ivan pronounced, more to himself than to her. "Maybe it won't take you a century or two. DelMonico. Maybe it'll just take three-quarters of one."

She had just been given a decent compliment, Ivan the Terrible style. She viewed it as one giant step in the right direction. "I'm going to knock that figure down to something manageable," she promised.

Ivan snorted. "You think that, DelMonico. You go right ahead and think that."

The tone he used clearly declared that while she might want to delude herself, he knew the truth and the truth, the way he saw it, said that she would never be capable of performing the kinds of surgeries he tackled on a regular basis. He just didn't see it being in her, no matter what she thought.

"I will," Bailey called after him as he began to walk away. "Because I have a good teacher." She raised her voice when he made no attempt to turn around and added, "You."

"Ha!" was Ivan's only response. He kept on walking until he disappeared through the opposite set of swinging doors.

Bailey turned on her heel, quickly heading around to the other side, to the locker room where her things were stored. For all the contact she'd had with the patient, she could have almost remained in the clothes she'd worn originally. The clothes she'd secretly hoped put her in a better light as far as first impressions went. She realized that she could have just as well worn a paper sack for all the difference it made to Munro, but it had been worth a try.

She grinned to herself. She'd seen her first brain surgery today. Despite the fact that Munro had relegated her to a far corner of the operating room, she had been able to witness the infinite skill with which he wielded the robotic instruments used to excise the tumor that had all but paralyzed the thirty-two-year-old patient.

She didn't care how much the neurosurgeon ranted and raved, how much he tried to get her to throw her hands up and scream "uncle" just before she quit. There was no way she was about to do that.

"Get used to it, Ivan Munro," she murmured under her breath as she walked into the locker room. "I'm going to stick to you like glue until I know everything that you do."

The second she entered the lockers she began shedding surgical livery. By the time she reached the locker that had been assigned her, she was in her underwear, ready to grab her street clothes and put them on.

The trouble with that was, someone, obviously thinking they were performing a good deed, had shut her locker door and flipped the combination lock. A lock to which she didn't know the combination.

"Damn," she muttered when the lock resisted opening.

"Problem?"

The question came from the other side of the lockers.

CHAPTER 9

Bailey's first inclination was to grab her discarded scrubs and cover herself up as much as possible.

The only thing wrong with that plan was that she'd tossed the scrubs into the dirty laundry receptacle and it was now approximately ten feet away from her. She sensed that a mad dash to retrieve the discarded clothing would undoubtedly amuse the chief neurosurgeon who seemed to have materialized out of thin air. She was willing to bet double her staggering medical school loan that if she did that, Munro would make some sort of humiliating, condescending comment about her pubescent reaction.

So instead of making a laughable attempt to somehow cover up the lacey pink bra and panties, and the skin that was above, between and below, Bailey raised her chin and turned around. She looked the neurosurgeon straight in the eye as if she were dressed from head to foot in a suit of impenetrable medieval armor. Only for a moment did she have the impression that he *wasn't* looking at her as if she were wearing impenetrable medieval armor. But at least he wasn't leering.

"Actually, yes," she replied as coolly as possible under the circumstances. "There is a problem. Someone seems to have snapped my lock shut."

She couldn't read his expression, but in her heart she just *knew* he was laughing at her. "That's why they make locks. To lock." And then he allowed a sigh to escape, as if this was all incredibly boring to him. "Use the combination."

"If I knew the combination, Doctor, that would be an excellent suggestion."

This time she saw his eyes slowly pass over her body. He seemed neither impressed nor disappointed. There appeared to be no reaction at all. She couldn't help wondering if he had spent too much time viewing people only as patients. At another time, she might have begun to speculate about his personal life, but right now, only hers, and how she was going to live this down, concerned her.

Goose bumps formed along her arms and legs in response to the lowered temperature. "Do you have any other suggestions?" she asked, her mouth growing annoyingly dry.

"Yes." He said the single word so slowly, it seemed to drip out of his mouth.

A beat passed. Nothing followed.

"Well?" she pressed, doing her best not to sound frantic. What if someone came in and saw her like this? Then what?

"Sorry." Ivan shook his head. "Nothing I can readily repeat out loud without offending the sisterhood."

Then he *was* reacting to her near nude state. She didn't know whether to be flattered for having gotten to the almighty Ivan or offended. Added to that, she hadn't a clue what he was referring to.

"The what?"

"Sisterhood," he repeated, then waved his hand as if to move the word aside. "Or whatever organization you and other females belong to that goes around bringing the male of the species up on inflated charges of harassment."

Frustrated, Bailey turned her back on him and gave the lock another tug, a harder one this time. It had the same results as the first one did. Nothing. The lock hung there, mocking her. Just like Munro.

"Really should have committed the combination to memory," he told her. He leaned forward just a touch, but not enough to actually come close to her. "Gnawing on it won't help, either."

She turned around, her anger eradicating her embarrassment. "Thank you."

He nodded, as if the exchange was of an ordinary nature. "I assume you don't intend to spend the rest of your days at Blair Memorial like that." For emphasis, Ivan's eyes slid down and then up along her torso.

She struggled hard not to shiver, even if she told herself his gaze was clinical. "No, I don't."

Raising her chin again, Bailey strode past him back to the laundry receptacle to retrieve the shirt and pants. She couldn't just continue standing here, talking to him while wearing only the amount of material used to produce a minor bikini.

About to take out the two items, the sound of Munro's voice stopped her.

"I wouldn't recommend that." She didn't turn around, but she did stop and wait for him to continue. "Germs, you know. Those scrubs were in the O.R."

He had a point, but so did she and as far as she was concerned hers trumped his. "Well, I don't really have a choice now, do I?"

In response, she heard him laugh. Tired of being his source of amusement, the high she'd sustained watching him operate completely dissipated, Bailey swung around to face him. Superior or not, she was ready to give him a piece of her mind, the consequences be damned. Someone needed to take this man down a peg and it might as well be her last act at Blair.

But whatever words she attempted to hunt up died in her throat as she saw what the neurosurgeon held in his hands. Neatly folded scrubs, both top and bottoms. "You could put these on." He raised one eyebrow quizzically. "Size small, right?"

"Right," she murmured, surprised. The scrubs had *not* been there before. And the ones she'd obtained earlier for herself had come from the supply area. "Where did you get those?"

"Magic," he informed her dryly. And then he nodded toward the closet behind him. "Scrubs for visiting surgeons are kept in there."

Something else she hadn't known. The list of things she needed to familiarize herself with was growing astronomically. And then she replayed his words in her head. "I'm not visiting."

"Yes," Ivan acknowledged with more than a tinge of sorrow, "I know." He looked down at the scrubs. "If you don't want these—" He raised the uniform blues up over his head and completely out of her reach.

"No!" she cried. Not knowing what the man was capable of, she made a lunge for the scrubs to retrieve them. Her body brushed up against his as she reached up as far as she could.

She felt the same way she had in physics class when she'd accidentally touched a live wire. Electrical current zapped through her body.

If her momentary panic amused him, he didn't show it.

Neither did he seem affected by the fleeting contact of her barely covered anatomy against his.

Instead, Ivan lowered his arm and very soberly presented the fresh scrubs to her. She snatched them up as if she didn't trust him to surrender the clothes to her.

"I'm making afternoon rounds in five minutes," he informed her as he turned on his heel. With that, he walked out of the locker room.

Bailey all but hopped into the blue scrubs while making her way to the door, grateful to finally put something on her body. Punching her arms through the sleeves, she caught up to him on the other side of the door.

"What about my locker?" she asked. She still had a problem.

His tone was completely disinterested. "What about it?"

She was beginning to understand why some residents used his picture as a dartboard. "I still need to open it."

Passing the nurses' station, he picked up a file without breaking stride. "Not now you don't."

"No," she agreed. Bailey glanced down and saw that one of her laces was untied. She knew better than to stop to tie it. That was going to have to wait for a lull, too. "But later—"

"Is later," he told her with finality, and it was obvious that as far as he was concerned, "later" had no place in the present. "It'll take care of itself."

Not without help, Bailey thought. She made a mental note to find either a janitor or a pair of bull cutters, preferably the former wielding the latter. She didn't care about going home dressed in scrubs, even though it was chilly outside, but her locker, the locker she'd purposely left with an open combination lock hanging from it, also contained her purse, her keys and all of her identification. She couldn't drive her car or get into her house without them.

She supposed, Bailey thought, shoving a loose pin back into her hair, she could hook up with either Adam or Jennifer and they could drive her home. But even if she did, that still didn't solve the problem of getting her things out of the sealed locker.

"You're panting, DelMonico," Ivan observed, making a left at the end of the corridor.

No, she wasn't, but she knew that arguing seemed pointless. "You've got on your seven league boots again, Doctor."

His glance was just short of belittling as he slanted it in her direction. "I guess you'll just have to get a pair, DelMonico."

She nodded as if he'd just made a perfect plausible suggestion. She had a hunch he got a certain amount of pleasure rattling people and she refused to accommodate him. "Just tell me where to shop," she replied without missing a beat.

Bailey thought she heard Munro mutter something under his breath but decided that she might be better off not knowing exactly what that was.

Christians, one. Lions, zero, she thought with a suppressed smile.

CHAPTER 10

"So, how is the great neurosurgeon doing?"

When the phone had rung a second ago, Bailey had debated between answering it and throwing it across the room. But because she was too exhausted to throw, she brought the receiver to her ear.

Hearing the voice made her miraculously sit up.

"Simon? Simon, is that you?" Even as she said his name, she brightened. Her older brother had always had that effect on her, bringing rays of hope into an otherwise gloomy atmosphere.

"None other. How're you doing, kid?"

She could hear the smile in his voice. "Great now that I hear the sound of your voice."

A tiny note of concern entered. "How were you before you heard the sound of my voice?" And then he became serious, ever the big brother. "They treating you all right?"

She didn't want him worrying or thinking that she couldn't take care of herself. She'd come a long way from that little girl who used to tag after him, shadowing his every move.

"By 'they,' do you mean the people at the hospital or my roommates?"

"Yes."

Good old Simon, she thought, always touching as many bases as he can.

"My roommates are great. They're both younger than I am, but I knew they would be." She'd known going in that she would be the oldest resident there, but she couldn't dwell on that. She was just grateful for the opportunity. "Part of me feels like I'm their den mother."

"Can't be that bad," her brother scoffed. "You're what—six, seven years older than they are? Maybe even less?"

"Something like that."

"Honey, five, six, seven years, that's nothing. You're hardly in the den mother league. Or even the baby-sitter league," he added.

She begged to differ. Bailey propped herself up on her elbows and moved back until she was resting against the pillows.

"You're seven years older than I am and you always acted as if you were my second father. Still do, sometimes," she added slyly.

"Rank has its privileges," he told her, unfazed. "Really, Bay, are you okay? Do you need anything? Don't be your proud, stubborn self. Tell me if you need something."

"Batteries."

"Batteries?" Simon repeated in disbelief. "Bailey, are you—"

She laughed, stopping him before he allowed his imagination to run away with him. "Batteries so I can keep going without crashing and embarrassing myself. I'm *way* beyond vitamins, coffee and energy drinks."

"You don't need batteries, Bay. What you need is sleep."

If only. Bailey laughed softly to herself. "Tell that to the attendings. As for the chief neurosurgeon, the guy I've been assigned to, he doesn't seem to sleep. Ever. He's there when I arrive in the morning and he's still there when I leave at night."

"Maybe he does it with mirrors," Simon quipped.

"Maybe," she allowed. "They call him Ivan the Terrible."

"That doesn't sound warm and toasty. He giving you a hard time?"

She almost responded with, "Is the Pope Catholic?" but given Simon's increased dedication to piety, she decided to skip the rhetorical comment. "Dr. Munro gives everyone a hard time. I think he might be lonely."

"With a name like Ivan the Terrible, I don't doubt it. Don't try to mend his broken wing, Bay." It was a reference to her always bringing home hurt animals when she was a little girl. "Just take care of yourself—and get that rest. You know what happens if you burn the candle at both ends—"

"—all you wind up with is a lump of wax in the middle," Bailey said, echoing her brother as she repeated the line she had heard more times than she could count. "All right, enough about me, how about you?" They cared about each other, but it was unusual for Simon to call out of the blue like this. "What's new in your life? How are you doing?"

"I'm doing okay."

Bailey sat up. She knew her brother inside and out, knew all the nuances. There was something just a little bit guarded about his answer, about his voice. She thought she'd heard him hesitate before he gave her the innocuous reply.

"Okay, give. What's up? Something wrong?"

"Nothing's wrong," he protested. "You couldn't be more off." And then Simon paused for a second, as if debating just how to frame what he was about to tell her. "I'm being ordained."

"Ordained?" That had always been her parents' dearest wish, to have their children follow in their footsteps. At least Simon hadn't disappointed them, she thought. "Oh, Simon, that's wonderful. Mom and Dad must be proud enough to burst."

"Pretty much," he agreed modestly. "But Mom calls it a mixed blessing."

"What's mixing it?"

He laughed softly. "Well, I'm going to need my own 'flock'."

"Which means you'll have to go off on your own," she concluded, understanding. "Poor Mom."

"Thanks. I was wondering where I was going to get my daily dose of guilt."

She knew he wasn't upset. Simon had always taken things in stride, upbeat, but with no false illusions. Unlike her, he didn't have an impetuous bone in his body. He thought everything through carefully before making a move. She used to call him "the turtle" when they were younger because his moves were so deliberate and slow.

"I just mean, first me, then you." She made an assumption as to where her brother's first ministry would be. "I suppose they could come back to live in the States."

He laughed at the thought. They both knew how settled their parents were, how dedicated to the life they had undertaken.

"Too savage for them," he quipped. They both laughed. "Listen, I'm going to have some time before I start and I thought I'd come out to see my favorite sister in the flesh."

"As I recall, I am your only sister," she reminded him.

"Good thing for you," he teased, sounding like the Simon she knew again. "If there'd been competition, you might not have made the cut. I'm not sure about the timing yet. How does the end of April, beginning of May sound to you?"

"Like it's much too far away," she told him wistfully. Talking to Simon had stirred feelings of nostalgia within her exhaustion.

"Know what you mean, Bay. I miss you, too," he told her with affection. "I'll call you again when I have something more concrete to offer, like flight number and time. You take care of yourself, hear?"

She had no idea why she felt so teary-eyed suddenly. "I will."

"And tell anyone who gives you a hard time to back off and leave you alone or they'll have your big brother to reckon with."

"Will do." The line went dead after a quick, "Goodbye."

Bailey found herself smiling down at the receiver in her hand. She could just hear Munro's response to that one. He'd tell her exactly where she could put her protective big brother. But she did appreciate the thought.

Appreciated her brother calling her, as well, even though the sound of Simon's voice had made her feel almost sad and definitely homesick. Sad even though she loved what she was doing, loved the prospect of getting up each morning, coming in and donning her hospital livery, even though she knew that she was going to be at odds with Munro the moment the man laid eyes on her.

She hadn't felt this homesick since that first week when she'd left home to get her undergraduate degree. After the first week, the intoxicating wave of freedom had swept her away and she'd gotten immersed in college life.

Until then, except for a week here and there, she had never been away from her parents or away from the continent of

Africa, not since she was ten and they had first undertaken the mission to which they were still so fiercely dedicated.

Maybe it was putting up with Munro that made her feel like a lone crusader, stranded in the middle of the forest. She'd been at Blair Memorial for almost three full months now, and he had yet to allow her so much as to hold a scalpel in her hand, other than lining it up on a surgical tray just before a procedure. Granted he allowed her in the operating room for almost every surgery he did, but to watch, nothing more. He just had her do a thousand and one errands. Busywork.

It was time for him to show her a little respect. She'd known that progress would be slow, but this was almost going backward.

Bailey bounced up, no longer tired. She knew what she was going to do, she thought. What she *had* to do. She was going to the hospital tomorrow morning and confront Munro. She would demand that he start teaching her something beyond how to dash to Radiology to fetch MRI films and rush them back to him. She hadn't endured all those years of grueling study and endless bills to be an errand girl.

She was going to be a neurosurgeon and if he couldn't mentor her properly, she would get someone who would.

CHAPTER 11

There they were again.

Nerves.

Every time she came anywhere close to Munro's vicinity, her nerve endings would come to life, conducting old fashioned games of hopscotch and leapfrog all through her system.

What *was* it about this man that inspired her to grab the nearest paper bag and breathe into it to forestall hyperventilation? It wasn't as if she was afraid of him, certainly not in the traditional sense. Granted, he was Ivan the Terrible, but he wasn't about to behead her if he found her offensive—

When he found her offensive, she silently corrected because the chief neurosurgeon apparently found everyone offensive in one way or another.

Regardless of that, nothing he said to her was going to cause her to regress to her early childhood and run into her closet, sit on the floor in the dark, sucking madly on her thumb. She didn't mind verbal confrontations. For the most part, she viewed them as sparring matches.

But there was just something about the man that rattled her. Something she couldn't put her finger on.

Something that had her bracing herself long before he or his office came into sight.

There was no avoiding this. If she shrank back, business would go on as usual. Which meant that she would continue her stagnant career as a slightly less than glorified errand girl. The longer that went on, the less confidence Munro would have in her.

As if the man had any now, she thought, mocking herself.

Okay, now or never.

She willed her knees to leave their watery state and solidify again as she took a deep breath. Knocking on the door to his office, she waited less than half a beat before opening it.

Ivan was sitting at his desk, a large, battered and scarred affair that was literally buried beneath folders, loose papers and books. A computer and monitor was relegated to one side.

For a second, she didn't think he'd heard her. He appeared lost in the pages of an unusually thick, well-worn tome. She was about to clear her throat when he glanced up in her direction. If he was surprised to see her, he didn't show it.

"You didn't say 'Simon, may I?'" he chided.

Bailey's mind went blank, and she fought back a panicky feeling. She had it on good authority that Blair Memorial's chief neurosurgeon could smell fear.

As she mentally scrambled to pull her thoughts together, she said the first thing that came into her head. "Funny you should say that. Simon's my brother's name."

"How nice for him." Ivan marked something down, then creased the paper he was writing on and put it into his top pocket. "Did you come in here to tell me that bit of earth-shaking information?"

Her memory mercifully restored, she wasn't going to allow herself to get sucked into a verbal dance. Yet. "Do you have a minute?"

Ivan glanced at the much-scratched surface of his watch. "I have sixty of them, if you're referring to the next hour. All accounted for," he told her with finality. Closing the large reference book with a loud thwack, he placed it on his desk.

She knew his body language by now. He was about to get up and leave. She needed to get this out before her courage wavered. "I want to talk to you."

Something akin to mild interest fleetingly passed through his eyes. "And here I thought you just wanted to gaze upon greatness before you toddled off to the Radiology department to bring back Dylan Wynters's latest CAT scan."

She pressed her lips together. *Don't falter now.* "That's just it."

He raised his eyebrows above the half glasses he wore whenever he did any extensive reading. "Dylan Wynters's latest CAT scan?"

"No." Her hands against her sides, she curled her fingers into her palms, as if that would somehow give her words more authority or her voice a stronger quality. "Being sent to fetch it."

"Well, none of my carrier pigeons seem to want to come back when I send them off, so you're my only other option."

She was getting used to his sarcasm and no longer took it personally. Or at least tried not to. "No, I'm not," she told him with feeling.

Ivan, about to rise, his hands splayed on his desk for leverage, stopped to look at her. "Trying out for the part of the Littlest Rebel, are we? I must say, Shirley Temple did a much better job of it, all those curls and dimples and things, you know."

He was trying to put her off, to bury her in clever remarks as he pulled in references she was only vaguely aware of, if that. But she wasn't about to be diverted. She needed to win this point. To move forward. "You have other interns to fetch things for you."

He made a face, as if the latter group wasn't worth consideration. "The interns don't like me."

Small world, she thought. "I doubt if that would stop you."

"You're right," he declared, approving her thought process without saying as much. He rose now. "I just like sending you."

"Why?"

Ivan caught her off guard by abruptly turning around and glancing down at her. He was accustomed to having his height alone intimidate people. That it didn't her was something he found both irritating and ever so slightly admirable. "Because Harold Bennett told me I had to mentor you."

"And you're going to teach him a lesson," she guessed.

"Something like that." He inclined his head in approval. "My, but you do catch on fast, Little Grasshopper."

She was vaguely aware that the reference was to some now obscure old television program that had once been a cult favorite. He was baiting her. But she had a greater goal in mind.

"How is wasting one of the best potential neurosurgeons you'll ever come across going to teach Dr. Bennett a lesson?" Bailey asked.

This time, Munro truly did look surprised. And then he laughed shortly. "Well, you certainly have the ego to become a neurosurgeon."

It was confidence, not ego, and it was slipping out of her grasp. She had to convince him before that happened, before she succumbed to his deep brown eyes and withdrew. "I have the skill, too. I've been here for close to three months now and in all that time, you haven't allowed me to even hold a scalpel."

He seemed utterly unfazed. "Didn't your mother warn you about playing with sharp objects?"

She was standing so close to him now, she was breathing his rarefied air. "No, but she did warn me about people who snap at everyone who comes close to them."

Ivan crossed his arms before him, the sleeves of his lab coat brushing against her bare arms. "And what is it she said, this wise mother of yours?"

She knew he meant for her to jump to her mother's defense, to take exception to his tone, but she didn't. *Eyes on the prize, Bailey.* "That all that snapping is just a defensive mechanism to keep people back so that they don't find out that there's a broken person hiding behind those high fences."

Ivan smirked, not giving even the slightest indication that she had hit just a little too close to home. "Believed in fairy tales, did she, your mother?"

Bailey sighed. This part was futile. "I'm not here to analyze you, Doctor."

"I'm glad to hear that." He unfolded his arms. "Because you're no damn good at it."

"Let me do something, Dr. Munro. Make an incision, make a stitch," she requested, the intensity in her voice growing. "Let me work on a live person, not fruit. I can't learn just by watching. I need hands-on experience," she concluded with feeling.

He paused, as if her words had made an impression. "Well, you have the passion for it."

"I didn't realize passion was required for neurosurgery." The moment the words were out, she realized she'd said them without thinking. They'd just emerged in response on their own.

Bailey held her breath. To apologize would be backtracking, but she had just insulted him...

The neurosurgeon watched her for a long moment, his eyes all but drilling holes into her. She didn't know if, in a moment of unbridled frustration, she had finally crossed the line.

And then he laughed in that distant, dismissive way she'd come to know.

Laughter's good, right? Bailey thought, desperate.

"Touché, DelMonico." Munro stood thinking for a moment, his eyes seeming to bore right into her. "All right, this time when you scrub in, I'll let you get your hands dirty."

Bailey felt almost dizzy. She'd won. Or was this just a cruel joke? "Really?"

"I just said it, didn't I?" He walked into the corridor. "And, DelMonico—"

She was right behind him, her heart hammering. If it wouldn't have gotten her thrown out of the program, she would have hugged him. "Yes?"

"Lose the wild-eyed enthusiasm, will you?"

It was a put-down, meant to ground her, she thought. She did what she could to look properly sobered but found she was too damn happy to pull it off.

"I don't think I know how, Doctor," she told him honestly. "Any more than you'd know how to cry."

The look he gave her made the very air back up in her chest. When he spoke, the expected sarcasm in his voice was absent.

"You'd be surprised, DelMonico," he murmured so so softly she almost thought she imagined it. "You'd be surprised."

CHAPTER 12

He had another brain surgery, the excision of a frontal lobe aneurysm that could rupture at any moment with serious, possibly fatal consequences. Despite that, it wasn't nearly as complicated as some of Munro's other surgeries. The aneurysm was not as entangled as the tumor had been in the very first surgery she'd watched the neurosurgeon perform. But left unchecked, the aneurysm was lethal and would easily kill the forty-one-year-old broker and father of three.

Some surgeons had music piped in and felt it helped them focus or perform. Munro demanded silence so, except for the rustling of instruments and swabs and the occasional instruction, the operating room was as quiet as a tomb.

Eerily so.

. It was as if the operating staff was afraid to breathe unless Ivan the Terrible expressly gave them permission to do so.

"Well, there it is, DelMonico, your very first aneurysm."

When he said her name, Bailey snapped to attention, her adrenaline rushing unchecked. Up until this moment, she'd stood on the sidelines, the way she had for all the other surgeries she'd witnessed Munro perform. Praying for a turn at bat, knowing it would be denied her.

Despite her earlier passionate plea, Bailey began to think that history was about to repeat itself.

Like all the other times, the chief neurosurgeon had not one but two other assistants standing by to close for him or to take over if he felt like being magnanimous—and critical. He never withdrew when he handed a scalpel over to another surgeon. Instead, he stood by, observing, making the other surgeon, no matter how many years of service the latter had under his or her belt, feel like an untried resident.

When the chief of staff took him to task Munro claimed that his running critique kept the surgeons on their toes. Legend had it that Bennett had finally given up arguing the point.

As a rule, Munro always made the first cut, dominating the operation for at least the first two hours if not more. He likened it to the game of baseball and maintained that he was in the same category as an old-fashioned pitcher, the kind that had the stamina and ability to last at least the first seven innings if not the entire nine.

So when he looked up in Bailey's direction and rasped, "Come here, DelMonico," after pronouncing this her first aneurysm, she was hardly prepared for it.

Aware that the other two surgeons, as well as the rest of the operating room staff, were looking at her, Bailey took the tiniest step forward.

"'Here,' sir?" she questioned, her voice cracking in the middle.

Piercing brown eyes looked at her over a blue surgical mask. "Am I not speaking your native tongue, DelMonico? Here. *Aqui. Hier. Ici.* Sorry, my Chinese is a little rusty."

The younger of the two assistant neurosurgeons, Alec

Springer, stepped aside, allowing her a space next to Munro. Pressing her lips together, she raised her chin, doing her best not to look as if she felt like chum being tossed out before a school of sharks. "English is fine, Doctor."

"Good. Here." This time when he said the word, Munro handed her the scalpel. Or rather, held it out to her. Bailey could only stare at the pointed instrument. "It's a scalpel, Del-Monico," he told her impatiently. "Take it."

She swallowed and prayed that her hand wouldn't shake. "Yes, sir."

"Now make the first incision," he instructed. "Preferably where it'll do the most good." He leaned his head in closer to her ear. "Hint, the man came in to have an aneurysm removed. That little blood-filled thing right there." Taking hold of her hand, Munro pointed the end of the scalpel at the offending growth.

Oh God, please let me do this right. "I know where it is, Doctor." Her tone gave no indication of the butterflies dueling wildly in her stomach.

"Well, good for you." Withdrawing his hand from hers, Ivan made an elaborate show of holding it up. "Now, you were so hot to get a scalpel in your hands, DelMonico. Show me what you've got."

She didn't know if he was trying to rattle her so that she would back away, or challenge her so that she would overcome the initial fear that stalked every would-be surgeon the first time they were faced with performing a surgery.

Whatever Munro's intent, she was determined to do her absolute best. Not to prove anything to the man who had become the bane of her existence, but because Wynters's wife and three children needed him back, healthy and whole.

Silently offering up a little prayer, Bailey began.

An eternity later, when she had completed the incision and exposed the aneurysm for better excision, her heart was racing so hard she thought it was going to break right through her solar plexus.

She was aware that the chief neurosurgeon was looking over her shoulder, not a difficult feat, given their height difference.

"Not bad, DelMonico. He's still alive." Munro's hand was out and Bailey gladly relinquished possession of the scalpel.

The rush didn't go away.

The wild, heady feeling remained with her for the rest of the operation. The fact that the procedure ended successfully only compounded the elation she was experiencing. At the end of the slow surgery, the intruding growth had been removed and the prognosis for a full, uncomplicated recovery was excellent.

Unlike all the other times, Bailey was the first to leave the operating room. Rather than push through the double doors and hurry off to the locker room to swiftly change into a fresh set of blue scrubs, she stood off to the side for a moment, drawing in the unchilled air and letting it travel slowly through her lungs.

Wow. The single declaration throbbed in her temple and through her veins. *Wow.*

She heard the doors open behind her and immediately sensed that they hadn't been parted by any of the other people who had been inside the operating room with her. She was right. It was Munro. There was no telltale cologne, identifying noise. She just knew. She was developing a sixth sense when it came to the man.

He was going to rain on her parade.

Well, he could try, she thought. But no matter what the neurosurgeon said, he wasn't going to steal this feeling from her. She'd waited too long to experience it.

Turning around, Bailey quickly headed him off before he could open his mouth. "Thank you."

Munro removed his mask and let it dangle about his neck. He looked at her as if she'd lapsed into Chinese. Bailey had obviously caught him off guard. It added to her sensation of triumph.

Recovering smoothly, Munro shrugged away her thanks. But rather than say something cutting or sarcastic, he floored her by nodding toward the surgical waiting area. "Why don't you go and tell Dylan Wynters's wife that her husband's going to be all right?"

Bailey could readily understand not wanting to have to tell a family member if the operation had gone badly. No one wanted to be the bearer of bad news, not even, she suspected, Munro. But why wouldn't the man want to be the one to deliver the good news? Gratitude, especially when merited, was a heady thing.

"Don't you want to do that?"

"If I wanted to do that, DelMonico, I would. Now be a good girl and do as you're told."

His words were a diversion from the point. She had no intention of rising to the bait. By now, she'd been around the man long enough to form her own opinion, independent of any of the talk that made the rounds of the hospital. Other than when he was operating on patients in the O.R., Munro avoided as much contact with them and their families as humanly possible. The handful of times she'd been around when he'd been forced to interact with either group, she'd been struck by how curt, how removed, he'd sounded.

"Why don't you like talking to patients?"

More questions. He'd known from the first that this one was going to be trouble. "Because I don't see the point."

The answer was so simple, she didn't understand why he didn't see it. "The point is that you might make them feel better."

He snorted at the very idea. "I don't care about talking to them so that they can 'feel' better. I'm here to *make* them better," he informed her with emphasis. "All I care about is getting the patient well, not making their Christmas card list."

Didn't the man have a heart at all? "You can't mean that."

She could have sworn there was pity in his eyes when he looked at her. "Trust me, I mean that. Now if you don't want to talk to Mrs. Wynters, I can get Springer or Hall to—"

"No." She held up her hand like a patrolman to stop him. "I'll be glad to talk to her." She smiled warmly at him, knowing it drove him crazy. He hated what he thought was irrational behavior. "And thank you again."

Ivan mumbled something as he waved her away. She caught herself thinking, as she watched him walk away, that his shoulders seemed to look broader somehow.

The next moment, she was hurrying off on feet that barely touched the floor to see Mrs. Wynters.

CHAPTER 13

It was just beginning to mist as Bailey let herself into the house she shared with Jennifer and Adam. Southern California's rainy season was more than several months away, but on occasion rain did make an appearance during the late spring and summer months. She sincerely hoped not. She liked these days of eternal sunshine, even if she was indoors, at the hospital for most of them.

Adam was sitting on the sofa. A sitcom was on the TV, but it didn't seem to hold his attention.

He looked in her direction and came to life. "There's a rumor going around that Ivan the Terrible finally let you hold something sharp and pointy in the O.R.—and actually use it."

Bailey grinned broadly. It was more than half an hour past the end of her shift and she still hadn't come down from her high. Bailey shook off the damp drops the mist had left on her hair.

"The rumor is absolutely true," she informed Adam happily. "He did and I did."

"He really let you operate?" Jennifer asked in awe, walking in from the kitchen. Her arms were loaded down with what looked like bags of every kind of snack food known to man.

Bailey raised a tempering finger in the air before her roommates could get carried away. "Munro let me make an incision," she corrected. Disappointment creased Adam's face. "Hey, it's a start."

Adam spread his hands wide to underscore his innocence. "I never said anything," he protested.

About to continue her story, Bailey stopped, her attention drawn to the large pile of individual-size bags that Jennifer had just deposited on the coffee table. Packs of chips, pretzels, cookies, various nuts littered the dull wooden surface. "What *is* all this?"

Jennifer was trying to bite her way into a bag, yanking at one corner with her teeth. The bag resisted tearing. "Food."

There was a better word to describe it. "Junk," Bailey contradicted.

Jennifer grew defensive. "I need to keep my energy up."

Bailey shook her head. After dropping her purse on the floor beside the coffee table, she shed her jacket and draped it on the back of the sofa. "You'll be dead before your residency is up," she countered. "You're a doctor, you ought to know that."

Adam had helped himself to a bag of nuts and tossed back a handful. "The shoemaker's children go barefoot," he quipped, chewing.

Hand clenched into a fist at her waist, Jennifer looked down at him and challenged, "And what's *that* supposed to mean?"

"I dunno." His thin shoulders rose and fell beneath his sweater. Five-eight and reed-thin, the neonatal resident looked even smaller than he was. "It sounded like it fit here."

There was only one way around this salt, sugar and fat fest. Ordinarily, she came home so tired, she latched onto anything to appease her hunger. But not tonight. "I'll make dinner," Bailey volunteered, heading toward the kitchen.

Adam craned his neck, looking after her as Bailey disappeared into the other room. "You can do that with what's in there?"

Already at the refrigerator, Bailey held the door open as she looked inside and took inventory. It wasn't a process that required much time. There was a carton of eggs, half depleted, a near-empty container of milk approximately a day away from turning. An untouched bag of spinach that had been purchased with excellent intentions but was presently in the process of wilting. Alone with sprouted eyes, there was some margarine in the butter compartment as well as some margarine *on* the butter compartment.

"Yup, I can do that," Bailey assured him. She had more than enough to work with. Ever since she was a little girl, she had always loved to cook and liked nothing better than having her creativity challenged.

Bailey took out the apron she'd stuffed in the tiny closet beneath the sink and tied it around her waist. Prepared, she cleared off the counter, ready to begin.

Adam had drifted in behind her and watched as she reached for the cutting board she'd bought the first week she'd moved in. "God, I'm glad you answered Jenny's ad," he told her. "Our last roommate was totally useless in the kitchen."

"Like you," Jennifer laughed, leaning her head in as she stood on the other side of the threshold.

"And you," Adam shot back defensively.

"Children, children." Bailey raised her voice to abort any squabble that threatened to erupt. "If you guys have all this extra energy, I could use someone to peel the potatoes." She set the potatoes down on the counter and looked from Adam to Jennifer.

Since he was closest to her, Adam sighed and took a knife out of the utensil drawer. Gathering the potatoes together against his chest, he deposited them into the sink and slowly began peeling.

As she chopped the prepacked spinach, Bailey glanced covertly into the sink to make sure that it was clean. Adam had a way of being oblivious to things and he could have just as easily dropped the potatoes into a dirty pot waiting to be washed. Fortunately, the only thing in the sink was the potatoes.

"So how was it?" Adam pressed. "Your first time," he added since the question seemed to have come out of nowhere.

Bailey raised an eyebrow in his direction, amused. "I'm assuming that you're still talking about the incision." Her words were punctuated by rhythmic chopping as her chef's knife hit the wooden block.

Adam grinned at her wickedly. Finished with one potato, he picked up another one. "Unless you want to tell me about your 'other' first time."

"Pass," Bailey declared. Deciding that she needed to put things into proper perspective for Adam, she began to give him a little background. "I went into Munro's office this morning—"

Adam shivered. He picked up a third potato and slanted a look in her direction. "Is that anything like Daniel walking into the lion's den?"

"No." Thanks to her parents, she knew every single story in the Bible backward and forward. Before she'd left to come to the States the first time, she'd taught Bible stories to the younger native children. "In the morning of the next day, the lions were rendered harmless and friendly. I don't think either term could be used in the same sentence with Munro."

He looked at her, puzzled. "So why did you go see him? Did he send for you?"

"No." Finished chopping, she began cracking the six eggs, depositing whites and yolks into a large bowl. "I went in on my own," she explained. "To ask Munro to let me *do* something in the operating room besides take root in the floor."

Adam's mouth dropped open and he narrowly avoided slicing his thumb. "You said that to him?"

"Not in those words," she admitted, "but that was the general gist."

"And he said yes?" Adam asked incredulously. As far as anyone knew, the chief neurosurgeon never paid attention to the wishes of anyone, let alone a resident, which to him was only a slightly higher life form than a single-cell amoeba. "Damn, Bailey, but you've got guts."

She poured the milk into the bowl and then began beating the mixture, adding a dash of paprika and then another. She didn't want Adam getting the wrong idea. "Munro didn't say yes when I made my request."

On his next-to-last potato, Adam seemed clearly confused. "But you just said he let you cut."

"He did." Having set the scene, she stopped mixing, took a dramatic breath and continued. "Just when I thought I'd never get a chance to do anything, Munro calls my name and tells me to come over to the operating table." She took another breath, a deeper one. "And then he told me to make the first incision."

"How did it feel?" Adam asked eagerly, repeating his initial query.

"Like, for five seconds, I was God."

Setting down the whisk, Bailey closed her eyes for a moment.

She could see the whole thing transpiring all over again, could feel the magnificent surge that overtook her in the operating room.

"It was just the most incredible, indescribable feeling. I can see why surgeons can get so full of themselves," she confessed. "It can happen without you even realizing it." She looked down at her right hand. The hand that had held the scalpel. "It's all there, the power of life and death, right there in their hands." She shook her head. "I don't know how I lived the first half of my life not realizing that I wanted to do this. To move along the giants."

Bailey looked at Adam to see if he understood what she was saying, but Adam's attention had been diverted. He was looking at the contents of the bowl that she had been beating. Picking up the almost-empty container of flavored bread crumbs, she added them to the mix, then deposited the spinach in, as well. She could almost read the thoughts going through his head. His hunger was obviously bigger than his interest in her story.

"It's going to be an omelet," she told him, not bothering to hide her amusement.

Adam looked from the bowl to the potatoes sitting among the peels in the sink. His imagination did not lean toward the creative. "With potatoes?"

"Hash browns," she corrected—and was rewarded with a wide, beaming smile.

Taking out a smattering of olive oil, she coated the bottom of the drying pan she'd placed on the stove. The everyday, with its needs and requirements, had clearly trumped glimmers of godliness, she mused, turning up the burner.

CHAPTER 14

It was another full two weeks before Bailey got a second opportunity to take part in surgery. Two weeks and one day.

She had a strong feeling that Ivan the Terrible was testing her. He had to be amusing himself by waiting for her to ask him to let her do something again. Depending on her mood and level of frustration, Bailey wavered between waiting him out and asking him to let her do something surgical again.

After all, the last time she'd asked, Munro *had* ultimately allowed her to take part in the surgery he was performing. Granted, it had been just the tiniest part, but every journey, her father was fond of pointing out, began with the first step, however small.

After mentally sparring with herself for the duration of the two weeks and one day, Bailey decided to go back into "the lion's den" to corner her mentor. But just as she'd made up her mind to head to his office in the hope of catching him, Munro stepped out of the elevator, right into her line of vision.

It was fate, she was sure of it. She opened her mouth, but his words came out.

"Scrub up, DelMonico," he barked as he walked past her. "It's showtime."

It took her a second to mentally change gears. She hurried after him. "Excuse me?"

"Showtime," he repeated, tossing the word over his shoulder. "Are you familiar with the term?"

In the beginning, she would have said his tone contained an air of superiority, but now she realized it was just his way of talking. He wasn't actively trying to belittle her.

"Yes, but—"

Not waiting for his resident albatross to finish her sentence, he elaborated, "It's a euphemism for 'you're on.'"

Catching up, Bailey had fallen into step with the chief neurosurgeon, still not completely sure where she was going. Guarded hope slowly sprouted within her.

Munro had had her studying MRI films of a man who had been brought to the hospital by ambulance from one of the few remaining farm fields that were still in Southern Orange County.

"Man versus tractor," Munro had announced dryly when he had handed her the films earlier. "Tractor won the first round."

By that he'd meant that the man had fallen off his tractor and through the macabre machinations of hard-hearted fate, had his hand severed by the same tractor.

Severed, but not mashed.

Packed in ice, it, along with the injured farmhand, had been quickly rushed to Blair Memorial amid flashing lights, sirens and squealing tires. His screams transcended them all until the paramedic gave him something to temporarily knock him out.

"On what?" Bailey asked the neurosurgeon, biting back impatience. Why couldn't he talk like a normal person instead of making her feel like she was blindfolded, feeling her way around an abyss?

Ivan Munro probably liked making people jump through

hoops, liked being in control and keeping everyone off balance and in the dark. "Keep 'em guessing" had probably been embroidered on the field of his family crest.

"On the hot seat, on center stage, on—fill in the blank," he told her with an indifferent shrug. And then he grunted. "Phillips had the audacity and utter ill manners to come down with the flu," he told her, referring to a fourth-year resident. "He claims he's too weak to stand up and assist. The slacker's probably too germ-laden to come within fifty feet of the O.R."

Bailey pressed her lips together. She wasn't about to get her hopes up just to have them dashed again. She wasn't about to give Munro the satisfaction. Struggling to keep up, she hazarded a guess. "And you want me to find someone?"

"I want you to *be* someone," Munro corrected impatiently, and then he stopped. He looked at her as if he thought her suddenly obtuse. "Do I have to spell it out for you?"

Bailey completely surprised him by nodding and saying, "Please."

For a second he looked as if he was just going to walk away, and then Munro appeared to think better of it. "Suit up, DelMonico, I need you to be one of my assistants."

She wanted this to be absolutely clear. "In the operating room?"

"No." His voice was saccharine-sweet and utterly sarcastic. "By the sink outside the O.R. I want you to wash my hands for me." He returned to his regular raspy tone. "Yes, in the operating room." And then he leveled one of his all-penetrating looks at her, the one she swore X-rayed her very bones. "Unless, of course, you're not up to it."

Oh God, he was serious. He was letting her assist. Assist!

"I'm up to it," she cried, clutching his arm without realizing it. "I'm up to it."

He looked down at her hand. Realizing she was clutching, she dropped her hand to her side.

"A little louder, DelMonico. I don't think they heard you in Seattle."

Bailey pretended to take in a deep breath. Holding it, she offered, "I can shout louder."

He closed his eyes for a second, as if searching for patience. When he opened them again, he shook his head. "There's no reason to get excited, DelMonico. It's just a severed hand."

"But it's my first severed hand." She made no effort to hide her eagerness. There were going to be a myriad of nerve endings to reattach and if anyone could get the poor man's hand to work again, it was Munro. He was every bit as good as he thought he was—and she was going to get to assist.

For once, Munro seemed mildly amused. "I'd wish you many more, but that sounds a little ghoulish, even for me."

So he *was* aware of his reputation, she thought. There were times that she wasn't sure. Other times, she was certain he was completely oblivious to the dark shadow he cast.

Her mind going in a million directions at once, like a shower of confetti at a ticker tape parade, Bailey heard herself asking, "How long do you think it'll take?"

The question obviously took him aback. "Why? You have some place to be?"

"No, oh, no," Bailey quickly cried, just in case the chief neurosurgeon used that to suddenly fabricate a reason not to use her, after all. "I was just curious, that's all."

"Killed the cat, you know," Munro replied flippantly, then

glanced down at her feet. "Make sure you wear comfortable shoes." It was the only form of answer he gave her.

The surgery was going to be long, she concluded. *Really* long. Rather than daunting, she found the thought exhilarating.

This was what she'd signed on for, the life-altering surgeries.

"Right away, sir," she told him, promptly turning on her heel and starting to hurry away. The locker room was at the end of the corridor. Happy enough to burst, she began to hum.

Munro snorted. Raising his voice, he called after her. "DelMonico."

She stopped in midstep and swung around, grinning from ear to ear like a child who had been told that there would be two Christmases this year. "Yes, sir?"

"You're humming, DelMonico." The chief neurosurgeon said it as if it was an offense that merited public flogging as punishment.

"I know, sir."

His eyes narrowed, dark eyebrows forming an even darker single line. "Stop it."

The grin on the resident's face appeared to grow wider. He didn't think that was possible. And her eyes were twinkling. Twinkling, for God's sake. And why the hell did that look so damn attractive?

"Yes, sir." The humming stopped. The grinning did not.

In a strange sort of way she was getting to him, and he didn't like it. Moreover, he wouldn't tolerate it. "And for God's sake, DelMonico, stop being so damn cheerful."

"Yes, sir." She did her best to wipe the smile off her face. And failed. She lifted her shoulders in a helpless gesture. "I can't help it, sir."

Ivan crossed to her, lowering his voice. It was all the more lethal for the lack of volume. "This is a serious surgery, Del-Monico. We are not going in there, skipping."

Bailey pressed her lips together, trying to blot out her smile. "I know it's a serious surgery, Doctor. I have no intentions of skipping."

"But you're not going to stop smiling," he guessed with what Bailey took to be more than just a touch of disgust.

She didn't bother telling him that she couldn't help it. "The mask'll cover that, sir," she promised.

"Make sure you put it on immediately," he ordered, then added, "And have Jessop bring the films into the operating room."

Bailey nodded, eager to comply. She was assisting. Hell had frozen over and she was assisting. She could call the intern from the lockers. "Anything else, Doctor?"

"Yes," he said icily, giving her another one of those looks that was meant to pin her to the wall. "Don't screw up."

No pressure here, she thought.

"I won't." And then, since he was looking at her, she crossed her heart and held up her hand as if she were taking an oath.

"Damn straight you won't," he growled as he turned away. He still had a call to make before the surgery. "It'll make me look bad."

"Can't have that, sir," she declared cheerfully before she disappeared into the locker room.

She didn't hear what he said in response. It was better that way for all concerned.

CHAPTER 15

The operation was grueling.

As hour melted into hour, it felt as if they had been in the operating room forever. Bailey marveled at the way the chief neurosurgeon remained so unshakably focused.

Typically, surgeries of this nature were shared, with one main neurosurgeon in charge. The other surgeons divided up the time each stood over the patient to join together the crucial, hairlike nerves that would, if done correctly, return feeling and movement to the patient's hand.

Whether Munro did not have enough faith in his team or felt a commitment to do most of the incredibly delicate surgery himself, Bailey couldn't tell. All she knew was that she was in awe of not only his concentration, but his stamina, as well. There had been no break, no stopping of the clock.

He was like a machine, a well-oiled precision machine.

She was also convinced that the head neurosurgeon at Blair Memorial had either forgotten about her or had decided that she was there simply as window dressing. He hadn't even looked her way in the past three hours. She began to believe that Ivan Munro was one of those extremely old-fashioned surgeons who took assistant surgeons into the operating room with him to be present in case he suddenly unaccountably collapsed, or had a heart attack, and was unable to complete his surgery.

If it wasn't for the cold temperature in the operating room, Bailey had an unnerving feeling that she would have fallen asleep on her feet, especially since she had just put in an eighteen-hour shift the day before.

"Think you can handle this one, DelMonico?"

The sound of his raspy voice jolted her out of her all-but-hypnotic stupor. Suddenly, all systems were go. Blood came rushing to her face, the product of an overexerting heart that had been startled into her throat.

Bailey blinked and stared at the chief neurosurgeon. The quiet operating room became even more of a tomb.

All eyes were on her.

"Sir?" she questioned, grateful that her voice hadn't squeaked.

Munro slanted am infinitesimal glance in her direction. "Falling asleep over there, DelMonico?"

"No. No, sir," Bailey answered with feeling, the volume of her voice growing with each word. She took a deep, somewhat limited breath beneath her surgical mask. Nerves jumped inside of her like dolphins playing leapfrog in the water.

"Glad to hear that." His voice was so dry, it could have broken in two. "I repeat, think you can handle this one?"

Bailey had no idea what he was referring to. "This one?" she echoed.

"This nerve. Do you think—if it's still within your limited power to think—that you can attach this nerve to its severed section?" he clarified.

She could visualize Munro clenching his brilliant white teeth beneath the blue mask.

Ivan stepped to the side just enough for her to see which of the isolated tiny nerve endings he was referring to. Threads were thick in comparison.

Fear gave way to excitement.

"Yes, sir," Bailey assured him with enthusiasm that only made the chief neurosurgeon shake his head.

"You're reattaching a nerve, DelMonico, not shouting out a cheer at a pep rally," he chided, but his tone was not as rough as it could be. "All right." Munro stepped back even further, his hands raised. "Show me."

"Yes, sir," Bailey repeated in a slightly more subdued tone.

Taking the instruments Munro had been using from him, Bailey stepped into his space. As she breathed deeply, she looked down. The patient was completely draped, except for his left forearm and the hand that they were reattaching to it. Through the benefit of the magnifying lenses imposed on top of the glasses she'd been given to wear, Bailey could see the minute whisper of a nerve she'd been challenged with.

Her hands didn't feel as if they were going to shake this time.

Thank God for small miracles, she thought as she began.

Time seemed to stand still, as did her heart.

Ordinarily, she would have been aware of Munro looking over her shoulder, standing on top of her shadow. But this time, she was so focused on what she was doing, on taking care that she did not "screw up," that all she saw were the two ends of the nerves that needed to be reunited and nothing more.

It was almost as if she were standing outside her own body.

Bailey watched as the nerve was reattached the same way she'd watched Munro reattach the other nerves. Except that this time, she was the one whose hand was holding the minute needle.

In what seemed like both an eternity and a blink of an eye, Bailey completed her assignment.

"Nicely done, DelMonico," Munro said. He reclaimed his instruments. Bailey eyed him, so happy she thought she was going to cry. "Glad to see that you didn't disappoint Dr. Bennett. He has such high hopes for you."

Bailey stepped back, moving like someone in a dream, a heady, mind-spinning exhilaration. Her heart began to beat again, hammering so hard she hardly heard anything else being said in the O.R. for the next five minutes. Part of her was surprised she didn't shoot out shafts of blinding light.

"GOD, EVEN WHEN HE GIVES you a compliment, he doesn't," Wayne Murphy, the other assistant surgeon, was grumbling as he removed his mask. He seemed clearly annoyed for her sake.

The patient had just been wheeled out after an exceptionally long surgery and Murphy, along with the rest of the operating room staff, was stiff and less than congenial.

In case she'd missed the intent of his comment, Murphy looked directly at Bailey.

"Nice touch, Bailey," Christina Nuygen, the anesthesiologist, told her with an approving smile. "You're a natural."

Because she was careful not to seem like too much of a novice around the others, Bailey tried to curb her enthusiasm. But it wasn't easy when she felt like running to the nearest rooftop and shouting. Besides, just because she'd reattached the nerve didn't mean that the feeling would return. That was going to take time and physical therapy to accomplish. A great deal of physical therapy.

So instead she met the kind words with a smile. "We'll see

how it goes. Hopefully, the patient'll regain full use of his hand."

Murphy rotated his neck.

"If he doesn't, it's not going to be your fault. That 'honor' will belong exclusively to the almighty Ivan the Terrible." When he frowned, Murphy's fair complexion turned a shade of angry red. "He hogged most of the operation."

She'd been annoyed with the chief neurosurgeon herself more times than she could count, but hearing him put down this way made her feel defensive for him. "That's because Munro's the best."

"Probably has something to do with the fact that he has a scalpel for a heart," one of the surgical nurses theorized.

The others laughed, agreeing. A few other equally sharp instruments were suggested, as well. A Munro-bashing session got under way, alleviating some of the tension they had all been under.

Bailey stopped listening and hurriedly changed into another set of scrubs. The surgeons' locker was directly on the other side. She wondered if Munro could hear them. Did it feed his ego in some perverse way, or did these comments hurt? If it was her, she'd know the answer to that. But, admittedly, Munro was like no other man she'd ever met.

Bailey no longer knew if that was a good or a bad thing.

She did know that Munro had rounds in a few minutes and she didn't want to miss them. There was no question in her mind that the chief neurosurgeon wouldn't wait for her.

As she quickly slipped on her shoes and tied them, it amazed her how she felt so compelled to take Munro's side when he was at times the devil incarnate.

She supposed that even the devil deserved his due and Munro might have been the perfect candidate to ask the wizard for a heart, but he didn't need brains or skill.

Heart still pounding from her experience, Bailey straightened her tunic as she hurried out of the locker room—and walked smack into the devil himself.

The devil was frowning.

CHAPTER 16

The unexpected bodily contact sent a hot surge through her. Bailey sucked in her breath as she took a step back. Munro had grabbed her shoulders to prevent her from falling backward, dropping his cache of folders in the process.

He released her as if his fingertips had gotten burned. "Do you have any idea how many accidents are caused by running?"

"Haven't a clue, Doctor." On the floor, Bailey quickly retrieved the fallen folders and rose again, offering them back to him. "Sorry."

His scowl didn't abate as he accepted the folders. "Sorry that you haven't a clue or sorry that you were running?"

Why did he make everything sound as if her very survival at Blair depended on her right answer to the question? "Both if it pleases you."

He glanced through the folders and reorganized them. "What would please me is if my resident wouldn't constantly come off like some addle-brained Pollyanna every time she opened her mouth."

She raised her chin and he could see the flash of annoyance in her eyes. Then he watched in mild fascination as it subsided. The woman had good control, he thought.

"I'll work on it, sir," Bailey promised.

He began walking again, and she fell into step beside him. Munro addressed his comment to the air. "Probably won't succeed."

"Probably," she agreed.

She had a feeling she'd surprised him. His jawline had grown less rigid. Maybe he was even in a favorable mood. After all, the surgery seemed a success. At least all the nerves had been reattached. That didn't always happen. Sometimes they were too damaged no matter how skilled the neurosurgeon was. She imagined that Munro didn't take those kinds of defeats well.

Bailey took a deep breath. "Thank you for letting me assist."

Munro snorted, but didn't bother looking at her. "I had no choice."

Now that she didn't believe. "You always have a choice, Dr. Munro."

The neurosurgeon abruptly stopped walking and glared at her. Bailey couldn't read his expression this time any more than the other times.

But then he nodded. He seemed to like the idea that she thought of him as a man who couldn't be ordered around. Or easily *gotten* around.

"Yes, I suppose I do." He had no idea why, but he felt as if he needed to give her an explanation as to why he'd used her. Maybe because he sensed she'd go on asking until she had an answer. "Bennett holds you in high esteem, for some reason. Not to use you would be an insult to him."

Though he didn't admit it to himself, Ivan watched her smile unfurl with interest. "Wouldn't want to offend Dr. Bennett."

Munro inclined his head. "Not without a good reason."

It suddenly hit her like a ton of bricks. They were getting along. She didn't want this to be a one-time thing. Which meant she needed him to admit, if only subconsciously, that he didn't mind her company. It would make working together so much better.

"Um, Doctor, after we finish with the rounds…" She faltered just a little.

Munro turned down a corridor. The ICU was at the very end. "Yes?"

Her courage flagging, Bailey tried again. "Would you like to get a cup of coffee at the café?"

He eyed her suspiciously. "Why? Because I let you take a stitch in time and now we're compadres? Amigos? Buddies?"

There was contempt within each word. But she was determined not let him make her back away. "Um, no. Because I always see you alone and I thought you might want company."

Damn, maybe he'd made a mistake, after all. She was obviously one of those people who, if you gave them an inch, they took a mile and tried to build a shopping mall on it. "If I want company, I'll tell you."

Bailey shook her head and smiled at him. She'd learned a few things in the last few months. "No, you won't."

They'd reached the Intensive Care Unit. Munro pressed a large button on the side and the double doors sprang open. Rather than enter the area where his first patient lay, the neurosurgeon looked down at his resident instead. "What did you just say?"

Her hands still weren't shaking, but everything inside her was. However, she'd come too far to back off. Besides, she believed in what she was saying. Munro was a loner and she was convinced that no one was happy being alone.

"I said 'No, you won't.'"

Ivan narrowed his eyes. To his growing displeasure, she didn't seem as if she was afraid of him. Just what he needed, a resident with guts.

"I had no idea that Mind Reading 101 was on the course agenda for this semester. Because if it is," he continued, leaning over her, his voice growing lower and raspier, "and this is a demonstration of your abilities, you, my little-resident-that-could, are in danger of flunking the course."

She stood her ground, keeping her voice as low as his. Aware that they were attracting the attention of the ICU nurses. "You're always lashing out at everyone."

"Did you ever stop to think that maybe everyone needs to be lashed out at?" he suggested.

"And maybe you think you need to keep everyone back."

"Good answer," he congratulated her. "Except for the word 'think.' I don't 'think' I need to keep everyone, with their humdrum problems, back. I *know* I need to keep them back."

"Why? Because you're afraid you'll let someone get too close?"

Munro took her completely aback when he said, "Yes." But then he returned to the colors he enjoyed displaying to the world. "Because when people get close, they suddenly feel compelled to share the most intimate, boring parts of their lives. I don't have time to get nauseous on a regular basis."

The man was a master at put-downs, but she wasn't buying it. There was a heart inside there, there *had* to be. She knew for a fact that he wasn't in it for the money. What had first caught her attention about him was the large donation he'd sent to the clinic where her parents had brought some of the native children. A man didn't give away money like that if there wasn't compassion at the core.

"I think it's for another reason."

"News flash," Munro announced harshly. "In case you've forgotten, what you 'think,' DelMonico, doesn't interest me." And then, just as she braced herself for him to come down really hard on her, the neurosurgeon said, "What you do, however, does. You did a good job in the O.R." She looked at him, wide-eyed. "You have, as they say, 'potential.' Do yourself and everyone else, especially me, a favor and don't screw it up by trying to play psychiatrist.

"Now, are you ready?" He didn't wait for her response, but merely declared, "Good," and walked ahead of her to do the part of his job that he purely disliked. Interacting with the recovering patient.

With any luck, Ivan thought as he approached the first bed, the patient would be asleep. If that occurred, he never bothered to wake said patient. After all, everything he needed to know was written down on the chart.

But to Munro's dismay, as he picked up the patient's chart from where it was hanging at the foot of the bed, he saw that his resident was gently shaking the patient awake.

Munro clamped his hand down on hers, drawing Bailey away. "What the hell do you think you're doing?" he snapped.

"Waking up the patient. You can't find out how he's doing if he's asleep."

"There are nurses' notes for that," Munro informed her tersely. "They are a fairly competent lot here at Blair as far as nurses go."

But it was too late. The patient was opening his eyes. In his late forties and not exactly at his best in a blue-and-white floral hospital gown, the patient seemed confused. He shifted his eyes from the neurosurgeon to the woman next to him.

Bailey smiled at the man in the bed. "How are you doing this evening, Mr. LaRue?"

Henry LaRue attempted to return a smile in kind. It was a weak effort at best, but he brightened at the attention and the question. "You tell me. They said that they got the tumor."

"They did," she told him with enthusiasm. Then, remembering her promise, she sobered just a touch. "That is, Dr. Munro did," she clarified, nodding at the tall, scowling man beside her.

LaRue glanced in the neurosurgeon's direction, then back at Bailey. "Doesn't look very happy about it," he observed weakly.

"Oh, but he is," Bailey assured the man with feeling, forgetting herself. That was the second time today she'd felt protective of Munro. As if the man needed someone to take up his cause, she upbraided herself. "That's Dr. Munro's happy face."

The patient's bushy brown eyebrows drew together. "How can you tell?"

"There're no furrow down between his eyes," she confided.

She saw her answer brought a mild look of surprise to Munro's face. *That* she could read.

Enough was enough, Ivan thought. He didn't have time to watch an episode of *Scrubs*. "Any complaints, Mr. LaRue?" he asked the patient pointedly.

The man in the bed moved his bandaged head slowly from side to side, as if to prove what he was about to say. "Headaches are gone. I'm a new man."

Ivan shut the chart he was holding. "Not quite," he responded. "But what you are is able to go home in a couple of days. As long as you make sure you don't overdo things for a while," Ivan added. He looked pointedly at Bailey just before he walked out. "Any comments or things you'd like to add, Dr. Del-Monico?"

Stunned, her mouth dropped opened. "No."

"Well, hallelujah for that," Ivan declared, walking out.

CHAPTER 17

Bailey didn't remember walking out of the area. One minute she was inside Henry LaRue's ICU room, the next she was standing outside it, dazed as she watched at Munro's departing back.

"Doctor." The title left her lips in a stunned, awed whisper.

The chief neurosurgeon stopped walking. She could see by the set of his shoulders that he wasn't in a patient mood, but then endless hours of surgery would do that to a person. Not that Ivan Munro was exactly famous for his patience.

"What?" he demanded irritably without bothering to turn around.

Bailey hurried to join him. "No," she corrected, "you called me 'doctor.'" Munro had told her that he would be the one to tell her when she was a doctor and at the time, she pretty much assumed that was his way of putting her down. She also was certain he would never affix that title to her. That he had almost made her feel giddy.

For a second, Ivan debated telling her that it had been nothing more than a thoughtless slip of the tongue, but he didn't believe in lying. There was no need for lies in a world that was cruelty itself. Most of the time, just telling the truth was harsh enough. Still, he had to admit, despite his negative view of life, seeing this young woman all but glowing from head to foot made it difficult for him not to smile.

"I told you I'd let you know when you were a doctor and despite being a major pain in the butt around patients, Del-Monico, you did perform admirably well in the O.R. today." He shrugged carelessly. "Probably a fluke, but for the time being, you've earned the right to be called 'doctor.'" He narrowed his eyebrows. "Now, any other annoying questions?"

She beamed so hard, he thought she was going to float down the hall like some maniacal pixie.

"None, sir."

Ivan rolled his eyes dramatically, as if savoring relief. "Thank God." And then he placed the next folder on top. "Patient number two," he announced. Just before entering the next room, he stopped abruptly. "And this time, if he's asleep, Del-Monico, I'd appreciate it if you *leave him that way*."

She grinned and it annoyed him that he found it much too distracting. "Leave sleeping patients lie?" she asked whimsically.

"Works for me," he declared, moving ahead of her into the tiny room.

CAUTIOUSLY, Bailey peered into the room.

Munro was still in his office, working. Immersed in a book that was half as thick as she was tall.

For a future surgery? she wondered. She had no idea. Behind her, some of the lights had dimmed. It was the hospital's way of trying to economize in a world where expenses always spun out of control.

Holding her breath, she ventured into the quiet office, all but crossing the room on her tiptoes so as to not disturb the neurosurgeon. She placed one of the two tall containers of coffee she held in the center of his desk, then slowly began to withdraw.

She managed to take two steps in retreat.

Suspicious brown eyes suddenly looked up at her, pinning her into place as effectively as if she were a butterfly immobilized on a corkboard.

"What's this?" Munro nodded at the container.

"Coffee, Doctor. From across the street."

Still holding his place in the vast tome, Ivan turned the container around to face him so that he could see the logo. Round Three, the coffee shop liked to call itself.

"Like throwing your money away? That coffee is three times as expensive as the coffee they sell at the hospital."

"It's also three times as good," she pointed out. He merely snorted. "Don't worry, you don't have to drink it with me," she told him, beginning to back out again.

His voice halted her in her tracks. "Sit down," he barked out.

She did as she was told, perching more than sitting on the lone chair that faced his desk.

After marking his place, Ivan closed the medical reference book and moved it aside, then reached for the coffee. He took the lid off to inspect what he'd been offered. It passed muster. He leaned back in his chair and regarded her for a long moment, as if trying to decide if she were fish or fowl.

"I think you've been sent to Blair Memorial for the sole purpose of annoying me," he said.

She grinned. Her hands wrapped around the container, she took a long, deep sip. "I've picked up on that."

Ivan took a long sip of his own. He wanted to dislike the

coffee. Wanted to, but couldn't. It was decent. More than decent, it was good and he knew good from sludge. The latter was what he normally consumed here at the hospital.

Briefly, he regarded the paper container, then looked at the woman who had brought it to him. He tried to second-guess her. "If you're thinking of bribing your way into another surgery, Del-Monico," he warned, "you should know that—"

Bailey shook her head, cutting him off. "No bribe," she assured him vehemently. She shrugged casually, as if her doing this was the most common thing in the world, something she'd done countless times instead of just once. "I just thought you might want some coffee since you were working late."

He took another sip before asking, "And how would you know that I was working late?" His eyes were looking right into her soul. "Spying on me, DelMonico?"

"You always work late. Everyone knows that." She raised her eyes to his. "People say you have no home."

He seemed mildly entertained. "Is that what people say?"

She couldn't tell if he was actually interested in the gossip that made the rounds, or if he was just mocking her. Her hands tightened around the container for warmth. "Some people."

Ivan leaned over his desk, managing to cut away the distance even though his chair remained where it was. He fixed her with an intent gaze. "And what is it that you say?"

She didn't hesitate, didn't try to buy herself some time by taking another long sip of coffee. "That you're dedicated."

It earned her a dry laugh and a reprieve. Munro leaned back in his chair, never taking his eyes off her. "Unlike some of my esteemed colleagues, I don't like someone who kisses up, Del-Monico."

She wasn't dumb enough to attempt to flatter him. The only thing that worked with Munro was the truth. "That's not possible with you, Doctor. I'd be in danger of having my lips cut off."

This time, when he laughed, it wasn't a harsh sound. She'd succeeded in amusing him. "Wouldn't want that, would we?" It wasn't a question that needed an answer. "As far as lips go," he told her, looking away as he took another sip, "they're a nice set."

Had there been the slightest breeze in the room, she would have fallen off her chair.

Bailey stared at the chief neurosurgeon as if she'd never seen him before. He noticed her lips? Dear Lord, did that mean Munro thought of her as a person? Had she actually succeeded in making it to that rarefied level in his world?

It took her a few beats, but she finally found her voice. "Thank you. They serve their purpose," she mumbled self-consciously, not having a clue as to what else to say.

"And that is what?" he queried, his expression unreadable. "Flapping in the breeze?" As if to punctuate the question, he tossed the empty container into his overflowing wastebasket. It fell out and rolled over to her feet.

Bailey bent and picked it up, then deposited the container carefully back into the trash.

Well, that moment had been short-lived, she thought, sitting up again. Time to go. Ivan the Terrible was back. Or maybe, she amended, just the illusion of the persona Munro thought he was channeling. As far as she knew—and she had done a little research on the subject in the scarce moments she had to herself—the original Ivan the Terrible had not had any nice moments. Blair Memorial's version of the despotic monarch did. She'd just experienced one with him seconds ago.

"My lips don't flap," she told him, rising to her feet. "They're not that big."

Bailey was aware of his eyes as they took stock of her, of her face, especially her mouth. She would have said it was purely clinical, but—and this could have been because of the late hour and the fact that they were both tired—she could have sworn that there was something more there.

"No," Munro concluded quietly, agreeing, "they're not."

CHAPTER 18

The groan came from her very toes, working its way up through her body and gaining volume and feeling as it progressed.

Bailey had brought her hand down on the alarm clock so many times, she'd lost count. The last time with a less than friendly slam right down on the so-called snooze button. Had the clock not been in the center of the nightstand, the impact would have sent it falling to the floor.

Four o'clock in the morning was an ungodly time to get up. So regarded, Bailey groggily thought, because God didn't even get up until at least five-thirty. Which was ultimately the time she was shooting for, except that the alarm clock wouldn't play along.

Exhausted last night, she'd set it for the wrong time and now it refused to give her a longer reprieve than ten minutes. Each time she shut it off, it rang ten minutes later.

Bailey grew weary of playing slam-the-clock after her seventh or so round.

Dragging herself into an upright position, she tried to buoy her energy and stumble toward the shower. Time to wake up for yet another grueling day.

Instead of getting up, she fell back against her battered pillow.

Drops, propelled by the wind, threw themselves against her window. It was raining outside.

Dark and rainy. A perfect day to stay indoors, to stay in bed with the covers pulled up over her head. Maybe even for the next twenty-four hours.

She knew it wasn't possible, but that didn't stop her from wanting it. Wanting the blissful opiate of sleep and with it, oblivion.

They'd lost a patient yesterday.

Not she, personally, but she had experienced the engulfing horror of it by proxy.

Bailey stared at the ceiling, immobile.

She'd been beside Munro, acting as his assistant. That had meant standing by as he worked feverishly to stem the unexpected bleeding of a burst capillary in the brain. There was no stopping the bleeding and no amount of joules applied from the paddles that would restart the patient's heart.

The silent anguish within the operating room was palatable. Three hours into her operation, Mae Sullivan, mother of three, grandmother of five, was dead, leaving a hole in the universe.

Bailey had felt Munro's frustration. More, she'd felt his anger. Not at any of them but at the invisible force that had taken this patient from him. After it was over and Mae Sullivan was pronounced dead, she'd tried to talk to Munro but the chief neurosurgeon had walked past her as if she were nothing more than random molecules scattered in the air.

When she'd hurried after him, even as Alice Washburn, the senior surgical nurse, had told her to stop, she'd discovered that the neurosurgeon had gone straight to the lounge where Mae's family was waiting out the surgery.

She watched them all rise to their feet as if they were connected by some invisible cord. Seen their faces, fearful, hopeful.

And then Munro began talking.

He was short, precise, prefacing his message with a distant apology that barely registered before he delivered the fatal words. And then he withdrew. She'd glimpsed a pained look in his eyes as he'd passed her again.

Bailey had been torn between going after him and going to speak to the family herself. Not that she thought she had any magic words to offer that would assuage the pain when it came to the latter. But she thought of how her own family would have reacted if they'd lost one of their own.

It tilted the scales for her and she walked into the lounge rather than followed Munro. Both needed comforting, of that she was certain. But she was also certain that at least she stood a ghost of a chance accomplishing that with Mrs. Sullivan's family.

The odds of her getting through to Munro were abysmally low.

She'd told Mr. Sullivan and his older daughter about grief counseling available on the premises and held Mrs. Sullivan's oldest grandson, an eight-year-old boy named Shamus, who cried.

At a loss for an answer when the boy asked her, "Why?" she could at least offer sympathy and show the Sullivans that the hospital staff really did care about the patients.

She did her best.

And when she was done, Ivan Munro was nowhere to be found. She checked his office, she checked the operating room even though there was no earthly reason why he would be there. She even checked the ICU area, all without luck. The neurosurgeon was gone.

Briefly, she entertained the thought of going to his home, but she had no idea where that was and human resources—not that they would tell her if she asked—was closed for the day. So she took her good intentions and her heavy heart and went home.

It only occurred to her as she pulled into the slick driveway that there was one place at the hospital she hadn't tried. The hospital morgue. She didn't know why she thought of that location, but it was where Mrs. Sullivan had been placed until her family sent a mortician to pick up her body.

Located in the basement, the hospital morgue was a desolate place. Perfect for a man who had come face-to-face with someone else's mortality and had been unable to rescue them from it.

Munro was there, she thought with sudden certainty. But she was too tired to turn her car around to verify her theory.

Leaving her car parked outside, she walked through the mist to the front door and let herself in. Adam was out on a date and Jennifer had pulled a night shift at the hospital, so she was alone. Ordinarily, it wasn't a state she enjoyed, but this time, she welcomed it. Bailey took advantage of the peace and quiet by taking a long bubble bath. A very tall glass of wine accompanied her.

Somewhere in the middle of the night, the rain came in earnest, pouring down in proverbial buckets. Somehow, it seemed appropriate. She knew that Mrs. Sullivan would have approved.

Angels are crying.

Her father had told her that when they had attended the funeral of one of the other missionaries. She'd been six at the time and it had rained that day. She'd always liked that explanation.

The last thing Bailey thought before she'd drifted off to sleep, was that she hoped Ivan wasn't out walking in the deluge. It seemed like the type of thing he would do.

Sitting up again, Bailey struggled to banish sleep and the uncustomary blanket of depression from weighing down on her. She thought of Munro.

God knew she probably needed to have her head examined, feeling sorry for him. If the man had a heart—and the jury was still out about that—there was armor plating around it. She was wasting her time and her sympathy on him, time and sympathy that could best be applied somewhere else. A great many people would have welcomed her sympathy, patients and staff alike. Munro had made it perfectly clear by his actions that he wanted none of that, from her or from anyone else. The man was a self-contained fortress.

What the hell had made him that way? she couldn't help wondering as she quickly toweled herself off from her two-minute shower.

And why did she care?

If the tables were turned, Munro wouldn't care about anything going on in her life. He was right. She had to stop these Pollyanna tendencies she had.

She smirked at herself in the cloudy medicine cabinet mirror.

As if.

The knock on the bathroom door startled her and brought her back to her surroundings. Bailey sighed as she moved even more quickly. She should have gotten up when the alarm clock had first rung, not almost an hour later.

"Hang on. I'm almost done," she called. Her words were met with another, sharper knock. "Damn it, I only took two minutes in the shower. Hold your horses, Adam," she cried, knowing that the person on the other side of the door couldn't be Jennifer. The latter had stumbled in at two and from the sound of it, had fallen face-down on her bed. "I looked at the schedule on the refrigerator. You don't have to go in this morning until nine."

Despite the fact that there were three hours until nine, more than enough time to shower, shave and get to the hospital at a leisurely pace, there was another knock on the door.

Now she was getting annoyed. Funny how she'd never been like this before she'd started working with Munro. God forbid she turned into a miniature copy of him, Bailey thought in horror.

The fourth knock on the door had her huffing under her breath. Her hair still wet, she grabbed up her hair dryer, the football jersey she slept in and had discarded on the bathroom floor and her wet towel. Loaded down, she swung open the door.

"A little patience would be nice."

"I was just thinking the same thing," said the tall, good-looking visitor standing before her.

CHAPTER 19

The man before her grinned broadly. "You know, Dr. Del-Monico, I've been having this weird sort of pain radiating right here—"

He began to lift his shirt, but never got the opportunity either to complete the movement or to finish what he was saying. Swaddled in the bath towel that she had hastily wrapped around herself and secured just over her breasts, Bailey threw herself into her brother's arms, genuine surprise and pleasure registering on her face.

"Simon, what are you doing here?" she cried, overjoyed. The promised visit in the beginning of April had been postponed three times already. It was now September and she had all but given up hope of ever seeing him.

Her older brother laughed. "Right now, trying not to lose my balance and fall down." He was holding on to her even as he said it, trying to keep both of them from landing on the floor. Releasing her, he looked Bailey over. "I see that nothing dampens that enthusiasm of yours."

Unable to resist, he gave her a proper hug, squeezing hard. He wasn't ashamed to admit that he had missed her since she'd left all of them to strike out on her own. Releasing her a second time, he held her at arm's length. This time, he shook his head.

"You're so thin." And then the import of his words hit him. "God, I sound just like Mom. Sorry. But how have you been, Bay?"

She tried to catch her breath. Seeing him here like this had caught her completely off guard. "I'm not sure, I've been too busy to notice," she told him honestly. And then she frowned. There were things she would have done with some warning. "I thought you were going to call me first before you came."

His smile was wicked. "I decided it was more fun to catch you by surprise. Besides, if I had to postpone it again, I wouldn't have to hear your disappointment."

Now that her brain had cleared a little, questions assaulted her. She asked the most obvious one. "How did you get in?"

Simon nodded in the general direction of the stairs. "A very sleepy-looking guy in drooping pajama bottoms let me in. Didn't look too happy about answering the door." He looked at her for a second and tried to sound nonchalant as he asked, "Boyfriend?"

She almost laughed out loud. If anything, she regarded her male roommate as a cross between a little brother and a walking teddy bear. "No, that's Adam, one of the roommates I told you about."

Simon seemed visibly relieved. "For a minute there, I thought I was going to have to listen to your confession."

She laughed shortly. Always the big brother. She could easily see him as a minister. He'd always had a need to protect someone. "You're a minister, Simon. Confessions are for priests." She grinned at him affectionately. "Haven't they explained your duties to you?"

He moved his wide shoulders in a vague shrug. "I thought about broadening my base." Simon nodded at the large white towel. "Why don't you get dressed? I'll wait in the hall."

Simon's sudden appearance had thrown everything else out of her head. She'd forgotten she was wearing only a rectangle of slowly drooping terry cloth. "I'll just be five minutes."

He grinned, nodding at the time frame. "You always were fast."

But instead of shutting the bathroom door, Bailey paused for a second to hug him again. With even more feeling than before. "God, it is *so* good to see you again."

And then, letting go, she stepped back into the bathroom and shut the door.

Simon crossed his arms before him as he leaned against the wall beside the door. "So I'm forgiven for dunking you in the river?" he asked, raising his voice so it would carry through the wood.

Bailey knew exactly what he was talking about. She'd been twelve at the time. As he pushed her into the water, he claimed to be practicing for the responsibilities of the ministry he someday hoped to enter. But she had known better. A devout practical joker, Simon was just playing a prank on her, destroying her very carefully arranged hairdo. She had labored over it for what seemed like hours in hopes of impressing a new doctor. She'd had a monumental crush on Paul Denton. Scrambling out of the river, she'd screamed at Simon, swearing she would never forgive him. *Never.*

Bailey smiled to herself. She'd always been passionate about things. No half measures for her. She thought about her profession. Nothing had changed.

"I'll think about it," she told him as she hurried into her jeans and the green pullover she'd taken with her into the bathroom. Dressed, she glanced into the medicine cabinet mirror. Her makeup ritual consisted of dabbing on a light eye shadow that brought out her eyes and applying a slash of pink lipstick. She was forced to allow her hair to dry by itself.

Done, Bailey opened the door in four minutes, not five.

Simon straightened and nodded his approval. "Fast, as usual. I like the hair thing. Going for the natural look?"

She could have said yes, but it would have been lying. "My hair dryer's broken. I thought I'd skip fooling with it this morning and talk to you instead. Besides, it might rain again later on."

Simon placed a hand to his chest. "I'm honored, especially considering how you feel about your crowning glory." And then his face softened from a grin to a big brother, I'm-proud-of-you smile. "You don't look very doctor-like," he teased.

She returned the compliment. He wore a flight jacket, black turtleneck and very worn-out jeans. "You don't look very minister-like."

"I guess that makes us even." Putting his arm around her shoulders, he hugged her closer. "Is it true what they say about medical students?"

She wasn't sure what he was alluding to as he directed her toward the stairs. They went down with his arm still around her shoulders. "What is it that they say about medical students?"

"That they're all starving," he told her as they came to the landing.

"I can still scrounge up breakfast for my favorite pest," she assured Simon. She was about to head toward the kitchen when her brother stopped her.

When she eyed him quizzically, Simon indicated the front door. "I thought I'd buy you breakfast, instead."

She didn't want to sit in some impersonal restaurant with her brother while food servers moved in and out around them. She wanted to talk to him right here, the place she'd come to regard as her home.

"Eggs Benedict." For as far back as she could remember, it was her brother's favorite way to have eggs.

"You have Canadian bacon?"

"I have ham, I'll fry it," she told him.

He flashed another grin. "You talked me into it."

"Good." She led the way to the kitchen.

It wasn't a state-of-the-art kitchen, the way she dreamed of having someday, but everything she needed to prepare basic meals was right here.

As she moved around, taking out the various utensils, pans and ingredients they had a chance to talk and catch up.

But all during the exchange, Bailey couldn't shake the feeling that her brother was keeping something from her. Whether it was good or bad, something he was saving for a dramatic announcement, or something he was refraining from telling her because he thought it would upset her, she hadn't a clue. She just kept the conversation going, nonstop, hoping that Simon would eventually tell her what seemed to be on his mind.

Opening up the cabinet door beneath the sink, she threw the broken eggshells into the trash and dusted off her hands. Bailey glanced over her shoulder as she asked, "So Mom and Dad are doing well?"

Simon was sitting on a stool at the counter, nursing the cup of coffee she had made for him. "Never better. They said something about coming to the States to visit you around Christmas, but you know them." He stopped to take a sip, then shrugged. "Good intentions and all that, but—"

Bailey nodded. She was well versed when it came to her parents' habits.

"Something always comes up." The muffin she'd put in the toaster popped. Taking it out, she slathered it in warmed butter. "I kind of figured you'd be the same way," she confessed, turning her attention to first the eggs she was poaching and then to the hollandaise sauce she was mixing. Timing was everything.

"What? And miss seeing you before—" Simon stopped abruptly, then cleared his throat. Bailey looked at him, alert. "Can I have more coffee?" He indicated his half-empty cup.

"Sure, you don't have to ask." Picking up the pot, she began to pour. "But I do." Their eyes met. "'Before' what, Simon?"

He picked up the cup and focused all his attention on it. "Before I start."

She shook her head. "That wasn't what you were going to say."

His expression was innocent. "Still claiming to be a mind reader?"

"I just know an incomplete sentence when I hear one," Bailey countered. The eggs were making noise in the pan. Easing them off with a spatula, she deposited them onto the open muffin and the ham slice she'd fried. The hollandaise sauce was drizzled over it.

Simon stared at the offering like a man entering rapture. "Before I start my duties, that's all. This looks terrific, Bay. Nobody makes Eggs Benedict like you."

"Thanks." She knew Simon wasn't ready to tell her his news. Consumed with curiosity or not, she would have to let him take his time.

But she wasn't about to have him leave without telling her what he'd really meant to say.

That, she thought, was a promise.

CHAPTER 20

Bailey had left Simon at the house, but not before securing a promise from him that he would still be there when she came home tonight. As she drove in, she couldn't help wonder what he wasn't telling her. She hoped it wasn't anything bad.

Leaving her car in the newly built parking structure, she frowned. Munro was rubbing off on her. Her thoughts didn't used to be so pessimistic. Walking outside, she hurried toward the hospital entrance.

Her pager went off the moment she pulled open the front door. Hurrying into the building, she looked down at the small screen clipped to her belt. The number was all too familiar.

Munro.

Now what?

She knew better than to take time to go to the locker room and change into scrubs. If Munro paged her, he wanted her stat.

Taking the elevator to his third-floor office, she quickly reviewed all of her actions in the last few days, trying to unearth what the chief neurosurgeon might be taking her to task for—because why else would he be summoning her first thing in the morning?

Bailey came up empty. But she had a feeling Munro wouldn't.

She walked by the administrative assistant's desk. All three doctors in the immediate vicinity made use of Alma Greeley's multitasking abilities. The desk was empty and from the looks of it, Alma hadn't come in yet. It wasn't like the woman to be late. Bailey had been hoping Alma could give her a clue why Munro wanted to see her, or, at the very least, an encouraging order.

Bailey went in cold. The door was ajar. Knocking once, she opened it and looked in. Munro was looking back.

This can't be good. "You wanted to see me, Dr. Munro?"

His scowl seemed to deepen right before her eyes. She told herself to remain calm.

He gestured her forward, his eyes holding hers. "I saw you with the Sullivans last night, talking to them after I'd left." Ivan allowed the words to sink in and find their proper level. "Why did you feel called upon to talk to those people?" Before she could respond, he fired more questions at her. His voice was deadly calm and all the more unnerving because of that. "Is it your considered opinion that I didn't do an adequate job informing them of Mrs. Sullivan's demise? Did you feel you had to 'clean up my mess'?" he suggested, sarcasm and cynicism woven in equal parts through his words.

Her very first impulse was to run. But she was standing in the middle of a frozen pond and the ice was cracking beneath her feet. If she ran, she'd go under. And he was waiting to watch her sink.

She wasn't about to accommodate him.

Bailey took a breath. "Adequate isn't a word that should readily come to mind when telling someone's family that they won't be seeing that person at the dinner table anymore."

He indicated that she should sit. "Please, enlighten me. What would be a good word?"

Bailey lowered herself down like someone who knew they were perching on a powder keg. "Compassion."

"Compassion?" he questioned irritably. "I don't know these people."

"Doesn't mean you can't have compassion for their situation, their grief."

"And you do." The words mocked her.

He wasn't going to make her back down, wasn't going to make her apologize. She was right, damn it. And it was about time he acknowledged that. "Yes."

In a strange sort of way, her bravado, her certainty, fascinated him. "Why?"

"Because I can feel," she told him simply, knowing she was venturing further and further out onto progressively thinner ice. But that couldn't be helped. Not if she was going to tell him the truth. "Let's face it, Dr. Munro, you might be the world's greatest neurosurgeon—"

He glared at her. "Are you patronizing me?"

Bailey pressed on as if he hadn't interrupted. "But when it comes to bedside manner, you suck."

"Obviously not trying to patronize me," Ivan concluded.

He leaned back in his chair, touching his fingertips together, looking at her with that gaze that some claimed could melt steel at ten paces. He maintained his silence for so long, she thought she was going to scream. And then, finally, he spoke, using a tone that told her nothing.

"Apparently, you're becoming braver, my little resident-that-could." Before she could respond, he continued. "There was a scene in an old sitcom that went something like this. The crabby old news producer looked at the young, pretty interviewee who'd come about the assistant producer's job and said, 'You know what? You've got spunk.' She blushingly attempted to thank him, looking fetching and demur, and he cut her short by telling her, 'I hate spunk.'" Munro watched her even more intently, if that was possible. "Do you get my drift, DelMonico?"

Bailey never wavered as she replied, "You're not old."

Stunned, Ivan blinked, as if that could clear his hearing. "What?"

"You might be crabby," Bailey told him, "but you're not old."

The sigh that escaped was more of a huff. "You're completely missing the point here."

She slid forward in her chair, her hands folded before her on his desk. He wasn't sure if she was praying or trying to restrain herself from grabbing him by the throat. Ivan was aware that he had that affect on people.

"No, Doctor," she told him. "I get the point. I just wanted to go on record as saying that." She paused, then added, "And the other thing—"

He knew exactly what she was referring to. "About me sucking at beside manner?"

"Yes." The word hurried out on a sigh. And then she looked down at her folded hands. "I wanted to go on record with that before you terminated me."

The neurosurgeon laughed then, completely taking her by surprise. It wasn't a full-hearted, jovial laugh, but it was, she surmised, probably the best Munro could offer, seeing as how he was probably out of practice.

"Don't think I haven't thought about it," he told her, adding the word "fondly" with such relish she wasn't sure just which "terminated" he was entertaining, the kind that placed her in an unemployment line or the kind that had her on a slab in the morgue.

In either case, she had to ask. "Then you're not terminating me?"

"No," he said with finality. "I'm warning you, DelMonico." And then he got to the heart of his warning before she could ask. "Right now, I own you, body and soul, at least within these four walls. If I had wanted you to talk to the Sullivans, I would have instructed you to talk to the Sullivans." He pinned her with a look meant to make her squirm. "But I didn't, did I?"

She didn't move a muscle, which annoyed him even as it impressed him. "No."

"There is room in this profession for innovation," he allowed, then snapped, "but not at your level. Do I make myself clear?"

She stared straight ahead, like a soldier called out on the carpet. "Perfectly."

"All right." He waved a hand dismissively. "You can go."

Bailey rose to her feet, wondering when her blood would start circulating again so that she could use them. "Thank you, sir."

Ivan snorted. "That might sound a little convincing if you didn't look as if you were trying to chew a mouthful of mold-encrusted cheese while you were saying it."

Bailey forced a smile to her lips and then inclined her head. "Better?"

"It'll do." She turned to leave and made it all the way to the door before she heard him say, "Oh, and DelMonico?"

Bailey stopped and braced herself before she turned around again. "Yes, sir?"

"You did good."

Her mouth dropped open. She was too young to be losing her hearing. "Excuse me, sir?"

"You heard me," he said tersely. "I listened to you." She looked, he thought, like Dorothy when she'd pulled aside the curtain in the wizard's chambers. "Don't look so surprised, how do you think I know you talked to them? My clairvoyance only goes so far," he quipped. He paused before finally adding, "You're right. You do have a knack for coddling and hand-holding. Nothing I'd want to cultivate," he informed her, "but I suppose it does have its place."

Bailey knew that it wasn't easy for Munro to admit any of this. Were her prayers being answered? Was he turning human on her? Probably too much to hope for, she thought. But this was one hell of a start.

"You get to talk to the next patient's family," Munro was saying, "should things not go well," he tacked on. "With any luck, you'll never have to speak to anyone unless spoken to."

Bailey didn't bother repressing the smile that rose to her lips. "Is that all, sir?"

"No." Shifting in his seat so that he could dig into his pants' pocket, Ivan took out a ten-dollar bill and held it out to her. "Get me some coffee. You seem to know where to get a decent serving."

The Lord giveth and the Lord taketh away, Bailey thought. With one breath, Munro raised her up, with the next, he pushed her down to the level of errand girl again. She supposed that in the long run, that balanced out.

Holding up the bill, she promised, "I'll bring you back change."

"Don't bother. Get yourself a container, too." He looked up and saw that she was still standing there, looking down at the bill he had handed her. "What? You're not moving."

Pocketing the bill, Bailey shook her head. Just when she thought she had a handle on things. "You are a very difficult man to figure out."

She saw a hint of a smile curve his mouth. "So I've been told. Save yourself a lot of grief, DelMonico, and don't try."

She didn't know how to respond to that, so she didn't. "I'll be back in a few minutes," she promised.

She heard him cryptically murmur, "Something to live for," as she closed the door behind her.

CHAPTER 21

Bailey didn't hear anyone walk up behind her. She was completely intent on double checking that all the reports that Munro had sent her to fetch were in the pile she held. So when she suddenly felt someone's arms going around her waist and then squeezing her, it took everything she had not to scream in surprise or drop the reports.

With an exclamation of protest and not a single idea who at the hospital would think to grab her like this, Bailey swung around to find herself face to chest with her brother.

She stopped trying to peel the strong arms away and relaxed. "Simon, you can't keep popping up on me like this," she protested. "You're going to wind up giving me a heart attack."

Simon laughed, his arms still lightly holding her in place. "Not you, Bay. You're like a bull."

Bailey huffed, feigning displeasure at the comparison. She knew what Simon really meant. "Very flattering."

"Maybe not," he allowed, releasing her. "But at the same time, very true."

Placing the reports on the counter for the time being, she looked up at him. An uneasy feeling began to thread its way through her. Something was off.

"*What* are you doing here?" she asked, putting emphasis on the first word.

He shrugged noncommittally as he looked around the area.

"I got bored," he told her. "Your roommate, Jennifer, offered to give me a ride when she drove in to the hospital, so I said yes."

"Jennifer offered," Bailey repeated, her eyes on his, knowing it couldn't have played out that way. Jennifer was shy and had trouble speaking to anyone.

Her brother's next words confirmed her suspicions. "Okay, I asked," he admitted. Shoving his hands into his pockets, he flashed the wide, guileless smile that was common to them both. "I wanted to see where you worked. Where you did your magic."

"I would have brought you," she told him. "Not today," she added quickly because the schedule on the board testified to a very hectic day, "but—"

He cut her short. "I don't have much time."

Bailey shook her head, not following him. "I thought you were staying for two weeks," she reminded him, clinging to the promise of fourteen days and secretly hoping that could be extended, not cut short. When they'd talked on the phone the last time he'd postponed his visit, she was certain he'd agreed to a two-week stay when he finally came to see her.

Simon sank his hands deeper into his pockets, as if he was trying to latch onto an excuse she would accept. He looked away, out through the fourth-floor window that showcased a sky filled with gray clouds. "Yeah, well, I might have misled you about that."

Bailey circled around him until she was back in her brother's line of vision. "How misled?" She wanted to know. The ominous feeling inside her continued to grow, taking on shape and form.

Avoiding her eyes, Simon glanced over her head. "It's going to be less than two weeks."

This didn't bode well, she thought. Simon had always been straight with her. He'd never felt it necessary to talk to her hair or to the air above her head before. Nerves began to tighten, pinching her stomach. Something was wrong. Something she wasn't going to like.

"How many days less?" she pressed.

Simon took a breath, still addressing the space above her head. "Eleven."

Tired of being avoided, Bailey grasped hold of his shirtfront, jerking his attention back to her. "You can only stay eleven days?"

Her brother shook his head. "No, eleven days less than two weeks."

It didn't take much to do the math. "Three days?" she cried. The noise on the other side of the lab alerted her that she was attracting attention. Bailey subdued her voice, but not her reaction to what Simon had just said. "You can only stay three days?"

His eyes were full of apologies. Maybe a little too much so, she thought. Her uneasiness continued to grow. There was more. "Afraid so."

Bailey felt immensely cheated. Unable to get away last year at Christmas, she hadn't seen her brother in a very long time. Three days wasn't nearly enough time. "Can't you get an extension? Tell them you'll be there later?"

Simon shook his head. This time he didn't try to look away. "Afraid not."

There was definitely something wrong. "Simon, I'm not liking this word 'afraid.'" She braced herself. "Are you trying to tell me something?"

"No." It wasn't a lie. He really didn't want to have to say this.

She was well-versed in word manipulation. She'd used it herself time and again on her parents when they'd asked how her marriage to Jeff was going.

"Okay, what are you not trying to tell me?" And then it hit her. This was about his vocation. "Just where is this new ministry of yours?"

He cleared his throat, then took hold of her hands. "Well, it's not a ministry, exactly."

Sincerely worried now, she pulled her hands free. Her stomach tightened another notch. "Just what is it, 'exactly'?"

His eyes held hers for a long moment. "I'm a chaplain, Bay."

"A chaplain," Bailey repeated slowly. She took a deep breath. "I'm taking this to mean you didn't suddenly find out that we belong to a long-lost branch of Charlie Chaplin's family."

A bittersweet smile played along his lips. Simon moved his head slowly from side to side. "No."

"And where is this 'chaplaining' going to take place?" He didn't answer her immediately. His silence told her all she needed to know.

Oh God, no. Please, she prayed.

She forced herself to form the question. "They're sending you where the fighting is, aren't they?"

He inclined his head. "There're no atheists in foxholes, Bay."

She was angry now. Angry and scared. How could he stay

safe out there, amid all that gunfire? Amid all those bombs going off? "Don't give me stilted old World War I sayings. Why are you doing this?" she demanded, her voice rising again. This time, she didn't bother lowering it. She was too upset to care if the lab technician overheard her. "Why do you have to go where people are shooting at each other?"

"Because," he told her simply, "that's where I'm needed."

"There're lots of people right here who need comforting, Simon," she insisted. "Who need words said over them and have their hands held. And they won't shoot you or try to blow themselves up when you come into a room."

"Bay, I have to do this."

"What?" she demanded, angry tears springing to her eyes. She tried to banish them, but one insisted on trickling from her eye. "Break Mom and Dad's heart? Never mind mine?"

He took his thumb and gently wiped away the moist track along her cheek. "Not fair, Bay," he told her softly. "Besides, Mom and Dad aren't exactly people who opted for the calm and tranquil life, either. Going into the heart of Africa to minister isn't the same thing as driving to a corporate office to sit behind a desk all day and make money."

Simon was right, and he was going to do what he was going to do. Bailey shook her head, and a soft laugh escaped. "Who would have ever thought that I'd be the most conservative one in the family?" The irony of it was overwhelming to her.

He put his hands on her shoulders and then raised her head with the tip of his fingers. His eyes met hers. "Mad at me?"

"Yes, I'm mad." To prove it, she doubled her fist and punched him in the arm. Hard. She felt his muscle tense just as she made contact. It was like hitting a rock. "And proud," she admitted reluctantly. This was a brave, good thing he was doing. Only she wished it was someone else's brother who was doing it. "Very proud. I want e-mail from you," she told him suddenly. It was an order. "Every day."

He looked skeptical. "That might not exactly be possible."

"*Make* it possible," she said firmly. "Or I won't let you go." He raised an amused brow at the declaration. "I have friends," she told him. "They have handcuffs. There are places in this hospital I could hide you where you'd never find your way out."

He laughed, hugging her to him. "Tough talk for a half-pint."

Half-pint. He hadn't called her that in years. Tears sprang to her eyes again, tears for all the years that were gone now. All the years she wouldn't get back. God, what if…?

Don't go there!

She looked up at him. "Three days, huh?"

They both wished it could be more. But it wasn't up to him. "Yes."

In the blink of an eye, Bailey made up her mind. "Stay here," she told him, turning on her heel.

"Where are you going?" he called after her.

Hand on the door, she looked back over her shoulder. "To ask for time off so I can spend it with you."

He took a few steps after her. "Do you have any time coming?" he asked.

"No."

He didn't understand. "Then how…?"

She'd already worked it out in her head. "They have provisions for family emergencies."

He had never been as optimistic as she was. "Showing your

older brother around Southern California doesn't exactly come under the heading of 'emergency,'" Simon pointed out.

She looked at him just before she took off down the hall. "No, but having him shipped out to the ends of the earth where people don't play nice is."

Her mind was made up and Simon seemed to accept that he couldn't argue with her.

CHAPTER 22

He was coming down with something.

He rarely did, his constitution being healthier than most, especially given the environment he worked in. But there was no other explanation for the way he was feeling, Ivan concluded. He *had* to be getting sick, because if he wasn't, then he wouldn't be experiencing this odd, stabbing...*emptiness* for lack of a better word.

Maybe emptiness wasn't the right word, but how else did you describe a black hole in the center of your abdomen? Nothing seemed to divert his attention from it, not even an impromptu evening at the L.A. Philharmonic.

Ivan felt his annoyance spiking. Looking down, he realized his hands were clenched into fists against his desk. With effort, he uncurled his fingers, resting his palms just above his center drawer.

He'd sent DelMonico to the lab, the word "stat" chasing after her in the hall. When she didn't return, he decided to find out for himself what the holdup was.

He wished he hadn't.

The "holdup" was that the resident was talking to someone. Someone who, he could tell even from where he was standing at the far end of the laboratory, mattered to her. Her body language told him as much. The fact that the tall and far-too-good-looking blond stranger had his arms wrapped around Del-Monico didn't exactly negate his assumption, either.

She had a boyfriend.

DelMonico had a boyfriend.

Disgusted, Ivan snorted at the very thought. The next moment, he told himself it was only natural. A lot of these so-called residents and fledgling doctors had people in their lives who they felt strongly about.

What wasn't natural was that he should care.

He *didn't* care, Ivan insisted silently. His hands were clenched again. Uttering a curse, he forced his hands open again.

Damn it, he didn't care, he was just surprised, that's all. Surprised because seeing her that way was unexpected. DelMonico never talked about having someone in her life in that capacity. And God knew, the woman did talk. Talk until he thought his ears were either going to self-destruct or fall off in self-defense.

That jerk who had his hands on her didn't know what he was in for, Ivan thought darkly. Either that, or he was stone deaf. Well, it made no difference to him as long as it didn't interfere with her work here at the hospital.

Ivan hit a few keys on the computer keyboard, looking for something. He accidentally shut down the program and cursed again.

Why *hadn't* DelMonico told him? he demanded silently. She told him everything else, told him things he had no remote desire ever to know or to hear. He knew all about her parents, her brother, her aunt and uncle who had taken her in when she was attending undergraduate college. She'd even touched on, briefly, the marriage that she wished had been even briefer.

This had to be someone new, he concluded. Angrily, he tried to open up the program again and found he had to reboot the computer. He fought a strong urge to "reboot" the computer across the room. Instead, he took his time and followed the necessary steps, closing his computer down and then turning it on again.

Grinding noises from the tower followed. It didn't sound promising.

DelMonico just hadn't gotten around to talking about this guy, he decided, his thoughts going back to her again. Which meant what? That this guy was something special in her estimation? Or was she one of those people who was afraid of talking about something because the very act of talking about it might jinx it?

Ha, he sincerely doubted that. The only thing that would get DelMonico to actually stop talking was strategically applied duct tape.

Ivan passed his hand over his forehead. It was cool, but he *had* to be coming down with something. His thoughts were bouncing around, just like one of her conversations did.

Damn, he didn't have time for this. The rest of his month was set. He glanced at his desk calendar. There were surgeries scheduled. Consultations all over the place. Things were set in stone. Ivan sternly forbid his body to succumb to whatever attempted to assault him.

An almost imperceptible noise at his door had him shifting his eyes in that direction, temporarily abandoning the hellish message on his computer screen that fairly screamed "Program not found."

Frying pan or fire? Neither was appealing. He didn't feel like tackling the problem with his computer, but neither was he in the mood to talk to anyone—even less than usual.

This job would be a hell of a lot more satisfying if he could just do it without having to interact with *anyone*, Ivan thought grumpily.

He decided to ignore whoever was on the other side of the door.

No such luck.

The doorknob began to turn. The next moment, the door was opening slowly.

"I didn't say you could come in," he snapped, turning his chair away from the doorway and toward the window with its dismal view. Rank had its privileges and right now, he was pulling it. "Go away."

"I will after I ask you this."

The sound of Bailey's voice undulated through him, creating havoc in its wake. He swung his chair around to face her.

A myriad of emotions ran through him.

Emotions, for God's sake. He wasn't supposed to have *emotions* anymore, Ivan thought angrily, scowling at their source. He'd banished them to some nether region decades ago so that he could operate without having them get in the way, impeding his skill.

What the hell were they doing here now, crowding him like this? Making him feel out of sync and very definitely off his game.

"Ask me what?" he snapped.

God, he was in a surlier mood than usual, Bailey thought, licking lips that had gone dry. Just her luck. Well, she was here, she might as well say this. "I know that I should actually go to Dr. Bennett's assistant with this—"

"'This'?" he questioned, pinning her sharply with a look.

What side of the abyss did he get up on this morning? "My request—"

Ivan smirked. "'Requesting' things now, are we?" The second that was out of his mouth, he had no idea why he said it. What the hell was going on with him? He was technically too young for dementia, he silently argued.

Bailey pushed forward. "Yes. I thought I'd let you know first."

He leaned back in his chair, never taking his eyes off her. "Go ahead." It wasn't an instruction, it was a challenge, as if he were daring her to continue, to say something that would wind up shattering the structure of his day.

What was his problem? She couldn't remember seeing him this nasty before. Why now, when she could have used someone to talk to, to understand what she was going through? She was fond of both her roommates and got along well with everyone in the neurosurgical program, but when it came to something like this, she needed someone who'd lived a little, who had experienced life. The other residents just didn't qualify.

Well, if she needed someone, it obviously wasn't going to be Munro, who was living up to his nickname more than usual today. "I need the next three days off."

He looked even more unsympathetic, if that was possible. "Is that enough time?"

The question seemed to come at her out of left field. She thought about how short a span of time that was in the sum total of things. "No," she answered honestly, "but that's all he has."

"'He,'" Munro repeated. It sounded to her as if the man was mocking her every word.

Just like that, her temper appeared, erupting like a can of

gasoline when a match was thrown into it. It nearly floored her and Bailey had to struggle to contain it.

Narrowing her eyes, she glared at the chief neurosurgeon. "Is there something wrong, Dr. Munro?" she asked, enunciating every word.

"No, there's nothing wrong," he told her coldly. But the distance he liked to maintain melted as he added, "Unless of course, by 'wrong,' you mean your behavior in the lab."

Instead of clearing things up, he'd only succeeded in making them more muddled. "Excuse me?" she demanded

"I don't expect any resident assigned to me to behave like some addle-brained adolescent, letting her boyfriend of the moment feel her up on public property just because his hormones kicked into high gear and she didn't have the good sense to stop him."

Dumbfounded, she stared at him. Fury entered her eyes, making them blaze. "What the hell are you talking about?"

No one talked to him like that, not even Bennett at his most annoyed. They knew better. Maybe this resident wasn't as long on intelligence as he had thought. "Don't play innocent with me, DelMonico. The ship has sailed on that one."

She didn't need any stupid metaphors, but because he seemed to relish them, she played along. "Well, the ship is obviously sailing out of a wrong port here. Now, I don't know what it is you 'think' you saw, but there was no one in the lab with me, besides Jenkins who gave me the results you wanted." Suddenly remembering she was still holding the reports, she threw them on Munro's desk. "Except my brother," she informed the neurosurgeon with fiery indignation.

"Your brother," he mocked.

Her voice was terse. "Yes. My brother. Simon. He's the reason I'm asking for three days off. My brother's in the army and he's being shipped off to where the fighting is. I want to spend some time with him before he leaves. Now, if you'll excuse me, I'm going to go request this through the proper channels."

And with that, she left.

Ivan had no idea how it was possible to feel the prick of guilt and be happy at the same time. It was as he had always thought, he snorted, getting back to work. Emotions were just too much damn trouble.

CHAPTER 23

She didn't know what to do with the ache inside her. It kept growing. Three days had never gone by so quickly.

She'd filled the time with everything she could think of, cramming it to the breaking point so that she couldn't dwell or anticipate. She took Simon to places she hadn't had time to go to herself. They went to Disneyland because that was traditional; she took him to Knott's Berry Farm for its charm and to the newly reopened Griffith Park Observatory for the sheer wonder of the place.

And all the while, amid the nonstop talking and laughter shared, Bailey could feel a clock ticking, bringing Simon's departure closer. Even when she didn't want to think about it, it was there, whispering along the outer perimeter of her thoughts, haunting her.

She'd never felt quite like this before. Bailey couldn't help wondering if it was some kind of omen, a premonition. Always close to her family, she'd never before had this haunting fear this might be the last time she saw Simon. The last time they ate together, shared memories together. Were together. As the three days raced to a close, the feeling was almost overpowering. She wasn't superstitious, but…

"You know, you could always change your mind, even at the

last minute," she told her brother as she stood in her doorway, watching him pack the single suitcase he'd brought.

Over his protests, she had insisted that he take her room while she slept on the fold-out sofa in the living room. The mattress was as thin as an individually wrapped slice of cheese, but a small enough price to pay for having Simon here. She would have gladly slept on the floor if it had come down to that.

Simon looked up at her and smiled. "I could," he allowed. His tone gently told her that her suggestion wasn't even up for serious consideration. "But I won't."

Putting the last of his toiletries into his suitcase, Simon zipped up the gray carry-on luggage. He placed it on the floor beside the bed and then crossed to her.

Simon took her hands in his. His eyes were gentle, as he tried again to make her understand.

"Did you ever feel in your heart that there was something you were meant to do? Something that you were brought into this world to accomplish, that was your actual purpose for existing?" He continued, not waiting for her to respond. "I always envied Mom and Dad. They were always so focused, so sure they knew what they were about. And you—" He eyed her affectionately.

For the third time in as many days, Simon had succeeded in surprising her. "Me?"

He grinned at her reaction. "You. I envied how you knew just what you wanted."

"No," Bailey corrected, shaking her head. "I knew what I *didn't* want. I didn't want to wander around jungles all my life, secretly lusting after hot water and electricity that didn't constantly give out." Some of the places that her parents had lived didn't even have the simplest of amenities. She supposed that growing up without them had made her strong but given a choice, that wasn't the life she wanted. "If you haven't noticed, my life up to this point hasn't been exactly stellar," she pointed out with a sigh. "A failed marriage isn't something most people strive for."

Simon's smile was full of love and understanding. "Not your fault."

"Ever the loyal brother." She appreciated him trying to whitewash her past for her, but the truth was the truth. "I could have chosen more wisely instead of rebelliously." It was her desire to leave her parents' life behind that had initially launched her into Jeff's arms and a shaky marriage.

"You were twenty," he reminded her. "And twenty is still more child than adult."

But she shook her head, contradicting him. "I was stupid."

"Okay," he allowed. "Not the wisest move someone could have made. But once you got rid of that dead weight known as your ex-husband, you sailed right into this." He gestured around the house, using it to symbolize her present, and binding, career choice. "Eyes wide open, doing everything you could to put yourself through medical school, along the way managing to get grades that would have made die-hard nerds envious."

Despite herself, Bailey laughed, affection brimming up within her. "You always did have a way with words, Simon."

"I'm hoping that's still true." He grew serious. "All I have are words, Bay. Words and faith. And that's what I'm planning on bringing with me to the battlefield."

He was being noble and selfless, and she was being selfish,

but she didn't want him out there, risking his life on a moment-to-moment basis.

"This is the age of computers, Simon," she insisted. "Couldn't you just teleconference all those comforting words in?"

He laughed, shaking his head. "Not the same thing, Bay."

"No," she agreed. "If they blow up the computer, you still go on living to 'comfort' another day. If they blow you up, you don't."

Still holding her hands, he wove his fingers through hers. "I don't have to get blown up," he pointed out.

"Your odds are a lot better if you don't go," she told him stubbornly.

Simon pressed their joined hands to his chest, his eyes intent on hers. "Honey, it's not in my hands. If my time is up, I can slip in the shower and hit my head on the faucet."

"Then take sponge baths," Bailey countered, and then sighed. It was hopeless. He was going. "You've practiced this, haven't you?"

He grinned again. "Pretty much."

"This the argument you used on Mom and Dad?"

"No, I practiced it to use on you. I didn't need to make Mom and Dad understand. After the initial shock passed, they were pretty much on board with my decision. They understand why I have to do this."

More than that, she thought, they could probably relate. But she couldn't. Not when it could mean Simon's life. "I guess they're braver than I am."

"You can't say that about my sister," he told her. "Bailey Del-Monico is the bravest woman I know." He kissed the top of her head, then hugged her to him. "For as long as I can remember, she's always been positively fearless."

"A lot you know," she murmured against his chest. Bailey blinked back tears, not wanting to make his shirt wet.

"YOU DON'T HAVE TO COME in, you know," Simon told her. Evening traffic was light as she drove him the short distance from her house to John Wayne Airport. "You can just drop me off at the loading-unloading zone." She took the right turn from MacArthur Boulevard into the airport a little sharply and he grabbed the strap above the passenger window to steady himself. "They won't let you go past the checkpoint anyway."

She didn't care. She wanted every second she could beg, borrow or steal. "I know, but I can still watch you as you disappear down the corridor beyond the security check."

Reaching the upper level where passengers were supposed to board their planes, Bailey went into the first lot to the right of the terminal. The search for a parking space was on.

"You don't have to," Simon insisted. "There's no parking, Bay."

"I want to," she countered. "And there is." Her heart leaped up as she saw a silver Honda pulling out of a space several feet ahead. She was there, in the car's shadow, in a heartbeat, beating out a black SUV by inches. Triumphant, she parked only marginally askew.

After getting out, Simon reached into the backseat and took out his suitcase. "You know," he observed, "I don't remember us being this close when we were kids."

Bailey hooked her arm through his and smiled up at her brother. The wind had turned chilly hours ago and now whipped along her face, reminding her that the holidays were just around the corner.

The holidays without her brother. Or her parents, most likely. She banked down the ache. "That's because we weren't. You're an acquired taste," she teased.

Simon laughed as they made their way into the terminal. "I could say the same about you."

Bailey heard the sound of his laughter in her head long after she could no longer see Simon walking down the long gray corridor that led to the boarding area.

CHAPTER 24

Bailey didn't sleep that night for more than a few isolated minutes at a time. Despite feeling like something the cat dragged in the next morning, she was determined to go back to work. She had no choice in the matter.

To stay home would mean to stay alone with her thoughts and right now, that wasn't something she welcomed. So, she got up early rather than lay awake in bed, made a huge breakfast for Jennifer and Adam and left just as they were coming down.

She didn't feel much like talking.

However, once she reached the hospital, it was unavoidable. Especially since she had made it her personal mission to get to know everyone on the hospital staff. Greetings and simple voiced pleasantries followed in her wake from the front entrance all the way to Munro's inner sanctum.

She felt obligated to check in with the chief neurosurgeon in case he had something in particular he wanted her to do.

Nodding at Alma, who looked as if she wanted to talk, most likely about Munro, she went right into the doctor's office, opening the door even as she knocked.

He was in.

Charts, CAT scans and MRIs were spread out over the surface of his large desk. He looked up irritably. "That is not a

revolving door. You stand outside until I tell you to come in."
The dire proclamation dissolved as a hint of a smile, cynical for
the most part, came to his lips. "Ah, so you decided to come
back."

If he was trying to bait her, he was going to be disappointed.
She didn't have it in her to spar with him today. "The leave was
for three days. Three days are over."

"And a lovely three days they were," he quipped. He rose to
his feet, reaching for the chart that was on the far side of his
desk. "You missed several impressive surgeries, DelMonico."

She sighed and nodded. The rain they'd been expecting never
materialized, she realized, gazing out of Munro's window. It was
hotter than hell where Simon was going. She'd checked the
weather on her laptop before leaving this morning. "I'm sure
there'll be more opportunities for me to see you being impressive."

The chief neurosurgeon looked at her sharply. "I said the surgeries were impressive, not me, but you're right, I was."

Bailey pressed her lips together. Her voice was low, devoid of
feeling when she spoke. "Nice to know some things don't
change."

Disturbed by what he was hearing, Ivan studied her for a long
moment. He peered more closely at her face. "Are you all right,
DelMonico?"

"Excuse me?"

"You seem…" He spread his hands wide, searching for the
right word. "Subdued. I'm used to you behaving like the bubbles
in a shaken can of soda, effervescing out over the top," Ivan
said. "Your brother get off all right?"

Her mind kept drifting in and out. She had trouble concentrating. Concern and lack of sleep conspired to bring her down. She looked past Munro's arm, focusing on nothing in particular.

"He got on the plane. It landed in the right place. I tracked it." She wished she could track Simon as easily, to make sure he was all right.

"Go home, DelMonico."

Munro's harsh voice broke through her thoughts. Her head jerked up and she looked at the neurosurgeon, stunned. "What?"

"Go home," he repeated, his voice even colder and more distant as he issued the command. "You're not here," he told her, tapping her temple with his finger. "I can't have you working at the hospital if you're not a hundred percent here."

Her shoulders snapped back. Anger pushed through the blanket of pain. "I'm here," she insisted.

Her protest didn't change his mind. "A hundred percent, DelMonico," he repeated. "I need the people I rely on to be here a hundred percent."

About to argue more aggressively, she suddenly pulled up short. "Rely?" she echoed in disbelief. "You rely on me?"

"Figure of speech." And then, because she didn't look as if she believed him, he tried again. "In a manner of speaking." Her eyes were still locked on his. Damn this woman for crawling under his skin like this. "All right, yes, 'rely.'" But he wasn't about to let her get smug about it. "What the hell would you call it?" he demanded, genuinely irritated. "I have you give me input and then I utilize it. To my knowledge, that would be one of the definitions of the verb 'to rely.'" He scowled at her as he issued his warning. "Don't let it give you a swelled head on top of swollen eyes."

Her chin snapped up indignantly. "My eyes aren't swollen."

Ivan took hold of her chin and angled her face so that their eyes locked. There was fire in hers again.

Better.

"That would be the first lie I've ever heard from you," he informed her. "Either that, or you are unlike any woman I have ever known and you possess no mirrors in which to endlessly check the condition of your makeup and your hair."

She'd forgotten just how much this man could annoy her. Bailey pulled back her head. "I have mirrors, Doctor," she snapped tersely, then added, "But I *am* unlike any woman you've ever known."

"Really." He sounded as if he was challenging her rather than questioning her.

"Really. You can't intimidate me or bully me."

She was probably right, he thought. That *would* make her different. And a challenge. "Careful, you're disassembling the only outside hobby I have."

They stood there for a long moment, two prize fighters weighing their options, one a veteran, the other a would-be contender.

And then Munro inclined his head, not conceding the fight, but only the moment. "All right, I'm going to do for you what I've never done for anyone else."

Her tone didn't betray the fact that she knew she'd ventured out onto less than solid ground again. How did Ivan the Terrible manage to do that to her, time and again? She wasn't confrontational by nature. "And that is?"

"I'm going to go back on something I've said. Change an order," he elaborated. And then he peered at her closely. "*Are* you up to this, DelMonico?" He held up his hand before she could answer. "Think carefully before you answer because I *won't* tolerate another lie."

Bailey didn't have to take time to think. When she'd walked in here, she'd felt dead from the neck down. Five minutes in Munro's presence and she was fighting fit again.

Her eyes met his, daring him to dispute what she was about to say. "I'm up to it."

"Good." He knew he could goad her out of her melancholy state. "Then I need Mr. Abernathy's films from the Radiology Department. Stat," he emphasized. "And then you can stop by the lab and get his blood and gases workup for me. I've got him scheduled for a craniotomy at two." Ivan sat down at his desk, his attention reverting back to the different films and charts he had spread out there. "You can scrub in if you're up to it."

The words sounded almost like an afterthought, but she knew better. Everything Munro said was calculated. Nothing was casual or off-handed. She squared her shoulders. "I'm up to it."

He looked up for a second, then back to his notes. "See that you are. There's no room on my team for the second-rate."

"I wasn't aware that you had a team."

She could swear that his mouth curved. It was hard to tell from the angle she was privy to. "Just proves that you don't know everything, little-resident-that-could."

It had never been her intent to pretend that she did. Bailey took a breath. "I guess not."

She was almost at the door when she heard him call after her. "DelMonico."

Now what? she wondered as she turned and forced a compliant look to her face. "Yes, Doctor?"

"He'll be all right," Munro told her in that authoritative, "do-not-question-me" tone she had become accustomed to.

Like an insect trapped in amber, Bailey made no move, stunned at the mortal moment Ivan the Terrible had just displayed. No one would believe her if she told them about this. Pulling herself together, she nodded. "Thank you."

Ivan waved her off. He was already back to considering another upcoming surgery, one that looked to be almost impossible at first review. One he intended to tackle, even if he had to battle Bennett and the board. Although he didn't really envision himself immersed in that kind of skirmish. He was far better at doing than talking. The battle would take place after the fact, he decided. If the patient lived, then his point about the procedure would be made. If the patient didn't make it, well, the odds of survival even if left untouched was so minimal it hardly registered on any chart.

His mind was already there, in the operating room, not here, talking to the resident he'd found himself thinking about during the three days that she had absented herself from the hospital.

With determination, Ivan deliberately plucked her from his thoughts now.

"Don't thank me," he told her gruffly, writing down a thought that suddenly came to him. "Just get those damn films before Abernathy expires waiting for us to do something for him."

Bailey opened the door. "I'm already gone."

"Promises, promises."

Or that was what she thought she heard Munro mutter as she closed the door behind her. That, at least, sounded like something Ivan the Terrible would say.

CHAPTER 25

To the casual eye, Administrative Assistant Alma Greeley looked far removed from possessing a soul. Wraithlike in appearance, she was, to Ivan's satisfaction, as quiet as a specter and performed like a robot dedicated to do the clerical work for the three doctors she reported to.

She succeeded admirably in keeping schedules, following up on notifications, never confusing one doctor's appointments with another and, in general, never falling behind in any of her work. In fifteen years, she had never claimed a sick day or taken any personal time. Some of the hospital staff felt this was due to the fact that Alma appeared to have no personal life outside the hospital's extensive walls.

Confident and self-assured, the woman could always be counted on no matter what.

But as she stood in the chief neurosurgeon's office doorway now, she looked more ghostly than usual and oddly unsure of herself. As if she was afraid to deliver her message.

Her knuckles against the door sounded like dried autumn leaves crunched underfoot. "Dr. Munro?" she queried hesitantly.

In the midst of heaping tasks onto Bailey's already crammed agenda, Ivan glanced toward the doorway. He never cared for intrusions and was annoyed as well as surprised that the rail-thin, almost angular assistant hadn't buzzed him on the telephone as was her custom.

Impatience echoed in his voice as he snapped, "Yes, what is it?"

Bailey turned in time to see Alma knotting her long, slender fingers together, glancing down at them like a penitent saying prayers. Asking for forgiveness. "You have a call."

Ivan scowled. Ordinarily, the woman put his calls through. "Will I like this call?" His tone only seemed mild to those who didn't know him. Each word had been dipped in sarcasm.

Alma took a breath, her shallow chest exaggerating the movement. "I don't know, sir. It's from your brother. John," she added in case there was more than one they didn't know about. The words were expelled from her mouth as if they didn't taste right.

At the mention of his brother's name, Ivan eyed the woman sharply. And then his features seemed to smooth out. No way could Bailey even guess at what was going on behind his eyes, but she had a feeling that none of it was peaceful. It was like witnessing the proverbial calm before the storm.

There was an unusually lengthy pause before the neurosurgeon finally instructed, "Put the call through, Ms. Greeley."

"Yes, Doctor." Alma backed out of the room, a death row convict given an eleventh hour reprieve by the governor. She shut the door.

Bailey turned back around to look at Munro. The words came out before she could think to stop them. "You have a brother?"

The sound of her voice roused Ivan, reminding him that he wasn't alone. For a second, his mind had taken him back, to another time and place far from where he was now. Ivan stared at the phone as it began to ring, but made no effort to pick up the receiver.

"I had parents, too," he muttered. "One of each." The phone rang again and he looked up at her. She was still standing there, frozen in place like his thoughts. He wasn't about to talk to John with her here. "You have things to do, DelMonico. Things that don't include listening in on my private conversations."

Nodding, Bailey made her way to the door. Her hand on the knob, she glanced over her shoulder at him. She knew it was useless to say the words, but she needed the offer to be out there. Just in case. "I'm around if you need to talk."

The neurosurgeon snorted dismissively. "I'm perfectly aware that you're 'around,' DelMonico." She began to leave. "And why would I need to talk?"

Pausing, she shrugged, her shoulders moving in a vague motion beneath the blue scrubs. "Just in case you do," she replied.

With that, she slipped quietly out of his office.

The third ring melted into the silence before Ivan finally lifted the receiver from its cradle and placed it against his ear. Mentally he braced himself. "Munro."

"Ivan." The voice on the other end was deep, weary. And he would have known it anywhere. "I need to see you."

No explanations, even though it had been more than five years since the last words had traveled between them. But then they were both like that, shunning explanations if they could possibly be avoided.

Ivan nodded to himself since there was no one else around to see. "When?"

There was no hesitation. The answer had been prepared before the receiver was even lifted. "As soon as possible."

Moving to the other side of his desk, Ivan looked down at his calendar. He paged through it and frowned. Every space was filled in, not only for that day, but for all the days that followed in the next month. He pushed the desk calendar aside. "All right, pick a time."

Again the answer came on the heels of his last word. "I can be there in an hour."

Ivan scanned at that day's notations. In an hour he had a meeting with three of the members of the board. Annabel Miller and two of her lackeys. He had been debating blowing off the meeting as it was. Now he had an excuse.

"I'll be here," he replied.

The call ended without further exchange.

Like a man moving through molasses, Ivan replaced the receiver in the cradle. He hadn't heard from his brother in five years and hardly much before that. They had never been close. They had grown up in the same house much like two passengers on a train who'd boarded from the same station bound for different destinations with nothing in common except their point of origin. John was ten years older than he was. It might as well have been a century.

Until after he'd hung up, it didn't even occur to Ivan that he had no idea how his brother had tracked him down. To the best of his knowledge, John hadn't even known what hospital he was associated with.

"Damn Internet," Ivan muttered under his breath. That was the only explanation. His brother had used the awesome reach of ever-evolving modern technology to locate him. And bring less than happy times back into his life.

The pencil he was holding snapped in two between his fingers.

"Are you all right?"

His head jerked up.

DelMonico stood in the doorway, the door only partially open as she peered into the room, a concerned expression on her face.

He felt invaded. "What the hell are you still doing here?" he demanded gruffly.

Bailey saw no reason to lie, even if it meant putting up with being yelled at. She was getting accustomed to it and she prided herself on being able to tell apart Munro's gruff tirades.

She nodded toward the outer office and Alma's desk. "I was watching the red light on Alma's phone. It went out, so I knew your call was over."

The explanation only made things worse. Munro glared. He didn't like having his instructions ignored. Free will was all well and good for God to bestow, but he was not that magnanimous.

"I don't remember red-light watching being one of the things on the list of things I told you to take care of this morning."

"I just thought maybe you'd need someone to talk to."

His irritation grew. "And why in God's name would I need that?"

When she'd been first admitted to the program, his tone would have been enough to send her cringing out the door. But she'd learned a lot in the last ten months. One of which was when to be fearless and when to run for cover.

"Because of the expression on your face when Alma said that your brother was on the phone. You looked…troubled," she finally elaborated, compromising on a word as his eyes seemed to bore small holes into hers.

He threw the word back at her. "I'm 'troubled,' DelMonico,

because I have a resident who doesn't seem to want to take orders but does think she's qualified to play Nancy Drew on my time." He jerked a thumb up toward the ceiling. "The Psychiatry department is two flights up if you want to dabble in voodoo and go intern with them. Just say the word and I'll have Alma get you the proper papers."

She knew what he thought of psychiatry, that it was a waste of space and didn't belong within the medical field. The man didn't believe in what he couldn't see, which went a long way toward explaining why he seemed to have no faith to speak of.

But this wasn't the time for that sort of battle. She held her hands up in surrender. "Sorry, my error." She crossed the threshold back out again. "I forgot you weren't human."

"Well, don't forget again," he called after her. Then frowned as he sank down in his chair. Deeply.

CHAPTER 26

To anyone observing them, Dr. Ivan Munro and his brother John looked like two strangers exchanging polite greetings because circumstances had thrown them together in a situation they might not have, given a choice, otherwise inhabited.

Since he was the one who felt minutely more comfortable, because the setting was his, Ivan gestured for his older brother to take the chair facing his desk.

John gripped both chair arms and lowered himself into the seat, as if he didn't trust his legs alone to support the action. Ivan watched and made a mental note. Taller by several inches, John Munro was thinner than his brother, his face gaunt and grave. To the casual eye, he might have seemed at least twenty years older, not the actual ten.

Sitting back in his chair again, not knowing what to anticipate, Ivan nodded at his brother. "You said you wanted to see me."

John slowly took in his surroundings without turning his head. There was no way to tell what he thought. About his surroundings or about anything. His expression was as set in stone as his brother's was.

"Yes."

The single word hung in the air. Ivan pressed his fingertips together, containing a wave of impatience that rose out of nowhere. "Well, since we're still three months away from Christmas, am I correct in assuming this isn't an early holiday visit?"

John met his gaze head-on. And gave the same reply. "Yes."

Ivan laughed shortly and shook his head. "And they tell me that I'm uncommunicative." He was in no mood to play twenty questions or to be kept in the dark any longer. If this was someone else, he would have pointed them to the door. But John never did things without a reason. His brother had never believed in wasting anything, not even time.

Something was wrong, he could sense it. "What is this about, John?"

John shifted ever so slightly, as if the topic, or even thinking about the topic, made him uncomfortable. "I need your professional services."

Ivan's eyebrows drew together in a single stunned line. "You're sick?"

"You tell me." John raised his pale gray eyes to his brother's face. "I have this tingling sensation along my spine and my legs go numb periodically."

Diagnoses crisscrossed through his brain. Ivan gave none any undue time. The symptoms were too vague. "Could be any one of a number of things."

John frowned and just for a moment, looked so much like his brother, it was uncanny and unnerving. His speech pattern mimicked Ivan's, as well. "I'm assuming you'll be more specific than that."

Instead of answering, Ivan eyed the door. He'd caught a movement. The door opened and Bailey stood just inside the threshold, a huge manila envelope in her arms.

He looked at her accusingly.

"I knocked," she protested.

"I didn't tell you to come in," Ivan informed her, but for once, his usual terse tone was absent.

If she hadn't known any better, Bailey would have said that the neurosurgeon was relieved to see her in the room. Relieved to have someone with him beside the man who eerily resembled him in so many ways. She had been outside the door long enough to hear the last exchange of words and was struck by how much the two men were alike.

Just what the world needed, two Ivan the Terribles, Bailey thought darkly.

Because the neurosurgeon began to glare, she came forward and thrust the manila envelope at him. "I'm sorry. But I knew you wanted these right away."

He'd sent her to the Radiology Department an eternity ago, before he'd taken his brother's call. Ivan glanced down at the markings on the oversize manila envelope housing the MRI. "In case you have no concept of time, 'right away' was over an hour ago."

She knew that. She'd half expected him to page her not once but half a dozen times. The fact that he hadn't told her that something was seriously wrong. "The Radiology Department was backed up. They just finished developing this five minutes ago. I ran all the way from there to here."

Ivan nodded. "Good." Taking the envelope from her, he placed it on his desk. "One way to keep you in shape and on your toes."

Bailey took that as a dismissal and began to retreat. She was almost at the door when he stopped her. "DelMonico, take my brother to the Radiology Department."

She blinked, then looked at his brother, sitting in the chair. The same stone face that she saw across the room was looking back at her from the chair. No enlightenment was forthcoming from either source. "Excuse me?"

Ivan was busy writing instructions on a preprinted form. Finished, he ripped the 8-by-10 sheet from the pad and held it out to her. She felt like a Pony Express rider, expected to take off at a second's notice.

"Radiology Department. Brother. Stat," the neurosurgeon ordered.

Her eyes shifted to the manila envelope. As far as she knew, the man whose MRI lay inside was scheduled for surgery this afternoon. Was there a change in plans? She was supposed to be scrubbing in for that. She did that more and more these days, but each surgery was a fresh, thrilling adventure to her, a life-and-death situation to be faced and conquered. She took none of it, not one second, for granted.

"What about Mr. Abernathy?" she asked.

"I'll take care of Mr. Abernathy," he told her, his voice leaving no room for either argument or query. He turned toward John. "We'll start narrowing down the reasons."

Bailey was certain the man would begin to protest. Instead, John Munro nodded complacently, as if he'd expected no other statement.

"Fine." As he rose, John Munro paused for a moment, once again holding on to both arms of the chair. His expression registered annoyance more than pain. The moment passed and he released his grip from the metal arms. Turning toward Bailey, he nodded. "All right, young woman, lead on."

"That's not a young woman, John, that's a doctor," Munro

informed him. There was no warmth in his voice, but neither was there any rebuke. "Address her by her title. She's worked hard to earn it."

Bailey's mouth dropped open. She stared at the neurosurgeon as if she had never seen him before. Because maybe she hadn't. This was as close to praise as he'd ever uttered.

John inclined his head toward her, accepting the correction. "My apologies, Doctor. No disrespect intended."

"None taken," she murmured.

This was completely surreal. She hadn't seen the frame when she'd walked into the office, but somehow, Bailey thought as she led the way out, she must have stepped through the looking glass when she'd entered. There was no other explanation for the chief neurosurgeon's sudden about-face.

IVAN FROWNED as he examined the MRI suspended on the backlit display before him.

He didn't like what he saw, the cause of his brother's discomfort and intermittent numbness. He'd left John waiting in his office. Since the news was not good, Ivan surmised that his brother wouldn't mind waiting a little longer to hear it.

The word "never" played along the perimeter of his mind.

Ivan knew the exact second she slipped into the darkened room behind him. DelMonico had been amazingly soundless, especially taking into account that she was a female, and females had a way of rustling, of disturbing things as they moved. But that ridiculous, teasing scent she always wore announced her presence as loudly as if she'd walked right into a tray overloaded with lab samples and sent it crashing to the floor.

He didn't say anything, feeling that to do so would only encourage her to remain and talk his ear off. Frowning at the offensive MRI, he waited for DelMonico to leave.

Instead, she spoke. "It doesn't look good, does it?"

"No," Ivan replied without turning around, "it doesn't."

She moved closer to the display. Closer to him. Bringing that damn arousing scent with her. "Does your brother know?"

"He suspects," Ivan replied evenly. "Otherwise, he wouldn't be here."

"You two don't see each other socially?" He turned to her. "Silly question," she realized out loud. "Being your brother, I guess he doesn't socialize with anyone, either." She turned her attention back to the tiny, innocuous-looking clusters of cells running up and down a section of John's lower spinal column. There was only one conclusion. "Do you want me to explain this to him?"

Ivan didn't bother disguising his surprise. "You're volunteering?"

She nodded. "I thought it might upset you, having to tell your own brother he has cancer."

"We don't know that for certain." Ivan turned back to the MRI. "They could still be benign."

It was the first time she had ever heard him entertaining a positive viewpoint, especially since it was in all probability an extreme long shot.

"Could be," she echoed.

The darkness mocked them both.

CHAPTER 27

For ten seconds there was nothing but silence within the small room. And then Munro narrowed his eyes, which brought his brows together in a dark wave. "Are you patronizing me, DelMonico?"

"I believe the word you're looking for is 'comforting,' Doctor, not patronizing." Her mouth curved. "I don't have a death wish."

Her correction only annoyed him more. "I don't need comforting," Munro snapped.

She inclined her head, as if allowing him the benefit of the doubt. "That would make you one of God's unique creatures," she told him simply. He continued to glare at her like a wounded bear about to lash out. "Even animals need comforting."

He snorted at her simple-minded innocence. The woman needed protecting, most of all from herself. "Warn me the next time you decide to cuddle a wolf."

Her eyes seemed to shine as she smiled up at him. "I promise you'll probably be the first to know."

He made no comment. Instead, he turned his attention back to the MRI highlight on the display. The neurosurgeon's frown deepened. She knew the more sensible thing was to get out while her head was still intact. But she didn't always believe in being sensible. Not when she was in the presence of pain and convinced she could alleviate it. "Are you going to operate?"

He continued to stare at the MRI, as if willing the films to become clear.

"That's up to John." There was no emotion in his voice. She wondered how he could keep it all inside him. She never once doubted for a moment that it was there, sealed in, needing a release. "Besides, even if I am the best one for the job, if he decides to have the surgery, it wouldn't be ethical for me to perform it."

"Ethical." The statement amused her. "When did that ever stop you?"

Her question caught him off guard. No one talked to him like that except, on occasion, Bennett. "When did you get this smart mouth?"

"I'm not sure." Her expression was innocence itself. And then the smile rose to her lips again. "Must be the company I keep."

After taking down the MRI, he slid the oversize sheet back into its envelope. "Then get better company," he ordered, crossing to the door.

"Couldn't if I tried," she replied softly to his back as he let himself out.

But he heard her.

IT SEEMED TO BAILEY that someone siphoned away a few minutes from each hour, leaving her less and less time to accomplish all the things she had to address within the course of a day. At times, she felt buried alive beneath the weight of responsibilities left unmet, assignments not completed. Sleep became a vague memory.

Classes and exams were still very much a part of her life, as they'd been in medical school, and yet she had a full schedule at the hospital practically every day of the week. They were always short-handed and needed her to cover.

Added to that, Ivan the Terrible was living up to his name these days, being even shorter with her and everyone else than usual. It took very little for his temper to erupt like a volcano.

She made excuses for him without explaining to anyone what she knew to be the cause of his worse-than-usual disposition. One of the first-year residents called her a lackey and it made her take stock of the situation.

A week had gone by under these conditions and they were all shell-shocked and battle-weary.

By the second week, it had gotten to the point where even Bailey began to doubt she could put up with Munro's abrasive behavior much longer. Since she was the only one who knew the cause, she took it upon herself to broach the subject with him.

She waited until she could get the chief neurosurgeon alone. It turned out to be in the same tiny room where he had first looked at his brother's MRI. Seeing him go in, she slipped in behind Munro and shut the door.

When she flipped the lock, he looked up. "I don't recall asking you in here."

The voice was cold, dismissive. It took all she had to stand her ground. "I think you should know that the residents are planning on rebelling and burning you in effigy."

Mildly amused for the first time in weeks, he nodded at the information. "But not you."

"Oh no, I'm leading the charge." Instead of exploding as she'd anticipated, he laughed. That unnerved her, but she pushed on, intent on clearing the air. "Have I done something to offend you, Doctor?"

"Other than breathe?"

"Yes." Without thinking, she took a breath to fortify herself. "Other than breathe."

He waved a hand at her as if her actions were inconsequential to him at the moment. "No."

"Then—?"

He was about to shout that it was none of her damn business why he was as angry as he was. Instead, he changed his mind and gave her a reason. "I find disease offensive, DelMonico. I find cancer offensive. I don't waste my time with people. They come and they go. Cancer insidiously lingers on like…like…" Frustrated, he searched for the word he wanted.

"A cancer?" she suggested.

There was no pun, no play on words intended. One look at her face told him that. He banked down the urge to yell.

"Yes," he pronounced with finality that boarded on defeat. "Like a cancer."

She knew that she was going where no man or woman had gone before, delving into Ivan the Terrible's private life, but she'd gone too far now to backtrack. "What did your brother decide?"

He watched her for a long moment and she braced herself for him to tell her off in no uncertain terms.

But he didn't.

"Odd that you should ask. He called me this morning to discuss the downside of the surgery." Forgetting about the

X-ray he had mounted on the display, Ivan sank his hands into his pockets and looked off into the darkness. "I told him that the very act of cutting the tumors out might cause the cancer to spread. That just one wrong move on the surgeon's part and he could be paralyzed for life."

"And?" she pressed.

Ivan laughed softly to himself, shaking his head. "And he told me not to make a wrong move. He wants the surgery." For the first time in his life, his brother had displayed a measure of optimism, choosing life instead of resigning himself to death. "I told him I couldn't do the procedure. He told me to find someone I knew was good."

"And you feel responsible."

His gaze was so intense, it felt almost physical. She had to stop herself from taking a step back. "Damn straight, I feel responsible." And then he hit her with a bombshell. "Especially since I'm recommending you for the surgery."

For a second, she thought she was hallucinating. But he continued to look at her, challenging her to refute him. Challenging her to live up to his expectations. "Me? I'm not ready. I mean, I've done procedures and you've been very generous to let me assist—" It had surprised her, really, when he began to put her on a rigorous schedule, allowing her to take an active part in more and more surgeries.

"Generosity had nothing to do with it."

She recalled the MRI, the cluster of tumors along the lower part of his brother's spine. "—But I've never done anything this complex."

"There has to be a first time." Munro scrubbed his hand over his face. When he dropped it to his side again, his eyes focused on hers. Holding her prisoner. "I'm only going to say this once and if you ever, *ever* repeat this, I will summarily deny it. Not only that, but I will have you recommended for a psychiatrist evaluation."

"I thought you didn't believe in psychiatry."

"I don't," he informed her impatiently, "but everyone on the board seems to swear by it."

She felt very shaky inside and desperately needed something to hang on to. "So what is it that you're going to summarily deny saying?"

He paused and she thought he'd changed his mind about telling her. But he hadn't. "That you have the best hands I've seen in a long time. You have an innate skill that can't be taught. You have to be born with it." He picked up her right hand. Something zigzagged through her, like an infiltrator trying to avoid getting shot. "The same can be said for these fingers. They're a perfect size for all the delicate work that's required." Realizing that he was still holding her hand, Munro dropped it suddenly. "Besides, you're the only half-decent surgeon around who'll let me bully them."

He'd lost her again. "Excuse me?"

He spelled it out for her, enunciating every word as if it came individually wrapped. "I intend to be in that operating room when you cut John open, looking over your shoulder every second that you're holding a scalpel in your hand. Yours will be the hands operating, but I'll be the one deciding the moves."

Oh God, what was she getting into? "Oh. Well, no pressure here, right?"

Ivan was in no mood for banter or lightness. "Wrong."

"It was a rhetorical statement."

"And it was wrong," he repeated. "Because if you think you've encountered pressure before, my little-resident-that-could, you have no idea what pressure is until you get into that operating room and hold my brother's life in your hands."

Was he trying to make her fold? Because the exact opposite was occurring. She felt herself rallying. "Are you trying to scare me, Doctor?"

"No. I'm trying to get the best out of you. Pressure makes the excellent reach their full potential. It's only the mediocre that cave." His eyes pinned her in place. Daring her to back down. "So, are you up to this?"

"Do I have a choice?"

"No."

"Then I'm up to it."

He nodded. "Keep it that way." Crossing to the door, he flipped open the lock. "And tell your little friends that the rebellion is off, or I'll have them all for breakfast," he declared, leaving.

CHAPTER 28

That morning, Bailey threw up twice. And recited every prayer she knew. Also twice since her cache of memorized prayers had dwindled over the years.

Just before she left for the hospital, a full hour before she was scheduled to go on duty and a full three hours before John Munro's surgery, she e-mailed Simon and asked him to use any pull he felt he had with God to get her a little added insurance.

She needed all the help she could get.

She'd met with John Munro several times since their initial introduction in the neurosurgeon's office. She'd covered everything about the procedure, but as she walked into the hospital this morning, she felt compelled to see the man one more time.

Passing the locker room, she went straight toward the surgical holding area. Per protocol, Ivan's brother had been admitted early that morning. After all the forms were filled out, he was taken to a general pre-op room, a holding area where all neurological patients waited to be taken in for surgery. Each department had a holding area like this. Because of the difficult nature of the surgeries performed here, most of the beds were usually unoccupied.

As they were today.

She made her way past the nurses' station to the back of the ward. All the other beds around John Munro's were neatly made. He seemed somehow smaller.

"You have the ward to yourself," she said cheerfully as she approached his bed.

John Munro looked uncomfortable to be out of his clothes. The blue-and-white hospital gown took away his identity, reducing him to the anonymous entity of "patient."

He glanced up when she spoke. There was neither pleasure nor displeasure in his face. "I like it better that way."

If she closed her eyes, she could have sworn it was the neurosurgeon talking. Her smile widened. "You're a lot like your brother."

John shrugged and she noted that he appeared to be far less broad-shouldered than the neurosurgeon.

"I never noticed," he replied. His voice didn't waver.

It struck her that Ivan Munro's brother appeared very calm for a man whose life could be altered within a matter of a few hours. The only telltale sign of his uneasiness were his hands. They were knotted together on top of the blanket, like a student's at his desk in an old-fashioned private school.

She didn't know why, but she laid her hand on top of his. John seemed startled at the contact. Bailey smiled. "Trust me, you're a great deal like Dr. Munro," she assured him. "Is there anything you'd like to ask me? Anything you'd like to go over?"

He never hesitated. "How much time will I have if this doesn't work?"

Bailey broke contact, withdrawing her hand. Searching for the right words. It was a stark, blunt question, something which she wasn't prepared for. She'd secretly hoped that the chief neurosurgeon had gone over this with his brother when he'd discussed the risks. Apparently not.

A technician entered, carrying a tray of vials and a small length of hose. Amid an apology, he said something about needing to crossmatch blood before the surgery, then went about doing just that.

"I don't know," she told John, answering his question honestly. The words stuck in her throat and she had to force them out. "Could be six months. Could be longer."

As he looked at her, she noticed his eyes were a different color. But they were Ivan's nonetheless. They had the same intensity, the same ability to pin her in place. "Could be less."

"Could be less," she agreed unwillingly. "But that's only if we don't get everything," she added quickly, refusing to have him facing a dismal prognosis.

There was a glimmer of a smile at the corner of his mouth. Or maybe she was just wishing it into existence. "And you intend to get everything."

She nodded. "Do my absolute very best," she promised her patient.

Her patient.

It felt so odd. And yet, at the same time, right.

The technician was filling one last vial, then slipped the needle from John's vein. Removing the hose from around his arm, the technician applied a Band-Aid to the tiny puncture.

"How good is your best, Doctor?" John asked her. Before Bailey could form an answer, he continued. And his next words took her completely by surprise. "Ivan thinks it's pretty damn good."

Was he talking about Ivan Munro? Ivan the Terrible? The

man who generally made her feel as if she had ten thumbs? True, he'd given her that compliment when he told her she would be the one operating, but she was beginning to think she'd imagined it. "He said so?"

"No, but he wouldn't be letting you operate if he didn't think so." John leaned against the pillows a nurse had fluffed up for him. "You know, I've been lying here, thinking, in between them draining all my blood from me." He eyed the lab technician. The latter nodded and withdrew. "I've drawn breath all these years without really living. Either way this surgery goes, when it's over, I'm going to change that." His eyes shifted back to her face. "Provided you don't kill me on the table."

"I won't kill you on the table." It was a solemn promise.

"I have your word?"

She nodded, masking the fact that her heart was now in her throat. "You have my word."

"Good enough." John pressed a remote control and the bed slowly leveled out. He lay back against the pillow like a man preparing to take a nap, not go into lengthy spinal surgery. "See you on the other side of the anesthetic, Doctor."

From your lips to God's ears, she thought. It was a saying she remembered one of her parents' friends, a rabbi, was fond of saying. At this point she was channeling every known religion she could.

Telling herself it was all going to be all right, Bailey left the pre-op ward.

"Why did you go in to see him?"

Startled, she realized she'd almost walked into someone. Bailey glanced up and saw Munro standing to the side of the entrance leading into pre-op. Was he there to see his brother? Or just to watch him from a distance?

Every time she thought she had him adequately pegged, Munro morphed on her.

"To see if your brother had any questions and to make him as comfortable as possible about the upcoming surgery."

Munro shook his head. Rather than go in, he began to walk in the opposite direction, out of pre-op. "Comforting again. What is it with you? We're neurosurgeons—or at least I hope you are." His tone was brittle, challenging her. "Our job is to go in, cut, resection and get out. The rest of it is for preachers and chaplains and such. Like your brother."

"Well, I guess then we have a difference of opinion, Doctor."

"No," he contradicted, "we don't." Before she could protest, he explained. "You haven't graduated the program yet. Won't for a number of years. You don't get to have an opinion."

The hell she didn't. He might fancy himself a dictator, but he had no say over her mind, her emotional approach to this discipline. Being cut off from humanity might be his way, but it wasn't hers.

"Too late," she responded, forcing herself to sound cheerful. "Patients need reassurance. They need to know that their surgeon cares about the outcome of the operation. That they're not just a slab of meat, a cadaver that just happens to still be breathing. A good state of mind can't be underestimated when it comes to having a patient face a difficult surgery."

The sneer was not quite convincing. "More psycho mumbo-jumbo?"

"No," she countered with feeling and conviction. "Common sense."

His eyes narrowed as if that helped him process the information. "So, let me get this straight. You'd rather have someone cry over you than be skillful?"

"I'd rather have both." She squared her shoulders, raising her chin. Joan of Arc off to fight the British. "I *am* both."

"There is room for only one ego in that operating room, Del-Monico," he informed her pleasantly, more pleasantly than she'd expected. "And it is mine."

"I don't have to have an ego," she responded. "I have a heart."

He laughed, but it didn't sound as if it was at her expense. "Well, Tin Man, if it's all the same to you, I'd rather see what you can do with your fingers and not your heart."

This could go on and on. Drawing in a breath, Bailey nodded rather than extended the debate. It would be time soon, time to enter the operating room. And she needed to concentrate. Needed to focus. Needed, she thought, to be the best she had ever been because this was the most challenging operation she had ever faced.

"That," she told him, "goes without saying."

Ivan nodded at her. "Good." He waved her on her way. "Go scrub in. I'll meet you in the operating room."

Though she knew he didn't like being questioned, it was on the tip of her tongue to ask him where he was going. It certainly wasn't to see his brother because he was still heading in the opposite direction, going down the left corridor.

It was only after a few minutes, after she had already reached the lockers, that she remembered.

The hospital's chapel was in that direction.

CHAPTER 29

Despite the masks they all wore in the O.R., Bailey could feel Munro's breath on the back of her neck, branding her. Making goose bumps form as her skin reacted to his warmth.

She supposed it was just her nerves—and maybe a very eloquent metaphor for the fact that she did feel as if the chief neurosurgeon was literally and figuratively breathing down her neck. It took effort to completely block him out and concentrate exclusively on the only thing she needed to do: excise the lesions embedded around her patient's lower spinal column. There were eight that had to be cut away.

If even one defied eviction, or exploded and spread, the operation would be a resounding failure.

The patient was draped and prepped.

Those were the beginning words of every single operative report. It seemed almost surreal that this time around, when the operation was all done and behind her, she would be the one dictating those opening words. But she was the neurosurgeon on record and she had witnessed John Munro being placed on his stomach, a sheet with a rectangular opening draped over his lower spine, exposing the area to be operated on.

John's MRI films were hanging inches from her left side, showing her where she needed to make her first incision to begin the painfully slow and arduous task of returning John Munro to the world of the well.

Bailey paused for half a beat, taking a breath. It felt as if she'd been doing this forever and she was only halfway finished.

"If you're getting tired," she heard Munro say curtly behind her, "Holt can step in." The chief neurosurgeon did not sound happy with the possible turn of events, or the fact that he thought she was flagging.

Gene Holt was one of the two neurosurgeons who had been tapped to act as assistant surgeons, the key words here being assistant surgeons rather than co-surgeons. He had placed the burden of the surgery, the burden of the responsibility, on her shoulders and it was clear that he expected her to live up to it.

Munro offered the suggestion during what she realized was the third hour of the surgery. Was he losing faith in her abilities?

It didn't matter what he thought, she told herself. All that mattered was that she focus on each lesion until they were all excised. Munro's "offer" only served to make her more determined to complete the operation.

Which was why, she figured, he'd done it.

"I'm all right," she told him without turning her head.

It was a lie. She wasn't all right. Her arms ached, her shoulders were as tense as a newly forged ironing board. Her neck was killing her and there was a headache the size of Boulder, Colorado, building behind her eyes. She fervently prayed that it wasn't a migraine in the making.

But all right or not, she was getting them, getting each one of the tiny pinpricks of cancerous and precancerous growths and painstakingly separating them from the complex spaghetti entwinement that comprised the human spine. So far, the excisions went without incident. The cuts turned out to be neat and clean. From what she could tell, John Munro's spine remained unthreatened.

She just wished there weren't so many of the tiny tumors.

The only time Bailey raised her eyes and looked away from the man's spine was to glance at the clock on the operating room wall to see how much time had passed. The minutes seemed to retreat at an incredibly slow pace.

Just as she felt that she couldn't take the stress any longer, that her hands and arms were going to literally begin trembling from the strain, Bailey managed to remove the last, most elusive of the lesions. A ninth one that had been hiding behind one of the others.

Feeling a heady surge of triumph, she scanned the area one last time to make sure that she hadn't left anything behind, that there wasn't another, even tinier lesion, hiding behind the serpentine network of nerves that wove in and around the spine.

There were none.

Like a diver removing her snorkel, Bailey took a long, deep breath into her lungs and held it for a moment before releasing it again. She retired her scalpel to the tray where it had originally been placed and took a step back. Away from the operating table.

"Done," she announced, spreading the single word around like a blessing on a Sunday congregation.

Bailey had never felt so relieved, so happy, in her entire life. She'd done it. She'd performed a delicate, dangerous operation and there had been no mistakes, no slips. No harrowing nicks that would result in permanent debilitation for the patient.

"Holt, close." Munro snapped out the order like a drill sergeant.

Bailey took another few steps back, clearing the way for Holt to do his work. She couldn't help glancing at Munro. If she was expecting the chief neurosurgeon to say something to her, to make a favorable comment on her work or to unleash a minute word of praise from his arsenal of words, she was disappointed. Munro acted as if she wasn't even there. His attention was completely riveted to the fourth-year resident who had taken her place at the table.

Exhausted, suddenly excruciatingly drained, she knew she should leave the operating room but she just couldn't bring herself to cross to the door. She had to remain in the O.R. to the very end of the surgery. Her sense of duty demanded it. This might have been Munro's brother but the man on the table was *her* patient and as such, she owed it to John Munro to remain until he was taken from the operating room to the recovery area.

Out of the corner of her eye she saw one of the masked attendants quickly gather together all the lesions she had so carefully excised from John Munro's spine. After placing the lot into a covered container, the attendant quickly picked it up and left the room. Bailey knew that they were being taken to the hospital's medical lab where they would be carefully examined, assessed and catalogued.

And, God willing, ultimately be pronounced benign, or at the very least, declared intact, which meant that the cancer hadn't spread.

She refused to even consider any other outcome.

And then, finally, it was over. The operation was finished. The last stitch had been taken, the wound satisfactorily closed.

The drape exposing the worked area was removed and a new, whole sheet was placed over the patient. He was left on his stomach.

An eternity after she had entered O.R. Number 3, Bailey watched her first neurological patient being wheeled out of the room and to Recovery where he would remain for several hours of observation. He would then go to the ICU area located at the very end of the first floor.

Dead on her feet, Bailey stripped off her mask. All around her, the rest of the staff followed suit, removing masks and gloves. Everything was done soundlessly.

The silence within the room was deafening.

It was as if everyone was afraid to speak, afraid of doing or saying something that would inadvertently set off Ivan the Terrible. The O.R. staff held their collective breath as they watched him walk toward the double doors through which, seconds earlier, his older brother had been wheeled.

His hand splayed on the swinging door, Ivan paused. He hadn't expected to feel this way. He hadn't expected to feel at all. He had almost succeeded in convincing himself that this was just another operation, just another patient. After all, it wasn't as if he and his brother were close, or had ever been close. He knew next to nothing about the way his brother was conducting his life. All he knew was that the man wasn't married, had remained single.

Just like him.

And yet, there was this…this *thing* inside of him, this restlessness, this inability to find a place for himself. It was as if his skin wasn't fitting right anymore and he was just out there, waiting for some impending doom, some calamity to strike.

Throughout the entire surgery, he'd been on edge, ready to move DelMonico aside and take over. No matter what he'd said to her, he didn't trust either of the two assistants he'd attached to the team to do a better job than DelMonico. Or even as good a job as she did. That meant that, ethics be damned, he was the logical one to take over the delicate part of the surgery if she wilted.

But, although he wouldn't say it out loud, DelMonico had performed admirably well. Her aptitude came as no surprise to him. He could feel the six pairs of eyes boring into him. Wondering why he hadn't left.

Ivan said the words without turning around to look at them. "Good job, people."

The silence only grew as he left the room.

CHAPTER 30

The voices rose spontaneously. The two surgical nurses looked at one another, stunned. No one could remember the last time they'd heard actual praise coming from the chief neurosurgeon's mouth.

"Was that Ivan the Terrible?" Julie, the younger of the two surgical nurses asked the other.

"Quick, someone check the lockers for a pod," Holt quipped, referring to the scene from the cult favorite, *Invasion of the Body Snatchers*, where people were kept immobilized in a garage while their cloned counterparts roamed around in their place.

"Never thought I'd hear a decent word out of his mouth," Sara, the other nurse, commented. She had been at Blair Memorial as long as Munro had.

Voices crisscrossed one another as opinions and comments were bandied about regarding the chief neurosurgeon's unprecedented behavior.

Only Bailey kept silent. The man was in pain, she thought. There was no other explanation.

She exploded out of the O.R. like a shot, intent on chasing him down.

She saw Munro going down the corridor, about to turn a corner. "Wait," she called after him.

Ivan stopped. Instead of turning around, he waited for the resident to approach him.

"What?" he demanded before she could say anything further. "You want your fifteen seconds of glory personalized?"

All the kind, understanding words she'd collected as she hurried after him evaporated. Obviously the direct approach was called for. "Stop it," Bailey ordered.

Her annoyed tone had Ivan raising his eyebrows in startled disbelief. "Did you just raise your voice to me?"

She hadn't realized what was coming out of her mouth until it did. But now was no time to backtrack and apologize. "Well, it worked, didn't it? You stopped for a second."

"Stopped what?" He had no idea what she was talking about and cared only insomuch as it was impeding him. "Did you breathe in too much of the antiseptic solution in there?" he asked.

"Stop pretending you don't have feelings."

The expression on Munroe's face would have made a stone statue turn tail and run. "There is no need to pretend."

Bailey dug in. "He's your brother, for God's sake. It's only normal that you should be worried, that you're afraid of the outcome. And you're frustrated because you can't be the one doing the operating, that you can only stand there like a puppeteer, pulling strings and barking out instructions."

"I'm frustrated because I have a resident yapping at me," he shouted, and then his brown eyes darkened. "And I do *not* bark."

The hell he didn't. "I'll bring a voice recorder in next time," she promised. Her eyes met his. It was, she thought, one of the bolder moments of her life. "Trust me, you bark. And you *are* worried," Bailey insisted. The man needed to admit that, if only to himself.

"Yes." He ground out the word as he lowered his face in close to hers, "that I made a mistake when I told Bennett that I agreed to take you on."

She wasn't going to let him hide behind rhetoric or divert her off the track. She would get him to admit he was worried about his brother if it killed her. "Let it go, Ivan."

His eyes narrowed. She had never addressed him by his first name and she had no place doing it now. It placed them on a different footing, one he had no desire to occupy. "I beg your pardon?"

The faint of heart would have fled by now, Bailey thought. But she was fighting for a good cause. Even if Munro didn't recognize it right now.

"You heard me. Let it go," she repeated. "It's not healthy to keep everything bottled up inside the way you do."

He took a breath, trying to compose himself. Trying not to shout at this annoying resident in the middle of the hospital corridor.

"Read my lips, DelMonico. There is nothing to bottle up." His scowl made him dangerous. "And I have already told you how I feel about this psychoanalysis bull."

"No, you expressed a disdain for psychiatry," she corrected, knowing it would only annoy him further, "and I'm not practicing either. I'm relating to you. You're human."

He didn't want her "relating" to him. Didn't want her opening doors that had been painted shut so many years ago, he couldn't remember things being any other way. "That's an ugly rumor, spread by my enemies."

"That's not a rumor," she told him softly, allowing a smile to curve the corners of her mouth. "That's my intuition."

The snort was contemptuous. Knowing what motivated it, Bailey took no offense. She made him nervous, she realized. Because she saw through him and he was beginning to understand that. She'd found the secret door to the mighty Oz's throne room.

"Contrary to popular opinion, the female intuition is not all it's cracked up to be and yours needs fine-tuning." He began walking away.

She had a feeling she knew where he was going as she hurried after him. "Want me to go with you?"

He looked at her for a long moment, as if trying to decide what her motives could have possibly been. "To the men's room? Come along if you want. But it's not the big adventure you think."

If he thought he was going to embarrass her, he was in for a surprise. The years she had spent with her family in the jungles of Africa had all but completely leached embarrassment out of her.

"After that. When you go the lab to breathe down the technician's neck to try to intimidate him."

He didn't bother denying his ultimate destination. "I don't try," he informed her. "I succeed."

"All the more reason for me to be the one to get the information," she countered. "Nervous people make mistakes."

His eyes held hers prisoner. "You didn't."

Bailey raised her chin. "I wasn't nervous." She'd been extremely careful not to give herself away during the operation.

Ivan smirked. "Lying doesn't become you, DelMonico. Your breathing was shallow. You were nervous," he concluded. Then he paused before adding, "And you performed admirably well. There. I said it. Satisfied?"

Is that what he thought she was after? Did he really think she was that self-centered? How egocentric was this world of neurosurgery that she was inhabiting of her own free will?

"Not that I don't live for your approval, Doctor," she replied, "but that wasn't the point."

"Well, I've lost track of whatever trivial point you were ineptly trying to make, so why don't you go to the lockers to change and let me go to the men's room?"

With that, he walked away. As she watched, he actually did enter the men's room. And when he came out again five minutes later, she was still standing there, waiting for him.

The discovery didn't make him happy. "Don't you have something more pressing to do than stand there, holding up the wall?" he snapped.

"Yes," she agreed, straightening. "I do. I've got to get to the lab to get the final report on my patient's lesions."

He'd had enough of this game she was playing. He didn't want her meddling in his life, didn't want her thinking she knew him. Because she didn't and he wanted it that way. "He's your 'patient' only because I authorized it."

"Doesn't change the fact that he is. And as the primary surgeon, I have the right to know first."

He drew himself up to his full height. There was no denying the man cast an impressive shadow. But she wasn't about to let it frighten her off. If she gave in now, she might never be able to regain her footing and as far as she could see, it was all about the dance with Munro. He had no respect for cowards even if he seemed to enjoy intimidating people.

"Don't get in a pissing contest with me, DelMonico," he warned, walking away from her. "I promise you'll lose."

"This isn't a contest, Doctor," Bailey answered, matching him step for step even if she had to stretch her legs as far as they could go in order to do it. "And for your information, you *need* me there."

She had an ego, after all, he thought. "I stopped needing someone to accompany me anywhere my first day in kindergarten."

To his surprise, she laughed at his answer. "Keep telling yourself that."

Enough was enough. He stopped walking and glared at her. "DelMonico, I am ordering you to stay put."

He'd raised his voice and was shouting at her. People in the hall watched them as they passed. She blocked them out and focused on sticking to her guns. In her heart, Bailey knew that she was right. That if the news was bad, if something had gone wrong and the tests showed it, then Munro shouldn't have to view it alone.

"Sorry, sir," she retorted flippantly. "Can't hear you."

"That's because the bats you have flapping around in your belfry are making too much noise."

She cheerfully shrugged his retort off. The euphoria produced by the completion of a successful surgery was still very much clinging to her. "Whatever," she answered, still matching him step for step.

They'd reached the laboratory. "Stay here," he snapped, walking in ahead of her.

But she was right behind him. "No."

He could have strangled her. And embraced her at the same time.

CHAPTER 31

From the recesses of her brain, Bailey remembered an ancient joke, the punch line of which was, "The operation was a success. Unfortunately, the patient died."

It echoed through her mind now, as she stood just a hairbreadth behind Munro and listened to the lab technician delivering bad news. The tumors were all cancerous. And although the multiple lesions had all been excised, what both she and Munro feared the most had come to pass.

The cancer had spread.

Bailey felt numb inside. And cheated, horribly cheated.

She knew she was being self-centered and selfish to make this about her instead of the patient, but this had been her very first difficult surgery. Her *first*. She'd done *everything* right.

Or at least she'd thought she did. And Munro hadn't filleted her with his tongue. That had to mean something.

Why wasn't the patient going to get well?

Ivan maintained a stone face as he took in the news. He put his hand out for the initial report. The technician's was shaking as he surrendered the paper. Ivan reviewed the results himself. It was there in black and white. There was no point in questioning the accuracy of the readings.

With a curt nod, Ivan let the paper fall back on the counter and turned away to leave. He was at the door before he realized that his shadow was missing.

Glancing back, Ivan saw her standing exactly where she'd been when the news had been delivered. His resident hadn't moved a muscle. Her face looked as if all the life had been drained out of her.

Why would she care?

It made no sense to him. Ivan had to call to her twice before DelMonico even looked in his direction. He didn't like the expression in her eyes, even from here.

"Get over here," he ordered. Responding after a beat, Del-Monico complied as if her whole being had just been placed on automatic pilot. He pushed the door open, planted his hand between her shoulder blades and pushed her out of the laboratory. "What the hell's the matter with you?" he asked as the door swung shut again.

The question penetrated the thick walls of the trance. Bailey blinked and watched him in sheer wonder. "How can you even ask that?" she demanded. "Didn't you just hear Jeremy?"

The name meant nothing to him. She was always doing that, tossing names at him as if she expected him to know. How the hell was he supposed to keep track of all these people who came and went at the hospital? They were all part of the fabric, the background. Knowing their names didn't make him a better surgeon and that was all that counted. "'Jeremy'? Who the hell is Jeremy?"

"The lab technician. Jeremy," she repeated impatiently. "He just said the cancer has spread."

"I know. I heard," he told her coldly. "My hearing's still intact." He was annoyed they were even having this discussion. "We knew that was one of the possible outcomes going in."

For a second, he left her speechless. Didn't *anything* faze him? Had he been right all along, that he was completely devoid of emotions? She just couldn't get herself to believe it.

"How can you say that?" she demanded, feeling herself very close to the edge. "This isn't some textbook case we're reviewing in class, this is your brother. Your *brother*." She pressed her lips together to keep her voice from breaking. But the pause did no good. Her voice cracked the second she began to speak again. "And I—I failed him." She took a breath. Tears filled her throat, choking her. "I did everything right and he's not going to get better."

Wide shoulders moved aimlessly in a careless shrug. "Happens."

"Happens?" Her eyes widened as she stared at him, stunned. "*Happens?*" she echoed in disbelief. "What are you, made of stone? He's going to die. Your brother's going to die." She was supposed to have made him better, she thought in mounting despair.

"We're all going to die," Ivan informed her, his voice distant, curt. "My brother just has an inside window on when."

That was so wrong, it took her breath away. Didn't the man *feel* anything? "I can't believe this. I can't believe you're reacting like this. How can you…?" Words deserted her.

Munro took hold of her shoulders. The grip was viselike and at that moment she realized the chief neurosurgeon was far from calm, far from removed. He just couldn't show an emotion other than anger.

Each word he spoke was carefully measured out. "I'm reacting this way because tomorrow I have to pick up a scalpel again. Tomorrow someone else will be lying on that table, someone else hoping for a miracle. Hoping his or her surgeon is clearheaded enough to focus exclusively on their operation and not allow a lot of useless emotions to clutter up his mind, detract from his work." Suddenly aware of the close proximity between them, he released her shoulders. "Now stop beating yourself up, DelMonico. You did the best you could. Better than most," he allowed grudgingly.

She shook her head. "But if I hadn't operated on him, the cancer might not have spread."

His eyes met hers. It felt as if he had a voyeuristic advantage. "You don't believe that. I don't," he told her, and then reminded her of another fact she'd overlooked. "And I was the one who initially recommended the surgery. So if there's a fault in this, it's mine. But there isn't one. And what you did was to buy John some extra time."

His scowl intensified until it seemed carved into his face. He minced no words. "Now if you can't handle this kind of thing, if you can't suck it up and move on, then maybe you shouldn't be in the program." She expected him to walk away on that, leaving the dramatic moment lingering in the air. Munro actually took a couple of steps before turning around again and adding, "Personally, I think if you do leave the program, you'll be making the biggest mistake of your life."

The man made her head ache. "Is that your way of telling me you think I'm good?"

The dry laugh told her he meant to praise her. "You've exhausted your limit of compliments, Bailey." And then he reconsidered. "But in case you have one of those notoriously short attention spans—yes," the word was grudgingly tendered "—I think you're good."

She'd barely heard the end of it. He'd trapped her right in the beginning. "You never called me by my first name before."

That, he thought, had been a slip on his part. He dismissed it with a vague nod of his head. "I guess we're both rattled. It won't happen again."

"No." That wasn't why she'd made note of it. She counted it as a breakthrough, not something that needed an apology for existing. "I like it." A smile came to her lips. "It makes all that shouting you do at me more personal."

Ivan could only shake his head, mystified. "You are a strange woman, DelMonico."

The smile spread. "But I am growing on you."

"Not really much of a recommendation," he pointed out as he resumed walking again, his destination the recovery room. "Fungus grows on things, as does bacteria. Neither being very appealing."

She had no idea why she suddenly found all this comforting, a space in time where she could take refuge. "I bet you didn't get many dates in medical school with that silver tongue."

He neither denied her assumption nor validated it. Instead he summoned an inscrutable expression and told her, "You'll never know, DelMonico."

He was grateful to her. She had managed, through her convoluted dialogue and quirky way of seeing things, to lessen the burden of the moment, lessen it enough for him to be able to deal with its meaning. With its sentence.

There was just one more thing he had to take care of. "I'll be the one to tell my brother." His tone left no room for debate or disagreement.

"He's my patient."

He cut her down with what he assumed was her kind of illogical logic. "I've known him longer."

She surprised him by contesting his statement. "Have you?"

He looked at her as if she'd lost her mind. The man was his brother, for God's sake. John had been her patient for—what, a week and a half all tolled?

"What's his favorite color?" Bailey challenged.

Now he was certain she'd lost her mind. "What? What the hell does that have to do with anything?" he fairly shouted.

"When you 'know' someone," she informed him, thinking that she'd won the debate, "you know details about them." She looked at him pointedly. "Personal things."

"His favorite color's blue," he growled out. "Like your eyes."

That floored her. Both that he knew and that he'd observed her long enough to know the color of her eyes.

"Wow." She blew out a breath. "I stand corrected." The next moment, she took the small victory away. "Okay, I'll compromise. We'll tell him together." And then she explained part of her reason. "You shouldn't have to face him with this kind of news alone."

Ivan found that his normally short temper was in even shorter supply. "You know that nurturing thing you do? That bit that you feel is so important in your relations with a patient?"

Since he was obviously waiting for a response, she gave him one. "Yes?"

"Stop it," he ordered gruffly. "I'm not one of your patients."

She didn't just treat patients that way, she thought, but now was not the time to bring that to his attention. "Yes, sir."

Her innocent tone mocked him. "You're not going to listen, are you?"

The smile was brief, as if acknowledging that he'd had a small breakthrough. "No, sir."

Ivan shook his head. "Like I said, DelMonico. You are a very strange woman."

"You didn't use the word 'very' before," she pointed out.

"I should have."

Bailey said nothing, only smiled.

CHAPTER 32

"You look like death," were the first words out of John Munro's mouth when he raised his head to see his brother standing over him. A full twenty-four hours had passed since the surgery and John had been placed in ICU until his condition was no longer guarded. "Is it mine?"

The question took Ivan aback. He'd come to talk to his brother about his prognosis. Thinking to avoid his annoying resident, he'd slipped into John's small, enclosed area early. Only to find Bailey already there. She'd smiled at him. He'd read a great deal into that smile, but before he could comment on any of it, his brother had opened his eyes.

And was now asking him something that sounded akin to a riddle. "What?"

John looked from his surgeon to his brother. When he spoke, his voice was raspy. "Are you here to tell me that the operation was a failure?"

Ivan slanted a glance toward the other doctor, remembering her expression yesterday, how upset she'd been about all this. The impression was burned into his brain. "No, the operation was a success. Dr. DelMonico removed all the lesions from your spinal column."

John never took his eyes off him. Waiting. "But?" he prompted.

Bailey beat him to it, not because she wanted to be the one to inform her patient but because she wanted to spare Munro from having to do it. "But the cancer has spread."

John's eyes shifted to her. She saw him moving his thumb back and forth over a small expanse of blanket. The man wasn't nearly as calm as he pretended to be, either. Something else the two brothers had in common, Bailey thought.

John nodded slowly, as if mulling over what she'd just told him. His eyes briefly passed over his brother's face before returning to the diminutive neurosurgeon. "How long?"

She wasn't sure she knew what he was referring to. "How long what?"

"How long do I have?" The expression in his eyes would not allow her to lie. Still, she wanted to soften the blow if she could.

But it was Ivan who interrupted. "That's hard to say."

John surprised them both by laughing shortly. "Everything was always hard for you to say. Give me a ballpark figure."

Bailey opened her mouth, but Ivan raised his hand, silencing her. "Six months. Maybe longer."

John nodded as if he'd resigned himself to that much. He glanced toward Bailey. "Same as before."

Ivan realized that his resident must have already covered this before the surgery had taken place. She was thorough.

"Same as before," Ivan echoed.

There was no apology in his voice, no attempt to comfort. Bailey looked at him, unable to comprehend how he could remain so reserved discussing what amounted to a death sentence.

"Medicine is making all sorts of advances every day," Bailey interjected with enthusiasm. "There are treatments you can begin that might very well send your cancer into remission. I can bring you reading material—"

Turning his head, John looked at his brother. "She always act like a cheerleader?" he asked, a trace of faint amusement in his voice.

Bailey felt frustrated. One ironclad Munro was hard enough to take. Two were next to impossible to put up with.

It was a moment. He couldn't remember the last time he and John had shared one. Probably because there had never been one before. A hint of a smile curved Ivan's lips. "You should try working with her. It's nerve-racking."

In response, John offered a weak smile. It softened his lined face considerably. "I can see where it would be. No," he said, addressing Bailey now. "No treatments for me."

She didn't want him giving up. She firmly believed that as long as there was life, there was hope and hope even on its own could do so many things. "But—"

John didn't seem to hear her protest. When he spoke, it was almost as if he was thinking out loud. "My life has been on hold for fifty-seven years. Suddenly, I can't remember why." He looked at Bailey. "I've been meaning to take a trip to England for years. This seems like the right time for me to go."

He was weak. He needed to recover from his surgery. And if he didn't seek treatment, he would get progressively weaker. Bailey shook her head. "Traveling might not be the best idea right now," she told him kindly.

"If not now, then when?" The question was innocent. And blunt at the same time.

There were arguments she could use, but Bailey knew they

would fall on deaf ears. Her patient had made up his mind. She knew stubbornness when she saw it. "You have a point."

John nodded, pleased. He looked at his brother. "She surrenders nicely."

Ivan snorted. "Not that I've ever noticed."

John examined her intently. She couldn't begin to guess what was going through his mind. When he reached out, she realized he wanted her hand, so she placed it in his.

"If I were ten years younger and had a little more time..." There was no point in finishing the sentence. There was no more time. All but a few months of his life were behind him, wasted.

He raised her hand to his lips and lightly kissed it in the courtly manner of eras gone by. The way he soon would go by.

"I WAS WRONG," Bailey said to Ivan several minutes later as she and the chief neurosurgeon walked out of ICU together.

He thought she was wrong on a great many counts. Wrong and yet somehow naively right at the same time. She struck him as a walking contradiction. But something about her made him almost anticipate the next day, the next encounter.

He said none of this. No one was ever brought down by his own words if he kept them to himself. So Ivan raised a speculative eyebrow and asked, "About?"

"You and your brother. You're nothing alike."

Ivan nodded. "I know. I was always considered the outgoing one."

The comment was so absurd she started to laugh. Once the sound was released, she kept laughing. Laughing so hard that all the emotions she was trying so hard to harness suddenly spilled out.

And before Ivan's horrified eyes, the laughter turned to tears. Tears even more uncontrollable than the laughter had been.

"Stop it," Ivan ordered.

When she didn't because she couldn't, he took hold of her arm and pulled her over into an alcove on the side of the corridor, a pocket of hallway that was overlooked and ignored for the most part. He was accustomed to being obeyed. But he had nothing in his arsenal to combat grief and tears.

"Damn it, DelMonico, stop it. Do you hear me? Stop crying like that," he ordered. "It's not going to help anything."

Unable to speak, to form a coherent word, all Bailey could do was shake her head. Because she knew the sight of her tears only succeeded in making him angry, she turned away from him. Bailey covered her face with both her hands.

She was completely unprepared for what happened next.

Lost in grief, in helpless, overwhelming despair, Bailey felt someone turning her around. And then she was being enveloped in a pair of strong arms. The comforting sensation of being held registered in the distant mists of her being even as she sobbed her heart out. Someone was stroking her hair, however awkwardly.

This time Ivan's voice was a great deal softer when he said, "Stop it, Bailey. It's not going to help him. You did what you could."

But there should have been more, something more, I could have done.

Bailey looked up at him. Her face was streaked with tears and the sadness in her eyes seemed bottomless. "I'm sorry. I'm so sorry."

Ivan had no reply for that, no words to offer. He had no idea what had possessed him to hold her to him. He had even less of an idea why he did what he did next.

Moved by her sadness, by the extreme sorrow he saw in her eyes, he tilted her head back ever so gently. Maybe with the idea of enlisting gravity, making her tears harder to fall. He didn't know. All he knew was that her grief touched him. Spoke to him. And he needed to strike it from existence.

No words of comfort came to him. He was desperate to alleviate the pain he was witness to in any way he could. But his mind went blank.

The next moment, his lips were on hers and he was kissing her.

Stunned, more prepared to have him push her away than to receive this display of kindness, Bailey found herself kissing him back.

The moment that she did, she felt a sharp connection coming to life within her. It was as if she'd just picked up a live wire and had the current shoot through her, leaving no part untouched, no part unchanged.

Reacting, Bailey rose up higher on her toes, entwining her arms around his neck, allowing the moment and the feeling to take her away. It blotted out everything else. Blotted out time, space and the very immediate world.

Who knew that a man who spit nails on a regular basis and was the closest thing to a semihuman robot could kiss this way?

Could melt every one of the two hundred and thirty-six bones within her body?

She had a feeling, as she felt her mind spinning off into oblivion, that not even Dr. Ivan Munro himself had known, until this very moment, that this possibility existed.

CHAPTER 33

What the hell was he doing?

The demand for an accounting, an explanation, echoed through his brain even as he continued kissing this woman he found himself unaccountably drawn to. For the first time in more than twenty-five years, Ivan Munro didn't have all the answers.

Or even a single one that stood up to the light of day.

He had not only veered off the narrow, guarded path he'd been on ever since Scott's death, he had completely lost his mind by jumping headfirst down a ravine.

And he was still free-falling.

The concept jolted him into awareness.

It was over in a heartbeat—if her heart had been beating. Which it wasn't. As a matter of fact, it had stopped dead. Frozen, no doubt, in shock. And wonder. An entire, breathtaking Mt. McKinley of wonder.

Neither one of them was the first to stop it, to pull back their head and send this kiss into the annals of history, most likely *Ripley's Believe It or Not*. The withdrawal into separate corners was simultaneous and mutual.

As was the silence that followed.

As the air slowly returned into her oxygen-depleted lungs, Bailey found herself completely tongue-tied. She was not altogether sure she hadn't hallucinated the whole thing. A decent night's sleep had eluded her since the night before John Munro's surgery and if pressed, she couldn't volunteer, with any degree of certainty, when she'd last thrown anything into her mouth, much less sat down to consume an actual meal. Maybe all that, along with the stress she'd been under all these months, had finally taken its toll on her and she'd experienced a momentary break with reality.

The silence echoed in her head until it almost became deafening. Bailey stared at Ivan now as if she wasn't able to swear to anything.

"Was that you?" she finally asked.

"What?" Ivan expected some sort of flippant remark from her, executed in self-defense. The woman before him seemed genuinely confused. And dazed.

That makes two of us.

Bailey cleared her throat. "Just now—" Her tongue tangled, she started again. "Did you just kiss me, or did I just have some sort of seizure?"

Was she comparing kissing him to having convulsions? That's what he got for momentarily losing control. "Why, was it that bad?"

He hadn't denied that he'd kissed her. Okay, at least she hadn't lost her mind. But she wanted to be absolutely sure. "Then you did kiss me."

"Yes," he snapped, "I kissed you." The words were ground out between his teeth.

Well, at least that sounded like him again. But explained nothing. She needed to know, to understand. Was he toying with her, or feeling something? "Why?"

"Damned if I know." And then a catch phrase from a classic comedy show he'd seen in passing on one of the cable channels came to him. "Maybe the devil made me do it."

"Oh." Was that good or bad? Damned if she knew. Everything was as clear as mud. "All right. As long as there's a plausible explanation." Maybe he was as surprised, as shaken up as she was. That had been one hell of a kiss. Worthy of risking eternal fire and brimstone. Bailey smiled. "Tell the devil he does nice work."

Ivan had absolutely no idea how to respond to that. "Yeah, you, too." It occurred to him that she had tasted sweet, like rich whipped cream. Like strawberries and whipped cream.

This thing with his brother had him completely turned inside out, Ivan thought grudgingly. And not making sense on any front.

"We've got work to do," he barked.

"Yes, Doctor."

It bothered him that she was grinning as she said it. As if she were more in control of the situation than he was. Hell, a june bug was more in control of the situation than he was.

But that would change, Ivan promised himself.

OVER THE COURSE of the next few weeks, Munro behaved as if nothing out of the ordinary had happened between them. There wasn't so much as a look, a glance, an indication that they had shared something more than mere cases.

It got to the point that Bailey was beginning to believe she really *had* imagined the whole thing, maybe breathed in too many fumes from the various chemicals used within the hospital. If anything, Munro was even gruffer toward her than ever. Initially she'd thought maybe he was embarrassed about that one moment, that one slip from his perch that had temporarily rendered him human. Embarrassed and angry that she and her lips had been on the receiving end of that lapse.

But as the days went by and Ivan continued to behave in a manner that by comparison made Attila the Hun seem warm and cuddly, Bailey stopped making excuses for the chief neurosurgeon. He'd apparently once again risen to his true level, or fallen down to it, depending on perspective. In either case she couldn't allow herself to dwell on it. She had work to do and precious little downtime in which to recuperate. The kiss was filed away as an anomaly of nature, a temporary break with reality.

She heard from Simon, which always made her breathe a little easier.

For every twenty e-mails she sent her brother, she received one back. Two if things were going particularly well and he had the downtime to answer her. She told him everything. Everything except about Ivan kissing her. It surprised her that in her mind the chief neurosurgeon and scourge of Blair Memorial had gone from being referred to by his last name to his first. She supposed that thinking of him as Ivan made their working relationship seem less formal, more personal.

So did being kissed by him.

But all that was now in the past. The very distant past by the way Ivan behaved. There seemed no point in mentioning it to Simon.

In contrast to her e-mails, Simon kept his missives short, upbeat and generally vague. She knew he did that on purpose so that she wouldn't worry. But she did anyway. It wasn't as if her brother had gone to spread the word of God at Club Med, but she knew better than to mention that.

The most recent communication from Simon arrived after a silence of almost three weeks. She was relieved to the point of almost being giddy when she'd found it on her laptop. Simon had written twelve lines in total.

Four per week, she'd thought wryly.

Bailey read and reread the twelve lines until she knew each word by heart. As always, her brother told her not to worry, that he was fine and would continue to be so. And he closed by saying that he was sorry he hadn't enough pull to pray Ivan's brother into good health. Even so, he assured her, there was a reason for everything, even if it wasn't clear.

"Ever the minister," she'd said out loud. She missed him terribly.

IVAN SEEMED TO BE in a particularly dark mood when she approached him at the hospital an hour later. Because she'd heard from Simon, it automatically had made her think of John and wonder if Ivan had heard anything from his brother. He hadn't mentioned anything since John had been discharged from the hospital, but then their conversations had been purposely professional since he had briefly made time stand still that morning in the corridor outside his brother's room.

There was no harm in asking.

Offering Alma a wide smile, Bailey swept into Ivan's office. "Hi. I heard from Simon today."

The neurosurgeon was on his feet and about to leave the room. When he saw her, he frowned. He couldn't deal with her brand of sunshine right now.

"Good for you." The words, as well as his manner, were dismissive.

"Actually, it was," she told him. "It put my mind at ease that he's still all right." Ivan said nothing. She decided to press just a little. He probably expected as much. "Have you heard from your brother?"

Crossing to the door, Ivan stopped and looked at her sharply. "Why would you ask that?"

"Well, I heard from mine and I just thought that maybe you'd heard from yours." Each word moved slower than the last until they became stillborn, refusing to emerge.

She didn't know what made her glance toward his desk, but she did. That was when she saw a postcard, picture side up, dead center. The picture was of the Tower of London.

It figured, she thought. The Tower and its history seemed in keeping with the gloomy perspective that both brothers were prone to.

"You *did* hear from John," she declared, pleased that the contact hadn't been broken this time.

"How…?" Anticipating his question, Bailey pointed toward the desk and the postcard on it. She saw a look she couldn't quite describe pass over his face before it became stony again. "Oh. That. That arrived over a week ago."

Something in his tone made the hairs at the back of her neck stand up. And his eyes…was that sadness?

An uneasiness began to take hold of her.

"You heard from him more recently?" she guessed.

He sighed before he answered. The words took effort and he resented this invasion into his privacy. "Not exactly."

"I don't—"

"The concierge from the hotel where John was staying called." Her stomach tightened in anticipation of the words she knew were to follow. And then he said them. "John's dead."

CHAPTER 34

Bailey felt the color drain out of her face. She thought of the way John had looked the last time she had seen him. Determined to make the most of whatever time he had left. She had estimated he had six months. He hadn't even had two.

She felt her heart twist in her chest. It just wasn't fair. "Oh God, I'm so sorry."

Ivan moved his shoulders in a dismissive shrug. He wasn't sure why he'd even told her. It would have been easier on him to lie. "It's not like it was unexpected. The trip to London was unexpected, but not his death."

Bailey studied his rigid face. Ivan was being stoic again, building that unbreachable wall all around himself again. Something rose up in her throat. Bile? It tasted more like frustration. She'd become very familiar with that because of him. With effort, she banked it down and concentrated instead on giving him support whether he wanted it or not.

"Is there anything I can do?"

"No."

But even as he refused her offer, Bailey realized exactly what she could do for him. With loans to pay off, her finances were squeezed so tight, they squeaked every time she opened her purse, but she knew she could always turn to her aunt and uncle. They were good people. They could be counted on for an emergency loan. And this qualified as an emergency. A big one.

Bailey harnessed the urge to hug him, to physically convey her sorrow for his loss. Instead she announced, "I'm going with you."

Dark eyebrows knit together over the bridge of an almost-perfect nose. "You always go with me on my rounds. It's part of the program."

"I mean to London."

His look darkened, warning her to back off. "The hospital's large but it doesn't extend that far."

"I am going to London with you to bring back your brother's body."

The look he gave her said he thought she really had gone off the deep end. "I'm not going to London to bring back his body."

But he had to go, she thought. How else would John's body be flown back to the States? "Isn't there some kind of law against shipping an unattended body from one country to another?"

He shook his head. It was obvious that he wanted the discussion terminated. "I haven't got the vaguest idea, but it sounds like the kind of red tape that would delight the heart of a bureaucrat."

"You're not having his body flown back here."

"You catch on quickly." He sighed. "Before you exhaust yourself—and me—by playing A Thousand and One Questions, I'll tell you. I'm having my brother's body cremated over there."

"Why?"

Why was he bothering to explain this to her? Why didn't he tell her that none of this was any of her damn business? But even as he wondered, he heard himself saying, "Because that's what he wanted. To be cremated and to have his ashes scattered at sea. He'd said something to the effect that at least that way, he'd finally get to travel around Europe—as long as there was the right tailwind," he added sarcastically.

He wasn't fooling her with that tone. He was trying to sound as if it didn't matter to him, but at bottom he'd just expressed a lovely sentiment. Lovely and overwhelmingly sad at the same time. That in death John Munro would pass through all the places that he had never allowed himself the opportunity to see while he was still alive.

"Aren't you going to go there for the ceremony?"

"No ceremony," Ivan contradicted. He had no plans for there to be one. Just something simple. "Just a man and a boat, the sea and the wind." Ivan eyed her for a moment. "You have some ulterior motive for getting me out of the hospital?"

"The only ulterior motive I have is to try to get you out of that prison you've constructed around yourself."

Damn it, there had to be a way to get this woman to back off, short of coming at her with a John Deere tractor. "If I constructed it, I must like it."

"Not necessarily." She didn't even remotely believe that. "You're just too stubborn to break out. It's also way too much trouble."

If it kept him in, it also was supposed to keep her out. And it was doing one hell of a poor job of that. He sneered at her. "And you're offering to dismantle it, brick by brick?"

She wasn't going to allow him to bait her. She felt like Daniel Webster, fighting the devil for possession of a soul. Except in this case, the soul's owner wasn't on her side. "I'm offering to help."

Ivan leaned into her. "Offer refused," he told her flatly.

She pretended she didn't hear him. "I can book two tickets to London for—"

"Offer refused," he repeated more loudly, saying the words into her face. And then abruptly, he said, "Phelps is operating at eleven. Tell him I sent you to observe. And *not* talk," he ordered emphatically. "Think you can do that?"

There were times when he really got on her nerves with his implication that she was too chatty, but she knew that he was just trying to blow a smoke screen, to lure her away from the true point. That he needed someone with him at a time like this.

"Yes, but—"

He yanked open the door and walked out. "Good. Go haunt Phelps."

She knew she couldn't directly disobey him when it came to the program. A helplessness draped over her as she watched Ivan walk down the hallway. "Where are you going?"

He didn't even bother to turn around to deliver his parting words. "If I wanted you to know, I would have told you."

HE WASN'T AT THE HOSPITAL the next day.

Or the day after that.

Bailey had Adam keep Alma occupied at the coffee machine long enough for her to secure Ivan's address and phone number.

He wasn't home, either. Or at least he wasn't answering his

phone. Or turning on the lights at night when she drove past his unit at the apartment complex where he lived.

Dr. Edward Phelps called them all together and announced that Dr. Bennett had made him temporary chief neurosurgeon until such time as Ivan Munro returned to Blair Memorial.

She raised her hand just as Phelps dismissed. About to leave, Phelps nodded toward her. "Yes, Dr. DelMonico?"

"Where is Dr. Munro?" She wanted to know.

Phelps sighed. "That is on a need-to-know basis," he replied.

Her eyes met his. As far as people went, Phelps was well liked and equally well respected. Both his approach to teaching and his manner were a breath of fresh air in comparison to Munro. But word had it that he was just not the better neurosurgeon. That honor belonged to Ivan and Ivan alone.

"I *really* need to know," she said, fervently hoping that was enough.

Phelps laughed, but in his own way, he was as close-mouthed as Ivan. It was a power thing, "them" against "us," and Phelps knew better than to cross the line. Or Dr. Munro.

"Sorry, Dr. DelMonico, but as much as I'd like to answer your question, I don't relish having my butt kicked whenever Dr. Munro gets back."

At least he'd answered that much. Ivan *was* gone. Finding that much out constituted a minor victory. There were others to be won before this was over, she promised herself.

WITH OR WITHOUT Munro, the pace was grueling. Rounds were made, patients reassigned. Each time Ivan's name was wiped away from the day board behind the Admissions desk, Bailey felt as if a little more of him was fading away.

She'd taken on the preponderance of his patients, keeping the records the way she knew Ivan liked them. And each day, after work, she drove by his apartment complex, by his unit, to see if there were any lights on yet. To see if he'd come home.

IF HE WAS EVER coming home, she thought in the shank end of the evening of the eighth day of his absence. He had been gone eight days and no one would confirm her suspicions. That Ivan had gone to London to scatter his brother's ashes.

From the little she actually knew about Ivan, John had been his only living relative. That left him alone in the world. As alone in fact as he had tried to seem in principle all this time. That might make a man do things that he normally wouldn't do. Might make him entertain thoughts he didn't ordinarily think.

Her speculation led her to a dark place, just as she entered his complex.

Oh God, what if his brother's death pushed Ivan over the edge?

She forced herself to stop letting her imagination run away with her. It wouldn't do any good to make herself crazy. Ivan was far too logical to terminate his existence.

But everyone had their limit. What if…?

Bailey abruptly stopped formulating scenarios and their accompanying questions when she approached his ground-floor unit and saw lights weaving themselves through the drawn drapes.

Ivan was back.

CHAPTER 35

Bailey sat in her car, idling a few feet away from Ivan's apartment, and stared at the drawn drapes. Here and there, a tiny stream of artificial light escaped.

She debated turning her vehicle around and going home.

But then she made up her mind. She'd come this far, she might as well knock on his door and say something. What, she wasn't sure. She hoped it would come to her once she was face-to-face with the man.

Or face-to-chest since Ivan was taller by about a foot.

It took a few minutes to find a spot to park. After leaving her vehicle in guest parking, Bailey got out and made her way to his door with slow, deliberate steps.

A corner apartment, the door and one window faced the parking lot while another, larger window and a tiny fenced-in patio with a sliding-glass door faced an artificial babbling brook. She had no doubt the soothing sound annoyed Ivan no end. Ivan was incapable of being soothed, at least by normal means.

As she approached the door, Bailey heard noise coming from inside the apartment. It sounded like someone had just broken a glass or a bottle. Startled, Bailey pressed the doorbell and heard nothing. The uneasiness she'd been harboring immediately mushroomed. Something was wrong.

"Ivan, let me in." She wouldn't put it past Ivan to disconnect the doorbell, so she knocked. The noise within the apartment stopped. But no one came to answer the door. Bailey knocked again with the same results. The third time she didn't knock, she pounded, wondering where she could find the apartment complex manager if Munro still didn't answer. "Ivan, please. It's Bailey, let me in."

The next moment, the front door was yanked open. Dropping her fist to her side, Bailey found herself looking up at a disheveled Ivan. His hair was uncombed, his clothes looked as if he'd slept in them and she was willing to bet he hadn't shaved since he'd last walked out of the hospital.

His body blocked the doorway and he looked only mildly surprised to see her.

"Well, well, well, if it isn't the hospital welcoming committee." Hanging on to the door with one hand, Ivan leaned into her so that his face was almost at the same level as hers. "Go home."

An alcoholic haze immediately enveloped her. "You've been drinking."

Straightening, he smiled as he shook his head. "There's that Johns Hopkins mind of yours at work again."

Now she knew something was completely off-kilter. Not because he was inebriated but because he was smiling. Bailey waved at the air just before her face. "My mind has nothing to do with it. My nose gave your secret away."

"Well, then…" He rephrased his order. "Take your Johns Hopkins nose and go home." To his surprise, she planted her hand on his chest and, catching him off guard, easily pushed him aside so that she could walk in. He turned on his heel. It made him dizzy and he almost sank down. "Hey, I didn't invite you in."

"No," she agreed, "you didn't."

Bailey quickly scanned the small apartment. It was in shambles. Something told her this wasn't the way he usually kept the place. There were bottles of wine lined up on the kitchen counter. Empty bottles. And a shattered glass on the floor by the sink. Had his vision played tricks on him and made him miss the sink?

"When did you get in?" .

Ivan followed her line of vision. Looking at the bottles he'd emptied over the last few hours or so, he smiled.

"Three bottles ago." He squinted and suddenly the number of bottles multiplied before him. He shut his eyes and then opened them again, refocusing on the counter. "Maybe six, I don't know." He turned to look at her and had to grab her shoulder to steady himself. The room had tilted. Again. "Why?"

"Have you had anything to eat?"

He began to shake his head, then stopped. The room continued to move around him. His grip on her shoulder tightened. "Not interested in eating, just drinking."

"Fine." She tried to move toward the kitchen only to find that he was still holding on to her shoulder. Tightly. "I'll make you some coffee."

"You'll make yourself scarce and leave, Bailey," he countered, pointing her toward the door. Or trying to. He found himself glued to the spot, his limbs refusing to obey him. "What kind of a name is Bailey, anyway?" He wanted to know. "You're a girl for God's sake, you should have a girl's name. Like Cynthia or Rachel or Babette."

Now there was a name to embrace, she thought wryly, then realized that Ivan looked as if his legs were about to buckle at any second. Shifting, she slipped her shoulder beneath his arm, providing him with a human crutch. God, but he felt heavy.

"I'll pass on Babette," she told him. Despite her efforts, she couldn't help being amused by his less than deeply controlled behavior. She would have never thought he had it in him to get this drunk. Grabbing on to his hand, keeping his arm across her shoulders, Bailey tried to hold him steady. "Bailey's my mother's maiden name."

Her explanation was met with a dismissive snort. "She liked it that much, she should have kept it." He took a breath, then attempted to look up. "Is it me, or is the room sinking?"

"Definitely you," Bailey told him. She was beginning to buckle beneath his weight. He put more and more of it on her and she wasn't sure how much longer she could keep him upright. "Where's your bedroom?"

He pointed behind him to the rear of the apartment. "That way." A wicked grin slipped over his lips. "You going to have your way with me?"

It was hard not to pant while she talked. "If by that you mean getting you onto a bed before you wind up crashing on the . floor, yes, I'm going to have my way with you."

"Good," he breathed, and then lowered his voice, all but whispering in her ear. "Because I've thought about that, you know."

It was really getting difficult not to pant. She considered herself fairly strong, but his weight swiftly shifted toward the "dead" end of the spectrum. Bailey had trouble maneuvering him across the threshold into the bedroom. The bed had a black comforter.

It figured, she thought.

Bailey slanted a look at him. "About what?"

His breath was on her cheek. Hairs along the back of her neck jumped to attention. "About having my way with you."

"I thought you were." She tried her best to sound nonchalant, business-like. "I jump through every hoop you hold up. There!" she declared in breathless triumph as she deposited her mentor onto the mattress.

And then she shrieked as she found herself tumbling on top of him. The buttons on her open jacket had somehow gotten tangled with his belt buckle. The momentum of depositing him onto the bed had managed to take her down with him, and she landed in a very compromising position.

His arms closed around her for a second. An engagingly silly smile graced his mouth as he gazed up at her. "Nice of you to drop in like this."

Heat immediately shot through her limbs as Bailey struggled to untangle her jacket from his buckle. But as she tugged, she realized that she would wind up losing buttons or tearing something. Frustrated, she managed to slip out of her jacket. The buttons remained coupled with his belt buckle.

Regaining her feet, she took a step back, still looking at him. Ivan seemed softer, she thought. Human, she amended. How awful that he had to get in this kind of state before he was able to reach this plateau. "You need to sleep this off."

His eyes were intense. She could almost feel something pulling her. "I need a lot of things," he murmured.

Banking down the self-conscious feeling that threatened to overwhelm her, Bailey turned her attention to his shoes. As she began to remove them to make him more comfortable, she felt Ivan reach out and lightly skim his fingertips along her hair.

"Have I ever told you you're pretty?"

She avoided his eyes, although something lit up inside of her. "The topic never came up."

"That's because I'm an anally retentive type-A workaholic bastard."

This time it was hard for her not to laugh. "I'd say that about covers it, yes," she agreed. With both his shoes removed, Bailey put them on the floor next to the bed and took a tentative step back. "Can I trust you to stay here and get some sleep?"

"You can always trust me," he mumbled. "I'm boringly trustworthy."

The words were out before she thought better of it. The only comforting thing was that she knew he wouldn't remember any of this conversation tomorrow. "There's nothing boring about you, Ivan."

He smiled at her, really smiled. "Funny, I was thinking the same thing about you. A lot." His eyelids were so heavy, he hadn't the strength to keep them up. He thought he felt something along his chest. Movement. With effort, he pried his eyes opened again. "Are you tucking me in, Bailey?"

She'd dropped a spare blanket over the length of his body. "If you want to call it that, it's fine," she answered.

"Okay." His eyelids began to sink again, weighing even more now than a second ago. Through the slits that were still, he thought he saw Bailey moving toward the door. Away from him. He fought to open his eyes again. "Don't go, Bailey."

Almost at the threshold, she stopped and turned around. "What?"

"Don't go," Ivan repeated. He thought he said it louder, but he wasn't sure. "I don't want to be alone. I'm always alone," he breathed.

She felt her heart twist inside her chest. Just as she'd suspected. He was lonely. Empathy filled her. "All right. I'll stay for a little while," she promised, crossing back into the room.

Ivan made no answer. He was already asleep. But there was a smile on his face and she was certain that on some level, he'd heard her.

CHAPTER 36

It took effort to pry his eyes open. The rays of morning sunlight streaming through his bedroom window hurt.

As did the anvil on his head.

The wool coat wrapped around his tongue didn't help, either. The last time he'd had a hangover, let alone one of these proportions, had been twenty-four years ago, when he'd been twenty-two. The quality of hangovers hadn't improved in all that time. He felt like something someone had scraped off the bottom of their shoe.

It took Ivan more than a few seconds to focus on what day it was and where he was.

And then it all came back to him at once, like heavy luggage being thrown square at his chest. For the last few days, he'd been in London. He'd gotten back to the States early yesterday morning. A taxi hailed at the airport had brought him home, but not before he'd had the driver make a pit stop at a liquor store.

Once home, he'd told himself that he meant only to toast John's departed spirit. He wound up finishing the bottle. And rooting out the others that people have given him over the years as gifts. Expensive bottles from grateful patients he'd stored in the back of his closet and then forgotten about.

Until yesterday.

It had been a stupid, stupid thing to do.

Ivan sat up in bed and then was forced to wait for the room to stop moving. When it finally did, he tried to focus on something.

Damn, his eyes were playing tricks on him. He thought he saw someone sitting in the chair by the window. The anvil on his head pressed down harder as he squinted and continued to stare.

Damn, there *was* someone in the chair.

He blinked twice. His hallucination didn't disappear.

"DelMonico?" The sound of his own voice hurt his head to the point that it made him wince. The woman in the chair didn't break up like so much vapor. Instead, she opened her eyes.

Startled, Bailey grabbed both arms of the chair she'd just spent an incredibly bad night in and shifted into a sitting position. Her back took her to task for not finding something softer to accommodate her.

She realized what had woken her up.

Munro.

He was sitting up. Looking miserable. Nice to know she could count on some things.

"Oh, good." She pushed back the blanket she'd used to cover herself. "You're not dead."

"Dead?" He lowered his voice because it hurt too much. "Why should I be dead?"

Against his will, he watched Bailey rotate her shoulders like a cat waking up from a nap. Except far more appealing.

"From all the empty bottles I found in the kitchen—" including the one she had to sweep up from the floor "—you drank enough wine to float a small battleship."

Ivan took her words as criticism and he'd never done well with criticism. "No, I didn't," he protested, allowing his anger to surface.

She folded the blanket and for the time being left it on the chair. "Okay, then I have some bad news for you. Someone broke in yesterday and drank all your wine." She made her way out of the room. "Didn't touch anything in the refrigerator, though."

"You were in my refrigerator?" Turning, he swung his legs over the side of the bed. It took him a moment to gain his feet. As he made his way out of the room after her, he realized he was barefoot. Where were his shoes? He'd had them on when he came in, hadn't he?

"Just long enough to take inventory," she reported. Taking the can of coffee out of the refrigerator, she proceeded to brew two cups. "For a doctor, you don't eat very well."

She was making herself at home. Who the hell gave her permission to do that? Damn, but his head hurt. "I didn't ask for your opinion."

She looked at him over her shoulder as she poured water into the coffeemaker. "Consider it a gift."

If he didn't feel as if his head was going to come off, he would have escorted the annoying woman out the door. Instead, he sank down at the small table in the corner of the kitchen. A minute later, a white tablet and a glass of water sat in front of him. "What's that?"

"It'll help you get rid of a hangover. Trust me, it works."

He stared at it grudgingly. "I don't have a hangover."

"Suit yourself," she said cheerfully, taking a spoon out and slamming the drawer shut. Out of the corner of her eye, she saw him wince and then swallow the capsule. Bailey smiled to herself.

Ivan set the glass down again. "What are you doing here, anyway?" he asked suspiciously.

"I came to check on you." She leaned a hip against the counter, waiting for the coffee to brew. "To see if you'd gotten back."

This woman was way too invasive for his liking. "How did you know I went anywhere?"

The smile she gave him was tolerant and he found himself resenting it. "Elementary, my dear Watson. The lights in your apartment weren't on the last eight nights. Until last night."

"You've been driving by here?"

The coffeemaker stopped making noise. She took two cups and placed them on the table, then filled them. "On my way home, yes."

He sat regarding her, his hands wrapped around the cup of black coffee. "Why?"

"I was worried about you." Slipping into the chair opposite him, she glanced toward the garbage and the empty wine bottles she'd thrown away. "Obviously, with reason." She took a breath, for momentum and courage, then asked, "So, how was it?"

He raised his eyes to hers, the very action cost him. "'It'?"

She nodded. "The cremation ceremony. Scattering your brother's ashes at sea."

He shrugged, looking away. He nursed the coffee for a moment, then took a sip. Bitter, just the way he liked it. "All right, I guess." It only occurred to him he had just admitted to attending a ceremony, something he'd denied wanting. She was good. And annoying. His eyes narrowed slightly as he appraised. "I don't remember letting you in."

She doubted he remembered anything. "You weren't yourself last night." She took a sip herself, then added, "It was an improvement."

Ivan snorted, trying to gather his anger closer. He found it was in short supply and that bothered him. "And you stayed the night?"

She nodded, taking another sip. "Seemed like the thing to do."

Ivan scanned the room and it suddenly hit him. The broken glass was gone from the floor. And the empty bottles on the counter were missing. "You cleaned the place up."

"Also like the thing to do," she told him, not bothering to hide her smile. "Besides—" she shrugged, nonchalantly "—I was restless and there was nothing to do."

"You could have driven home."

"I could have," she agreed, and her eyes met his. "But I didn't."

None of this was making any sense to him. He still didn't really know why she'd even bothered to come in. "Why?"

Bailey shook her head, retiring her cup for a moment as she regarded him. "You know, for a man nursing a bad hangover, you seem hell-bent on giving me the third degree."

He saw no point in denying the hangover, or mentioning that it seemed to be dissipating—probably because of whatever pill she'd given him. "I just want to know why you went out of your way like this."

She beckoned to him and leaned over the table. He leaned

in, as well, not knowing what to make of her. "So I could blackmail you."

This was getting worse, not better. Exactly what had happened here last night? Had he allowed his guard to completely disintegrate? "About?"

She straightened again, giving him an enigmatic smile she knew would drive him crazy. "That's for me to know and use at my discretion."

Ivan tried to stare her down. He'd done it before, with other residents. Easily. "You're bluffing."

Bailey toyed with her near-empty cup, debating as she paused. The expression on her face alternated between smug and innocent. And then she said, "You called me pretty."

"No news flash there," he told her dismissively. "You are."

"I didn't think you noticed earthly things that didn't involve neurons and nerve endings," Bailey told him honestly.

His cup empty, he set it down. "Forgive me for pointing out the obvious, but you have neurons and nerve endings."

"Not where you can readily see them without first applying a scalpel," she countered.

He laughed and shrugged. "I have a great imagination."

Her eyes met his again and something in her stomach tightened in anticipation. Her mind told her she was crazy. This would never go beyond wordplay. Her heart told her not to be so hasty. "Do you, now?"

He leaned back, his eyes sweeping over her. "You should see what I'm imagining right this minute."

She felt herself growing warm beneath his gaze and it took effort for her to keep up the banter, the charade of nonchalance. The air in her lungs grew scarce. "Do I get a hint?"

The next thing she knew, he'd gotten up and pulled her to her feet. Framing her face with his hands, Ivan brought his mouth down to hers. Hard.

Things broke loose inside of her. All the emotions that she had kept fettered broke free and rather than frantically pull them all back into confinement, Bailey let them escape, let them rise to their own natural level. Let herself go and sink into the kiss, just as she had the first time.

Just as she had wanted to ever since that first time.

Her head was spinning, her body temperature rising and she savored every second of it, not allowing issues like right and wrong or the threat of damaged working relations harness or impede what was happening this second.

She just wanted to feel, to have him feel, and to live and die within the moment that she had grasped.

She moaned with pleasure as her enjoyment continued to escalate.

CHAPTER 37

Just when Bailey was certain lines had been crossed and borders had finally breeched, she felt Ivan drawing away from her.

Opening her eyes, she found him looking at her. There was no way to read his thoughts. "We have a situation here."

Only Ivan would refer to this as a "situation," she thought, amused. She humored him, although if it were up to her she would have used a different word. "Yes, we do."

He didn't appear to be a man on the brink of passion, but one about to engage in a negotiation. "If we go forward with this, I don't want you expecting a bunch of flashing lights and lightning crashing in your veins like in those romance books you women like to read."

He was serious, she thought. Performance anxiety? Her heart warmed. "Too late," she whispered against his mouth, "they're already here."

Amazement creased his forehead. He watched her closely, most likely to see if she was putting him on. "Really?"

"Really," she assured him. "Now shut up and stop stalling."

Bailey didn't give him a chance to reply.

Instead, she sealed her lips to his and shattered any resolve he might have had left, arousing him to the point that he forgot that he was a doctor first, a man second. Order was completely reversed.

He took her then and made love with her.

And surprised her beyond all measure. Because as rough, as abrupt as Ivan Munro was, as egocentric as he could seem, he was a very passionate and yet very tender, attentive lover. Sharing, not taking. And extremely capable of creating the very electrical storms he had shrugged off only minutes earlier.

Somehow, they found their way back to his bedroom, to the bed barely disturbed that night.

Now was a different story. The bed was subjected to the full impact of two people enfolded in the throes of a passion the magnitude of which neither had expected nor thought to find.

He stole her breath away and completely erased her memory. Time, space, her own history. With possessive, strong strokes along every part of her body and long, languid, openmouthed kisses, Ivan communicated with her soul, making her fervently pray that this interlude would never end.

Even as climax dovetailed ecstatically into climax, causing explosions inside her body, making her simultaneously eager for more and craving a respite in which to regain her strength, Bailey couldn't quite get herself to fully believe that this was happening with Ivan.

But it was. Deliciously so.

Her heart brimmed with an emotion she didn't want to put a name to. Not just yet.

And when it was over, when Ivan lay beside her and they were both spent, searching for the breath they'd lost an eternity ago, she turned her head toward him and smiled into his eyes. "I think they're going to have to change your name."

There'd been a moment back there, just a solitary moment, when he'd lost control. When feelings had possessed him instead of the other way around. It had shaken him down to the core. Because ever since the accident that had ultimately taken his best friend from him, he'd been in control of every waking minute of every day.

But not with her.

Because he'd only partially heard Bailey, he looked at her now in confusion. "What?"

"We're going to have to change your name." Her amusement grew as she thought about it. "From Ivan the Terrible to Ivan the Magnificent."

"You don't have to flatter me."

"I don't 'have to' do or say anything, Ivan. But that is the truth." Bailey raised herself up on one elbow, modestly tucking a sheet around the body he'd savored over the last hour, and smiled as her eyes skimmed along his body. He was quite muscular, something she hadn't expected. "You are a surprise, Doctor."

Ivan clearly didn't know what to make of that. Or her for that matter.

"Why?" he pressed. "Because you didn't think I knew which end was up?"

"No, but, for one thing, I really didn't expect you to be nearly this well built." She ran her fingertips along the ridges of his biceps and pectorals, marveling how well he'd hidden his torso beneath the lab coat. Even the scrubs hadn't given her much of a clue as to the definition she saw there. "You work out," she concluded. "Bodies like that don't fall off the assembly line."

He waited for more. When she didn't say anything, he asked, "Your point?"

"I just didn't think you the type to bother with weights and things." Her eyes were smiling as they swept over the length of him again. "I guess still waters really do run deep."

He didn't know why that should pleasure him so much, but it did. He did his best not to show it. "I don't believe anyone has ever accused my waters of being still." Ivan shifted, dragging over the other end of the comforter and covering himself before he continued talking. Modesty had nothing to do with it. He just wasn't an exhibitionist. "You're not going to start expecting this to be a regular thing, are you?"

By "this" she assumed he was referring to lovemaking. Or maybe he thought she was after some sort of commitment from him. Nothing could be further from the truth. She needed to process what had happened first and come to terms with it. "No expectations."

He nodded, as if she'd given the right answer. "And I just want you to know that I'm not about to behave like some smitten adolescent, eager to carry around your medical books, shadowing your every step and following you to the ends of the earth."

She couldn't even begin to imagine him in a role like that. And then it hit her why he wanted all the ground rules defined. "Understood."

His eyes narrowed as he looked at her accusingly. "You're smirking."

She was nothing if not the personification of innocence. "Am I?"

If anything, her smirk intensified. "You know damn well

you are. Why?" he demanded. Was the woman laughing at him now that their lovemaking was over?

Bailey splayed her hand across his chest, her fingers skimming along his chest hair. "I don't think you really want to know."

He was scowling now, sinking into the black look that she had come to know so well. "Just because our flesh has rubbed together doesn't mean you have the inside track on anything, DelMonico. Certainly not the inside track on my thoughts. Now, just why the hell are you smirking at me like that?"

Her confidence did not waver in the face of his obvious ire. "Because I think the great Dr. Munro is afraid."

"Afraid?" he repeated incredulously.

Still holding the sheet to her, Bailey rose to her knees and looked down at him on the bed.

"Afraid," she repeated. "You felt something back there, Ivan. Felt something stirring inside of you. Just like I did," she added so that he didn't feel as if this was just one sided. "You discovered that you're not as invulnerable as you think you are and it's shaken up the very foundations of your world."

There wasn't even a glimmer of a smile about him. "You think you were that good?" he challenged.

In contrast to his dour behavior, her eyes were laughing at him.

"Yes. I do." It wasn't pride but confidence. *He* made her feel confident. As if she had something of consequence to offer him.

The shrug was almost imperceptible. "You have potential, DelMonico," he allowed casually. "But there's room for improvement."

"Oh?" Moving in a tiny bit closer on her knees, Bailey allowed the sheet that was wrapped around her to fall. "Show me," she whispered.

Bailey held her breath, half expecting Ivan to gruffly say something about being overdue at the hospital. That they were *both* overdue at the hospital. But the other half expected him to do exactly what he did. Grabbing her arm, Ivan pulled her to him, causing her to land squarely on top of him. She could feel his body grow rigid beneath hers.

"If you insist," he grumbled thickly just before he kissed her again. And spent the next hour making love both to her and with her.

If the first time had been a joyous surprise, there were no words to describe the second time around.

Or the third.

The morning melted into early afternoon before either one of them had the presence of mind or the strength to finally leave the bedroom.

CHAPTER 38

He avoided her.

And when Ivan couldn't avoid her, he spared her only a few words, biting them off and snapping them in her direction. Bailey swiftly garnered the pity of the staff, particularly the other neurosurgical residents who gratefully began to find virtues in the attending surgeons they were assigned when comparing them to the snarling chief neurosurgeon.

Because she knew what was happening, Bailey made excuses for him, saying that Munro was dealing with the loss of his brother, that losing the last living link to his family had been very hard on him.

In addition, she'd discovered that the chief neurosurgeon was in the midst of preparing to go to court regarding a wrongful death lawsuit that had been filed against him. The failed surgery had occurred more than a year before she ever came to Blair Memorial. The first time she'd heard about it was from Bennett when he'd stopped her to ask how things were going. The chief of staff hadn't seemed satisfied when she'd replied, "Fine," and seemed bound to tell her about the lawsuit.

Beyond dealing with the death of his brother and the lawsuit, she knew that Ivan was also trying to come to terms with what had happened between them in his apartment. More specifically, he was probably wrestling with the realization that he was human and in need of one-on-one contact.

Because she was doing a little wrestling of her own on that very topic, Bailey gave him time and tried not to take anything the chief neurosurgeon barked at her personally.

"HOW DO YOU DO IT?" Jennifer asked, retrieving a small string of colored lights out of the worn box of decorations. Everyone was pitching in to decorate the hospital for the holidays, using whatever time they had available to them. The Christmas tree, in Bailey's opinion, still looked woefully underadorned. "How do you manage to go around smiling like that with Ivan the Terrible as your mentor?"

Because she had her memory to sustain her and she had seen a side to the man that no one else was familiar with. But she kept that answer to herself, making a statement in the man's defense. "He's having a tough time of it right now."

Jennifer seemed dumbfounded. "*He's* having a hard time? From what I hear, he's spreading it around everywhere."

Taking the string from her, Bailey stood on her toes and attached the chain near the top of the tree.

"His brother died and he's being sued." Lights in hand, Bailey walked around the tree, securing them wherever she found a suitable place. "It's not exactly the way he pictured life at this point, I imagine."

Jennifer took the string from her and worked on her side. "Welcome to the real world. Didn't John Lennon say that life was what happened while you were making plans?" Jennifer prided herself on her extensive knowledge of pop culture trivia. "Except I don't see Ivan the Terrible making any plans other than trying to find different ways to make everyone else miserable."

Taking the string, Bailey worked on her side. "He has his moments."

"When? When he's sleeping?" Jennifer's head suddenly jerked up in her direction. Her roommate looked at her, her eyes widened. "You're not...?" Her voice trailed off as she finished the sentence in her head. "Oh my God, you are," she declared, clearly in shock. "You're infatuated with him, with—" Suddenly aware that her voice was carrying, she lowered it. "Ivan the Terrible. It's like the Stockholm syndrome, isn't it?"

Bailey laughed, masking her surprise at how close to home Jennifer had actually gotten. "I think you have your labels confused. The Stockholm syndrome is when a kidnapped victim falls in love with her captor because she's so dependent on him."

"All right," Jennifer conceded, going back into the box to dig out another decoration before her break was over and she had to get back to work. "So he hasn't kidnapped you. But the key word here is 'victim.' The rest is pretty much the same—a thug holding the power of life and death over you—"

"Munro's not a thug," Bailey told her and then stopped dead as she saw the person standing directly behind her roommate.

"Thank you, Dr. DelMonico," Ivan said, coming between the two residents, "I'll try to live up to those graciously flattering words." He looked coldly at Jennifer. "You. Don't you belong somewhere else?"

Jennifer seemed as if she was praying the floor would swallow her up. She nodded her head vigorously, her dark ponytail swishing back and forth. "Yes."

"Then go there." He didn't need to say anything further. Turning on her heel, Jennifer all but ran from the station. He turned his cold gaze in Bailey's direction. "What is all this?"

He was wearing a suit, Bailey noted. She'd never seen him dressed up before. Or clean-shaven for that matter. Every time they were together, he appeared to have two days' growth on his face.

She hadn't, until this moment, realized just how extremely good-looking Ivan Munro actually was.

Bailey pulled her thoughts together. He seemed to be waiting for an answer. "It's a Christmas tree."

Ivan blew out an annoyed breath. "I know what it is. What's it doing here?"

She raised her eyebrows innocently. "Being decorated?" she offered.

"Why?"

She could almost hear him declaring, "Bah, humbug." She wanted desperately to bring him around, at least a little. "Because it's Christmas. Or will be in a couple of weeks," she amended.

Christmas was her very favorite time of year, linking her even more closely to her family and to all the times they'd shared. Christmas was warmth and love, and Ivan needed both.

She saw his frown deepen. "And before you tell me to take it down, I have permission to do this."

"Whose?" Ivan demanded suspiciously. "Santa Claus's?"

"Close." She grinned, taking out another decoration and placing a hook through it. She hung it on an upper branch. "Dr. Bennett's."

He looked at her incredulously. "You bothered him with this?"

"I wouldn't use the word 'bother,'" she told him. "And for your information, Dr. Bennett told me he was happy I asked. He agreed that having the tree and decorations up would be good for the patients' morale. As well as the nurses'." Another decoration in her hand, she turned to look pointedly at the chief neurosurgeon. "He told me that you've been biting off more than your usual share of heads, but that he's cutting you some slack because of everything."

"'Everything'?" Ivan repeated, waiting for her to elaborate.

She jumped to a conclusion, anticipating his anger. "Don't worry, I didn't tell him about us."

She only succeeded in getting him to look more annoyed. "There is no 'us,' DelMonico."

She decided to take the high road on this. Bailey continued taking decorations out, one by one, and placing them on the tree. "Well, in a general sense, that's not strictly true. There's you, there's me, there's the burned sheet."

His eyes warned her not to continue. She stopped talking and smiled. Resting her case.

Damn, but he both hated and loved the way a smile seemed to filter into her eyes, all but making them shine as they touched him. "The sheet," he told her, his voice lowered, "was not burned."

"Whatever you say, Doctor." He could tell by her tone she was humoring him. "You look nice, by the way." Taking out a length of garland, she set it aside. One of the nurses came up and the woman looked as if she wanted to join in. But one glance at Ivan and she retreated. "How did the case go?"

Ivan was surprised she knew about the case, but then why wouldn't she? The woman seemed to stick her nose in everything. "The attorney wanted to settle out of court."

Bailey stopped decorating and looked at him, hearing the slight hesitation in his voice. "But?"

She knew that much about him, Ivan thought. He didn't know if he liked that. "But I said no. If we settled, it would be an admission of guilt. I did everything I could to save that woman's life."

She nodded, resuming decorating the tree. "Yes, I know."

"How do you know?" he asked, stopping her hands so that she was forced to look at him when she gave her answer. "You weren't there."

"I know you. It's not in you to do anything but your best." She smiled wider. "No matter what you're undertaking."

Releasing her hand, he snorted. "Too bad you're not on the jury."

"Tell your attorney to bring in character witnesses on your behalf. That might help."

He couldn't think of a single person willing to say something favorable about him. "I doubt it."

"And that is what makes you 'you,'" she concluded. "Suggest it to your attorney anyway. I'm sure Dr. Bennett would be willing to come forward. As well as some of your past patients." His success rate was amazingly high, especially given the nature of the surgeries he performed. "That would carry even more weight."

He crossed his arms before him as he watched her work. He was very aware of the time. "So now you're a lawyer, too?"

"No. I just know what would impress me if I was in that jury box. Right now, they just see your personality and you do come across as arrogant and self-centered." It pained her to be this honest, but he had to know the way people reacted to him. "They probably don't like you."

She was shooting straight from the shoulder, he thought. "Flattery certainly isn't your long suit."

She ignored the cryptic comment and continued with her thought. "But they can be made to respect you."

Ivan supposed it was worth a shot. Thus far, the twelve people in the jury box appeared less than genial when they regarded him.

He nodded a concession. "What are you doing tonight?"

Her mouth curved. "I don't know. Why don't you tell me? What am I doing tonight?"

"Having dinner with me."

"Sounds like a plan. Here—" she held out a decoration to him "—want to help me decorate?"

The look in his eyes told her he thought her question indicated that she'd just had a temporary break with reality. Turning on his heel, he walked away. "I have patients to see."

He heard her laugh softly. The sound seemed to follow him down the corridor.

CHAPTER 39

He gave her no special treatment. If anything, at the hospital Ivan made a point magnifying all her missteps and bringing them to her attention.

Bailey knew why he was doing it. To prove to himself—since no one else knew they were sleeping together—that his judgment wasn't impaired and that he wasn't allowing what happened in their off hours to color the way he saw his obligations as chief neurosurgeon.

Offering no apologies, no excuses for his behavior, Ivan seemed to go completely out of his way to find fault with her. And it was beginning to wear on her. As was not speaking up in her own defense.

"I thought Mr. Hale was the one in a coma, not you." Ivan delivered the terse statement as they walked out of Andrew Hale's intensive care unit during morning rounds. Bailey felt his ice-brown eyes boring right into her. "When I give an instruction, I expect it to be adhered to—to the letter. Do you understand, or should I resort to the use of puppets to get it across to you?"

Bailey raised her eyes to his, biting her lower lip to keep back an equally acidic retort. If she got into it with him now, in front of the other residents, it would only lead to a free-for-all. Ivan was *not* the type who retreated from any sort of verbal confrontation.

She stifled a sigh and kept her thoughts from registering on her face. "No, no need for puppets, Doctor."

"Bailey, who *is* this man?"

The question was uttered behind her.

For a brief second, both of her worlds, that of a neurosurgical resident and that of the daughter of two prominent missionaries, suddenly and unexpectedly collided.

Because a part of her thought her ears were playing tricks on her, Bailey swung around to verify what her heart already knew to be true.

"Daddy," she cried, throwing her arms around a tall, distinguished-looking man who, despite the touch of gray in his hair, had a very boyish face. A boyish face that nonetheless registered more than a drop of disapproval as Reverend Miles DelMonico looked in Ivan's direction.

Even as she hugged her father, Bailey looked around his embracing arm to the slight, petite woman who stood just slightly behind him. To the passing eye, Grace DelMonico looked more like her older sister than her mother, a woman who only occasionally enjoyed the comforts of the modern world.

"Mom." Bailey beamed at her mother, surprised to see either one of them here in the States. She stepped away from her father's warm embrace, for the moment ignoring what she knew had to be Ivan's less than patient presence. Instead, she glanced from her father to her mother and back again. Neither had changed so much as an iota. She found that infinitely comforting. "What are you two doing here?"

The answer was very obvious. Her father gave it, turning his body so that it blocked out the man he had taken a disliking to. "We came to see you."

Simon had initially told her they would be here for the holidays, but she had doubted, even after letters were exchanged, that her parents would actually show. Last-minute cancellations were the norm, not the exception. She couldn't help beaming at the pair. "But you're not due until the end of the week."

An enigmatic smile curved Grace's generous mouth. "Plans changed. We caught an earlier flight." She feathered her long, sun-bronzed fingers through her daughter's bangs, moving them away from Bailey's face. "We thought that we'd stop to see you before we went on to see your aunt and uncle—and your brother."

She knew that time was limited. Her parents rarely took more than a week off at any given period. "Then you're not staying for Christmas?"

Miles shook his head, his smile warm, encouraging. "'Fraid not, pumpkin. But you can come with us."

"'Pumpkin' has to work," Ivan informed the couple, even as he looked directly at Bailey. It was a crisp reminder in case she was getting caught up in this impromptu reunion.

Bailey could feel her father stiffening ever so slightly beside her. Miles DelMonico might feel compelled to preach the word of God, but he was a closet knight in shining armor and he only needed to perceive a threat to anyone he considered under his care to cause him to saddle up in full regalia.

She needed for her father to know that this was Ivan, the man she'd written them about. "Mom, Dad, this is Blair Memorial's chief neurosurgeon, Dr. Ivan Munro." She turned toward Ivan, sounding as formal as she could with the man who, just last night, had stripped her nude and made her rejoice that she was a woman. "Dr. Munro, these are my parents, Grace and Reverend Miles DelMonico."

Ivan nodded, his expression unreadable. "Your plaintive exclamation of 'daddy' and 'mom' gave it away," he informed her dryly. Because they were extended to him, Ivan shook first her father's hand, then her mother's, offering the latter what in some circles passed as a smile. Had he been an infant, Bailey would have called it gas.

The ritual satisfactorily completed, Ivan gazed expectantly at Bailey.

She remembered what the neurosurgeon had just said to her father and echoed the statement. "I have to work," she apologized. Bailey dug into her pocket and took out a set of her house keys. "Listen, why don't you take my keys and go to my place?" she suggested. Both Adam and Jennifer were on duty, so her parents could have the run of the house. "Make yourselves comfortable," she urged.

Neither parent attempted to take the keys from her. Her father shook his head, explaining, "We didn't want to impose, Bailey. Your mother and I already have a room reserved at the Four Seasons hotel."

There was no way she was going to accept that as an excuse. If her parents stayed at a hotel, that just robbed her of more time with them. Taking her father's hand, she placed the keys in the center of his large palm and closed his fingers over them.

"Unreserve it," she instructed, then grinned. "You're staying with me and I am *not* about to take no for an answer."

"Please, just say yes before she gets violent," Ivan deadpanned.

Miles glanced in his direction, then said to his daughter, "That's the Bailey I know and love." To underscore his remark, he bent and kissed her cheek. It was obvious, as he regarded the chief neurosurgeon fleetingly, that he was less than pleased by the kind of man she was taking orders from. "Don't forget who you are," Miles whispered in his daughter's ear.

"Miles, please, can't you see we're interrupting?" Grace prompted. Briefly hugging Bailey, she promised, "We'll be waiting for you at your house." Releasing Bailey, her mother looked at Ivan. "So nice meeting you, Dr. Munro."

"Same here," Ivan mumbled in response.

"I'll be home right after my shift ends," Bailey called after them as her parents walked away. She turned toward Ivan and flashed him an apologetic smile. She knew how much he hated having things disrupted. "Sorry about that."

His expression seemed exceptionally dour. She had no way of knowing that beneath the bluster was a trace of envy. Because she had family and he did not. "As well you should be. Any more relatives coming out of the woodwork today?"

Out of the corner of her eye, she saw the other residents were moving on with their attendings. This left the two of them alone for a moment and she fully intended to take advantage of it.

Bailey pinned him with a look as she struggled to keep her voice low despite the emotion brimming inside of her. "All right, I get it. My parents shouldn't have stopped by the hospital to see me. But we haven't seen each other in more than eighteen months. My parents miss me and I miss them," she informed him heatedly. "You don't have to be such an ass about it."

She'd never spoken to him that way before. To his recollection, no one had and he was stunned. "I beg your pardon?"

"Maybe you should." And then it all came out, all the hurt at the slights, the offenses she'd perceived and quietly withstood. "Ever since we've started sleeping together, you've made me into your whipping boy at work." She saw one of the residents glancing her way and lowered her voice even more. Her throat felt tight with emotion. "And even you have to admit that's not fair."

"Are you through?" he asked.

"Yes." She braced herself.

"All right then." He launched into his rebuttal. The very fact that he did told him this woman was someone who mattered. To the hospital and to him. He chafed at both. "'Fare' is what you pay for a public transit ride. It has no bearing in a place that deals with life and death on a daily basis. Get over it. And for the record—" he lowered his head so that his words were only audible to her ear "—we are not 'sleeping' together. There has been no sleeping going on during our 'non-hospital' time together. Moreover, if you're actually referring to yourself as a 'whipping boy,' indicating that you cannot tell the difference between male and female, perhaps taking a basic anatomy course at this point wouldn't be entirely out of order."

He was insufferable. Bailey struggled for composure and just barely managed to grasp onto it. "I don't know what I see in you."

"Other than my brilliance and my skillful touch?" he queried innocently.

"Yes." She ground the word out.

He nodded, as if he'd expected no other response from her.

"When you find out, be sure to let me know. Until then, we still have rounds to complete. Unless, of course, you've decided on a career change. I hear the local fast-food restaurant near the hospital is hiring."

She squared her shoulders, clutching the charts she had picked up earlier. "No career change."

"Pity." Turning on his heel, Ivan led the way to the next room. "All right, proceed."

She took a breath, trying to remember why her father had told her that hating a person was a bad thing. "The next patient is Prudence Beck—"

CHAPTER 40

For once, Bailey made a point to leave the hospital the moment her shift was over. Ordinarily, she lingered. She loved being a doctor, being a neurosurgeon-in-training. Loved every part of it. But she loved her parents equally and she wanted to make the most of the time they had together.

Shouting a greeting to her parents as she hurried into the house, she promised to be right down and then raced up the stairs. Life at the hospital had taught her how to change and get ready in the space of time most women used to apply a new coat of lipstick.

"Okay," she declared, coming back down to the living room where she'd left her parents, "I'm ready. Let's go. I intend to treat you both to the best meal in town."

"You're a struggling, starving medical student," her father told her pleasantly. "We'll be the ones doing the treating."

"Dad," Bailey protested.

Her father did what he could to look stern. "Bailey."

"Now that we all know one another," Grace announced, "let's just go out. The matter of who's paying can be settled later."

Bailey knew what that meant. Her father would be covering the meal. In his own, gentle way, he was every bit as mule-headed as Ivan was. "Okay, this is your first day here. I won't argue," Bailey relented.

"That's a good girl," Miles told her. "But I'm not above compromise. I'll let you drive."

"That's because you have no car," she pointed out. A taxi had brought them to the hospital and another had taken them to her house.

"Don't quibble over small points, dear," her mother told her.

Bailey took them to an Italian restaurant in the neighborhood. Both her parents had a weakness for Italian cuisine, something they didn't come by very often in the part of the world where they lived and worked.

The evening had barely begun to unfold before it turned to her work at the hospital. And to the chief neurosurgeon who, her father declared, behaved more like a warlord than a physician.

Her mother, Bailey quickly learned, was of the same opinion. Unlike her husband, Grace DelMonico was less dramatic and more to the point about her feelings. "He's dreadful, Bailey."

Bailey smiled. She could see where they might form that opinion, given the short amount of time they'd had to interact with the man. "You have to make allowances for his genius."

Grace frowned over her half-finished serving of tetrazzini. "Being a genius doesn't automatically give the man a free pass to be verbally abusive."

"He's gruff," Bailey admitted. "But he's just trying to make me into a better doctor."

"From where I'm standing," her father interjected, taking a sip of the solitary glass of red wine, "you're turning out pretty darn well."

Bailey grinned at him. "You have to say that. You're my father."

"I might be your father, but nowhere is it written I have to lie to you. Besides—" he deliberately narrowed his eyes as he looked at her "—I can recall times when you seemed to be quite bent on self-destruction."

In reality it hadn't been all that bad, but she had no doubts that, back then, her parents had viewed things a little differently than she had. Simon had been perfect from the moment he first opened his eyes. In comparison, she supposed that she'd seemed like a little hellion. But it was more of a matter of her needing to feel her own way rather than accept everything her parents said as gospel.

In the end, the conclusions drawn were the same. They all wanted to make a difference, to minister to people. Only their paths were different. Her parents and Simon all ministered to the soul while she took on the body.

"All that's behind me now," Bailey promised just before she took a forkful of the veal scaloppine she'd ordered.

Miles chuckled. "And they say God doesn't answer prayers."

Bailey basked in her father's warmth, in the warmth both her parents generated. They spent the evening talking more like old friends than parents and daughter. They touched on the past and the present, judiciously, for the time being, avoiding the future and the day when their paths would once again separate.

That would come all too soon.

BAILEY HAD A LITTLE TIME coming to her, three days to be exact, and she took them all together so that she could spend that time with her parents. They played tourists and she showed them around the Southern California that she had barely gotten to know herself. They did all the amusement parks and her parents, she noted with pleasure, behaved more like children than the somber adults she'd always thought of them as being. It struck her as ironic that the older she became, the younger they seemed to grow.

Three days disappeared in the blink of an eye and then, suddenly, it was the weekend. Ordinarily she worked Saturday and Sunday. This time, however, she managed to trade for them, giving up Christmas Eve and the morning after, in exchange for having one of the residents cover for her over the weekend.

Because she wanted to avoid an immediate confrontation, Bailey had broken protocol and asked the neurosurgeon's administrative assistant, Alma, to rubber-stamp her request rather than run the matter by Ivan. She did not want to be put in the position of having the chief neurosurgeon turn her down.

The two days sped by even more quickly than her three vacations days had. And on the last day, a full week before Christmas, she drove her parents to her aunt and uncle's for a short one-day visit. The next day they were boarding a flight that would take them to where they had arranged to meet with Simon who, like her, had managed to wrangle a few days off.

"It went by much too fast," Bailey lamented as she drove her parents to the airport.

"Much too fast," her mother agreed. It was hard to miss the sadness in her voice.

She wasn't going to let herself cry, Bailey silently swore. She wanted them both to remember her smiling.

"It doesn't have to end," her father told her suddenly.

Did that mean they'd changed their minds? That they were going to stay longer? But what about Simon? Wasn't he meeting them in Greece? "Excuse me?"

"Come back with us," Miles entreated eagerly.

He knew better, she thought. Why was he saying this? "Dad, I can't. I'm in this residency program, you know that." She had written them all about the program and how long it would take her before she could finally call herself a neurosurgeon. "It'll be years before I'm finally done."

"But that's if you become a neurosurgeon," Miles pointed out.

"Yes." But that was what she was going to be, what she'd set her heart on being ever since she'd first applied to medical school. She glanced briefly at her father. Where was this going?

Her father answered her silent question in the next breath. "What if you decide to be a G.P.?"

She smiled at the old-fashioned terminology. It took time for things to reach her parents' part of the world. "They call them family practitioners now."

"All right," Miles conceded good-naturedly. "What if you become one of those instead? Could you leave the States then?"

"Oh, darling, you know how scarce doctors are where we are," her mother chimed in. "It would be so wonderful to have you there with us."

They were both looking at her. Hoping. Bailey felt torn and selfish for feeling that way. "I still wouldn't be able to go away. I have a ways to go before I can be fully accredited."

"But it would take less time for that to happen if you didn't go into neurosurgery, right?" her mother asked.

"Right." She heard her father shifting in his seat, turning to her.

"Why don't you do that?" he suggested. "And then you would be able to work with us. Bailey, you have no idea how much your services are needed there."

She recalled the name of the doctor who had run the clinic when she'd left for school. "But what about Doc Preston—"

Her father shook his head. "Jon Preston retired last year."

"Retired?" she echoed incredulously. "I thought for sure he was going to die with a stethoscope around his neck."

"Technically," her father told her, "he did."

Bailey's mouth dropped open. She vividly remembered the man. He had been old, but he had also been vital—and seemingly tireless.

"When?" she asked. "How?"

"The beginning of the year," her mother answered. "He was seventy-seven. The poor man came down with cancer of the esophagus." She sighed sadly. "There was nothing to be done."

"I'm sorry to hear that," Bailey said. "He was a nice man."

"Yes, yes, he was." Her father was quick to jump into the opening. "And an even better doctor. He left behind a hole, Bailey. One you could easily fill."

She shook her head as she entered the far end of the airport. "Not for a few years."

"I know someone who could fast-track you. Dire times, Bailey, dire times," he told her in response to the quizzical look she gave him.

Her mother leaned forward from the back seat. "Stop pressuring her, Miles."

"I'm not pressuring," her father protested, his booming voice filling the interior of the vehicle. "I'm appealing to her better instincts." He looked at her pointedly. "The same instincts that used to bring all those stray animals home. What do you say, Bailey?"

"I'd—I'd have to think about it." She wanted to be a neurosurgeon, but the need to do good was deeply ingrained in her. Not to mention that part of her felt as if she owed it to her parents for all the times she'd made their lives miserable when she was growing up.

"Can't ask for anything better than that, pumpkin," her father told her, settling back in his seat. "Just so you know, I'm going to need an answer by Christmas. You can e-mail it to me if you can't reach me by phone." He smiled as he said it. "You know, I hate to admit it, but there are some very rewarding things to be found in technology."

She gave him a perfunctory smile, but her mind was elsewhere.

Christmas Day.

That gave her a week to agonize over whether or not she was going to make a life-altering decision or continue on the path she was on. It didn't seem like nearly enough time.

CHAPTER 41

Because he was proficient at hiding his thoughts, Ivan felt confident that Bailey DelMonico had no clue his heart had allowed a few erratic beats to break free. She was walking down the hall to the nurses' station and him.

On the surface, he kept his expression stony. "Ah, DelMonico, you're back. I was beginning to think you'd abandoned us and just forgot to leave a note in your wake." Closing the file he'd been perusing, he placed it next to the computer.

She braced herself for whatever was coming. God help her, but the sight of that rigid, unshaven face made her pulse accelerate into double time. She'd missed him and couldn't help wondering what he would say if she told him that.

If you go off to Africa, you're never going to see that rigid face again.

Bailey waited for instructions. And further chastising. "I took a few days off to spend with my parents. I'll make it up."

"Of course you will. Parents gone now?" he inquired mildly.

Bailey nodded. One of the nurses smiled a greeting at her as the woman hurried by to answer a call button. "I took them to the airport. They're flying to meet Simon."

"The chaplain brother," Ivan recalled.

Something was up, Bailey thought. Ivan's voice sounded too even-tempered. The calm before the storm? "Yes."

Ivan thought about the dynamics of Bailey's family. Damn different than his had been. Where he had grown up, survival from one end of the day to the other had only fifty-fifty odds.

"Looks like you're the black sheep of the family." He saw her raise her eyebrow in a silent question. "Unless, of course, you'd like to pray over me," he added. "Try to save my soul."

Now she understood. He was referring to the fact that her parents were missionaries and her brother was a minister. It wasn't all that different from what she'd been thinking the other day. "I only take on battles I can win."

To her surprise, he laughed. Or at least the sound was a reasonable facsimile of a laugh.

"Touché. Although," he philosophized, lifting a handful of manila folders and unceremoniously dumping them into her arms, "you never know. From what I gather, having faith involves believing in miracles."

Hugging her folders against her chest, her eyes narrowed as she scrutinized the chief neurosurgeon. He didn't look any different. "Is it my imagination, or have you suddenly gotten mellower?"

"Your imagination," he fired back gruffly, sounding more like himself again. "Now, if you're ready to work, DelMonico—"

"I am," she responded.

And she was. Because she didn't want to think about her decision, she was determined to submerge herself in work. That was why she'd come to the hospital straight from the airport despite the fact that technically, she had the rest of the day off.

"Good, then I have work for you." He nodded at the folders he'd given her. "Read all those and get back to me within the half hour. We have rounds to make."

She looked at the load. There had to be ten folders there. "I take back what I said about you getting mellower."

"Good," he told her as he walked away. "It was a rotten thing to say."

THE HOSPITAL was eerily quiet, the way it usually was in the middle of the night. Except that this was only seven o'clock in the evening. Because it was Christmas Eve, they were running on minimum staff. Most of the others had gone home to their families or loved ones.

As he made a notation in the chart of a patient just released, Ivan could actually hear his pen scratching along the paper.

Footsteps were easy to detect. He glanced up and found himself on the receiving end of his own minor surprise. Bailey. He'd thought for sure she'd left an hour ago. "What are you doing here?"

She'd ducked out for a quick dinner in the cafeteria. Back, she slid her shoulder bag from her shoulder and temporarily placed it on the nurses' desk. "Working," she told him brightly.

"But it's Christmas Eve." The woman had been decorating everything that wasn't moving since she'd gotten back from her impromptu family holiday. He would have bet a month's salary that she had plans for the evening. "Aren't there parties for you to go to?"

"Yes," she replied slowly, wondering if he was setting her up for a caustic remark. Feeling somewhat wistful and left out of things. "But I traded Christmas Eve and Christmas Day for last weekend."

"Oh, right," he remembered now. "The parents." He was sure that at the time, it had probably seemed to her like the thing to do. "Are you sorry now?" he asked. "You strike me as the type who likes to do warm, fuzzy, useless things on holidays. Being here—" he gestured at the semi-darkened corridor "—must make you feel lonely." Even the decorations had taken on a somber appearance. It didn't bother him, he thought, but it probably depressed her a great deal.

"Why are you probing?"

He frowned and glanced at the call board. But none of the lights were on. Not a creature was stirring, not even a mouse, he thought. "Just making conversation, DelMonico."

"Conversation?" she echoed. Something *was* up. "Something else you don't concern yourself with," she didn't hesitate to point out. She peered at his face. "Are you all right?"

No, he thought, he wasn't all right. Ivan supposed that by some standards, he might be having a midlife crisis. He'd thought himself impervious to the holidays, he always had been before. But now he felt something was lacking. He supposed it had to do with John's death, with looking down the double barrel of mortality, a mortality that would eventually wipe him away from the face of the earth—without a single indication that he had ever drawn breath.

For the first time in his life, he actually disliked the idea of being alone.

He blamed her for that. Somehow, some way, Bailey Del-Monico had turned his well-ordered world on its side. Because being with her the handful of times that they had made love had showed him just how alone he was when she wasn't there.

And how he didn't like it anymore.

But he couldn't bring himself to admit it to her. Not yet. With luck, not ever.

"Yes," he snapped at her. "I'm fine. Why?"

She shrugged, drawing her purse over to her again. "No reason. You just seem…different, that's all." There was no other way to describe it and for now, she didn't try. She raised her eyes to his. "You weren't at the staff party yesterday."

He didn't see the connection. "And you find that different?"

"No, I guess that's being true to yourself." Reaching into her cavernous purse, she closed her hand around a rectangular box. "They had a gift exchange."

Why would he care? "And?"

She backtracked. "We drew names of people to give gifts to a couple of days ago. Kind of like a Secret Santa thing."

"Santa Claus." His tone was dismissive and belittling. Nowhere evident was the small boy who'd waited in vain for the sound of sleigh bells and toys that did not come. Ivan had buried him before he'd ever reached his preteens. "Another plot by the department stores to sell merchandise."

She loved everything about Christmas, including the legends and she refused to get drawn into a dark discussion about society's follies for allowing children to dream. "I swear, if you say, 'Bah, humbug,' I might not be responsible for my actions."

It was difficult to say which of them was more surprised by the smile that rose to his lips. "I'll try to contain myself."

"Anyway, I drew your name." It was a lie. She had drawn Stacy Eldridge's, one of the day nurses on the floor. Ivan's name had not even been thrown into the hat. Everyone knew how he felt about the season. But it was easier segueing into what she was about to say if she began with a lie.

Ivan snorted, contemptuous of the custom and the need for

strangers to have to run out to stores at the last minute to buy a gift no one would ever use. "I absolve you of any responsibility to buy me anything."

Her eyes were smiling at him. "Too late. Here." She handed him the box she'd pulled out of her purse.

Because she'd pushed it into his hand, he found himself holding the gift. And staring at it. There were penguins on ice skates making figure eights and skating into one another. "What is it?"

"Why don't you open it and see?"

He looked up at her. "Now?"

This was harder than leading a horse to water. "Seems like a good time to me."

Ivan couldn't remember the last time someone had given him something at Christmas. And that was fine with him. But this sensation went through him, eagerness for lack of a better word, and he didn't know what to do with it.

He didn't like his peace disturbed.

Muttering under his breath, he tore the penguins asunder. Ivan stared at the dark rectangular gift box beneath the wrapping paper. Reaching over him, Bailey removed the lid so that he could look at his gift.

Ivan raised his eyes to her, needlessly identifying the present. "An electric shaver. Is this a comment on my appearance?"

She sighed. The man saw the negative in everything. She should have known. "No, it's a comment on efficiency. You don't have to waste time with shaving cream or buying blades."

He regarded the gift for a long moment that seemed to stretch out endlessly. "And you don't think if I wanted one of these, I would have bought one?"

She refused to let him daunt the spirit of gift-giving. She'd wanted to give him a present he needed and could use. "I think it never occurred to you to buy one. By the way, the proper response is, 'Thank you.'"

He frowned, slipping the lid back on the box. "Thank you."

Never had the words been more grudgingly uttered. Bailey laughed softly and shook her head. "It kills you to be nice, doesn't it?"

"I have no idea," he said truthfully. "I've never tried it, but now that you mention it, maybe I shouldn't take the risk."

Well, she'd tried. Maybe taking on the holidays was just too much for him. She shrugged, this time putting her purse in the bottom drawer and shutting it. "Suit yourself."

When she glanced at him, he looked a little lost, something she had never associated with him before. "I don't have a gift for you."

It had never even crossed her mind that he might. "No surprise there."

His scowl deepened. "You didn't expect one?"

"No."

"I see." Still, he felt he had to reciprocate somehow. "Do you have plans after your shift?"

She got off about 3:00 a.m. Bailey considered the question for a moment. "I suppose the party at my house will still be going on."

"Oh."

He sounded disappointed. Or was that just her imagination? "Would you like to come?"

"No." Ivan paused, looking off into oblivion. His thoughts oddly jumbled. "I don't suppose you'd like to come to mine."

She wasn't sure what he was referring to. "Your party?"

"My house—apartment," he amended. "You don't have to if you don't—" He didn't get a chance to finish.

Delighted, warmed, Bailey brushed her lips against his cheek. "Since you put it so temptingly—yes."

She left him speechless.

CHAPTER 42

They spent the night together. And made love. Dawn came to find them in each other's arms, drifting off to sleep, only to have to get up several hours later and return to the hospital.

She made him want to go out and buy a Christmas tree. Ivan realized that he was in serious trouble but the effort to disentangle himself from the situation seemed too much of an effort. So was pretending that none of this meant anything.

For one thing, she made him want to smile.

All in all, as far as he was concerned, it was surreal.

At the hospital, to his relief, Bailey behaved professionally and he treated her accordingly. Until he found her crying softly in one of the empty single-care units.

"What's the matter?" To the best of his knowledge, none of the remaining patients on the floor had died or received a poor prognosis.

Bailey took a deep breath. She'd been grappling with her thoughts all morning. "My parents want me to become a family practitioner and leave the program."

He didn't see what the problem was. "You told them no of course." And then his eyes narrowed as he watched the tracks of her tears. He knew that women cried for a variety of reasons and he hadn't a clue here. "You can't be considering it."

She told him what her father had told her. What made her feel guilty standing here in the land of conveniences. "There is a shortage of doctors where they are."

"Anyone entering medical school can become a family practitioner." He took hold of her shoulders, ready to shake some sense into her if he had to. "Very few have the talent or skill to become neurosurgeons."

She'd never heard him this adamant before. "Are you giving me a veiled compliment, or just stating something in general?"

"Both," he growled.

"Then you're asking me to stay?" She wanted to hear him say it. More than anything in the world, Bailey realized, she wanted to hear him say the words to her.

"I'm telling you I don't feel like going through the tedious process of finding another neurosurgical resident to train."

He *was* asking her to stay, she thought, her mouth curving. "As I recall, you didn't. Dr. Bennett conducted the process—and until I came along, rumor has it that you did not deal with neurosurgical residents on a daily basis."

Why was she twisting things around? Was she trying to get him to bare his soul to her? "I'm dealing with you."

"As a way of making you more humane, more accessible," she said, remembering what Bennett had told her in private. Her smile intensified. "How's that going, by the way?"

His scowl was all but black. "Miserably."

Somewhere deep inside of her, lights went on. Lights on the end of sparklers. She touched his face ever so lightly. "I wouldn't describe your personality as miserable, Ivan."

He knew he should be drawing back, but somehow, he couldn't make himself do it. "You'd be the first, then."

"You're hard on everyone," she told him. "Even yourself."

"Your point?"

"Maybe you shouldn't be. Maybe you should lighten up a little. Toward everyone." It had been a joke in the beginning. And a warning. But now, she didn't like the fact that people referred to him as Ivan the Terrible. And she wanted him to do something about it.

She still touched his face. And brought him perilously close to a meltdown. Who knew? "Is that your way of seducing me?"

Her smile had risen up into her eyes again. And was now in the process of reaching out to him. "How'm I doing?"

There were still hours to go on their shift. It didn't matter that the floor was close to empty. He had to remember that. "We're getting off the topic."

She caught her lower lip between her teeth, making him struggle with an uncontrollable urge to nibble on it himself. "I wasn't aware that there was a topic."

"You said you were thinking of leaving," he reminded her.

"I am."

Damn it, the uneasiness he'd been experiencing returned. "Thinking or leaving?"

"I'll let you know when I decide."

Ivan kept his hands on her shoulders and they tightened now. "Decide now."

He was being gruff again. She'd pushed him too far. "What?"

"If you're leaving," he said tersely, "I want to know now."

Tell me you want me to stay. "Why? So you can tell Bennett to start looking for a replacement?" She held her breath, expecting him to say yes.

"So I can tie you to the bedpost."

Relief came flooding out of nowhere. She mattered to him, she thought. He wouldn't have said that if she didn't. "I've seen your bedroom. You don't have a bedpost," she reminded him.

He never hesitated. "I'll get one."

Bailey tried very hard to maintain a straight face. It took a great deal of concentration, especially when she felt like laughing. "I can't be at the hospital if I'm tied to the bedpost."

His look was intense, no smile. "But at least you'll be here."

"And that matters to you?" she prodded, holding her breath, studying his face. Searching for a sign that she really was right.

He released her then, frustrated. "What do you want from me? I already told you that you were a skilled surgeon."

Bailey unconsciously ran the tip of her tongue along the outline of her lips. Ivan felt his gut tighten as he watched. "Maybe I want more."

"All right," he declared. Ivan added a word. "You're a very skilled surgeon."

"Maybe I want something more than an adverb," she clarified.

"Such as?"

Bailey moved closer to him than a whisper, drawing the length of her body along his so that he felt every muscle, every fiber, tightening in anticipation. He'd been a doctor so long, he'd forgotten what it was like to be a man. She had brought that world to him, front and center.

And now, he knew, he didn't want to do without it. Didn't want to do without her.

"Guess," she breathed.

He filled his hands with her hair, framing her face. "I don't guess."

Her mouth curved. Tempting him. "Then I suppose that rules out game show contestant as a second career."

He sighed, shaking his head. Wanting her. "You know, half the time I don't know what the hell you're talking about."

She rose up on her toes, tantalizing him. "And the other half?"

"How long do you plan to keep talking?" he asked.

"Until you find something better for my mouth to do," she challenged.

"I think I can manage that." The next second, his lips covered hers.

But just as she began to sink into the sensation he created within her, she felt Ivan drawing back again.

"What's wrong?" Logic, she knew, was prevailing. But she did so want to go on kissing him. "You were doing so well."

His eyes searched her face as he gathered courage to him. Something he would have, until this moment, sworn he didn't lack. But saying this cost him. Not saying it, he knew, would cost him more. It would cost him her. "I don't want you to go."

"You're asking me to spend the night again?" she guessed.

He pushed on, before his nerve deserted him. "I'm asking you to stay at the hospital. To stay with the program."

"And?" She waited, holding her breath. *Say it. Say it.*

Ivan took a breath. "To stay with me."

She smiled into his eyes, satisfied. "There. Was that so hard?"

She had no idea, he thought. "One of the hardest things I've ever done."

"It'll get easier," she promised, lightly brushing her lips against his.

"Yeah," he murmured sarcastically, "in about twenty years."

Twenty years. Twenty years with Ivan. She liked the sound of that. "Sounds about right."

Taking no chances, he wanted Bailey to spell it all out for him. "Then you're staying? With the program?" he tacked on.

"With the program." She nodded, then looked up at him. The look in her eyes instantly took him prisoner. "With you."

Relieved, Ivan still felt uncomfortable letting his feelings out like that. Maybe he'd said too much. "Look, the more important thing is that you stay with the program."

"Is it?" she challenged. "The more important thing?"

He supposed that it was too late to backpedal. Or lie. "All right," he surrendered, "it's equal. Okay? I want you to stay for the program and for me. With me," he amended.

"Because?" she coaxed.

"Because…because…" What did she want, blood? Apparently, he thought, looking into her eyes. Okay, he'd come this far, blood it was. "Because when you were gone those five days, I missed you." Ivan was almost shouting now, as if the only way the words would come was if he physically forced them out. "All right?"

Her eyes crinkled. "Very all right. And someday, Ivan, I'm going to get you to say those three little words that'll have me walking on air."

"Go hang yourself?" he suggested innocently.

She laughed. "Not even close." And then she became very serious as she threaded her arms around his neck. "I love you."

"I know what the words are."

"No," Bailey shook her head. He didn't understand. "I love you," she repeated intently.

Stunned, dazed, he took a breath without being conscious of it. "You're saying that you…?"

Her smile reached into his chest, into his heart. Into his very core.

Very slowly, her eyes on his, she moved her head up and then down. "Yes."

Bailey DelMonico had everything going for her. She was pretty, she was vivacious, she was intelligent. Skilled, highly skilled. Moreover, he'd seen the way other men looked at her. Like she was the reward at the end of the rainbow. While he…he was just Ivan the Terrible.

It didn't make sense to him. "Why?"

He never stopped dissecting things, did he? Even this. Bailey began to laugh. "I'll give you a written three page report tomorrow." As her body leaned into his, she felt the electricity beginning again. "Now shut up and kiss me."

He had every intention of doing that. But on his terms. "I don't like bossy women."

"Learn." She was dead serious.

Ivan leaned into her, conceding. "There might be something to that," he allowed, never taking his eyes off her. Just before his lips touched hers, he remembered. He hadn't said this to her yet and he sensed that it was important. "Oh. Merry Christmas."

And it certainly was. For more reasons than one.

* * * * *

Don't miss Marie Ferrarella's next novel
REMODELLING THE BACHELOR,
available from Special Edition
August 2007.

*Be sure to return to NEXT for more entertaining
women's fiction about the next passion in a woman's life.
For a sneak preview of Hank Phillippi Ryan's FACE TIME,
coming to NEXT in October 2007,
please turn the page.*

It's statistically impossible that my mother is always right. So why doesn't she seem to know it?

Besides, it's demonstrably true that I'm not always wrong. I have twenty-one Emmys for investigative reporting.

But, at this moment, struggling for balance on a cushily upholstered chair at Mom's bedside in New England's most exclusive cosmetic-surgery center, somehow I no longer feel like the toast of Boston television. I feel like toast. Once again, I'm a gawky, awkward, nearsighted adolescent, squirming under the assessing eye of Lorraine Carpenter McNally. Two months from now, provided her face heals in time for the wedding, she'll be Lorraine Carpenter McNally Margolis.

"Charlotte," Mother says. "Stop frowning. You're making lines."

Millions of viewers know me as Charlie McNally. I'm not Charlie to my mother, though. As she's repeatedly told me; my news director; my producer, Franklin; my ex-husband, Sweet Baby James; admirers who hail me on the street; and as she'll certainly tell Josh when she meets him: "Nicknames are for stuffed animals and men who have to play sports." After that pronouncement, she always adds: "If I'd wanted a child named Charlie, I would have had a boy and named him that."

Mom and I do better by long-distance. Most of our conversations begin with me telling her about something I've done. Then she tells me what I should have done. But here she is in my hometown, swaddled in a frothy peach hospital gown, surrounded by crystal vases of fragrant June peonies, reclining against down pillows. "All the pretty girls are doing it," she says. "And if you don't make an appointment with the plastic surgeon at your age..." her voice trails off. Apparently she's been rendered speechless by my continuing to face reality. She settles into her plump nest of pillows. "Charlotte, you know I'm right and..."

Keeping my face appropriately attentive, I begin a mental list of all the things I should be doing at 9:30 on a Monday night, instead of babysitting my mother. Thinking about a blockbuster story for the June ratings. Calling my producer, Franklin, to see if he's come up with another Emmy winner. Making sure I have a bathing suit that won't freak out my darling Josh, who has only known me since November and has not yet encountered my forty-six-year-old self in anything but sleek reporter suits or jeans and chunky sweaters or strategically lacy lingerie. Under dim lights.

"And local TV is so—local..." Lorraine is reprising one of her favorite themes. Why is it, she wonders, that I've never wanted to move to New York and hit the networks? Or at least move home to Chicago, where she could set me up with a handpicked tycoon who would convince me to abandon my television career and become a tycoon wife?

I look dutifully contemplative, nod a couple of times and continue my mental should-be-doing list. Feed Botox, who's probably already ripped the mail to shreds. Dig up a book about young girls and see how experts suggest I deal with Josh's daughter, Penny.

Penny. Right.

I've been to war zones, chased politicians through parking lots, wired myself with hidden cameras, even battled through the annual bridal-gown extravaganza at Filene's Basement, but spending a month of vacation weekends with a surly eight-year-old and her blazingly attractive father? This may be my toughest assignment ever. Not counting the bathing suit.

"Look in the mirror," Mother urges. She starts to point but, happily for us, there's a knock at the door. As it opens, Mother's expression softens from imperious to flirtatious.

"Miz McNally?" A romance-novel-cover-model wannabe in a white oxford button-down and even whiter pants consults the chart clamped to the foot of Mom's bed. He's just one of the pill-dispensing glamour boys I've seen wearing the center's fashionable nursing whites.

"Charlotte, dear," Mother says. "I hope you're going to be on the news tonight. We'd love to watch you."

"Nope," I say, smiling as if this isn't a ridiculous question. And, I grudgingly realize, she's just being a proud mom, which is actually very sweet. "I do long-term investigative stories," I explain to the nurse, as though I'm just an amiable daughter joining the conversation. "I'm only on the air when we've uncovered something big. So, nothing tonight." I shrug, smiling. "Sorry."

The nurse's face suddenly changes from sweet to a scowl, which is baffling until I see he's pointing at my tote bag. Which is ringing. I dive for my beeper and push the kill button, but the illuminated green letters that pop up are inescapable. CALL DESK, it demands. RIGHT NOW. NEED U LIVE FOR ELEVEN PM NEWS.

Mom was right again.

TV journalist Charlie McNally is about
to snag the scoop of a lifetime—proving a
confessed murderer's innocence. Through
all this Charlie has to juggle the needs of
her professor boyfriend and his little girl,
face time with her pushy mom who just
blew into town—and face a deadly
confrontation with the real killer....

Look for

Face Time

by

Hank
Phillippi Ryan

Emmy® Award-winning
television reporter

Available October
wherever you buy books.

www.TheNextNovel.com

REQUEST YOUR FREE BOOKS!

2 FREE NOVELS
PLUS 2
FREE GIFTS!

There's the life you planned. And there's what comes next.

NEXT07R

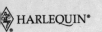

HARLEQUIN®

EVERLASTING LOVE™

Every great love has a story to tell™

An uplifting story of love and survival that spans generations.

Hayden MacNulty and Brian Conway both lived on Briar Hill Road their whole lives. As children they were destined to meet, but as a couple Hayden and Brian have much to overcome before romance ultimately flourishes.

Look for

The House on Briar Hill Road

by award-winning author
Holly Jacobs

Available October wherever you buy books.

Silhouette®

Romantic
SUSPENSE

**Sparked by Danger,
Fueled by Passion.**

When evidence is found that Mallory Dawes
intends to sell the personal financial information
of government employees to "the Russian,"
OMEGA engages undercover agent Cutter Smith.
Tailing her all the way to France, Cutter is
fighting a growing attraction to Mallory while at
the same time having to determine her connection
to "the Russian." Is Mallory really the mouse in
this game of cat and mouse?

Look for

Stranded with a Spy

by *USA TODAY* bestselling author

Merline Lovelace

October 2007.

Also available October wherever you buy books:

BULLETPROOF MARRIAGE *(Mission: Impassioned)*
by Karen Whiddon

A HERO'S REDEMPTION *(Haven)* by Suzanne McMinn

TOUCHED BY FIRE by Elizabeth Sinclair

Ria Sterling has the gift—or is it a curse?—
of seeing a person's future in his or her
photograph. Unfortunately, when detective
Carrick Jones brings her a missing person's
case, she glimpses his partner's ID—and
sees imminent murder. And when her vision
comes true, Ria becomes the prime suspect.
Carrick isn't convinced this beautiful woman
committed the crime...but does he believe
she has the special powers to solve it?

Look for

Seeing Is Believing

by

Kate Austin

Available October
wherever you buy books.

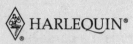

COMING NEXT MONTH

#93 FACE TIME • Hank Phillippi Ryan
TV journalist Charlie McNally's reporting is about to prove
a confessed murderer's innocence and set her free. But just
as she's snagging the scoop of a lifetime, Charlie's mother
hits town for a little plastic surgery. Now Charlie has to
juggle the needs of her professor boyfriend and his little girl,
as well as face time with her pushy mom—and brave
a deadly face-off with the real killer....

#94 SEEING IS BELIEVING • Kate Austin
Ria Sterling has the gift—or is it a curse?—of seeing a
person's future in his or her photograph. Unfortunately,
when detective Carrick Jones brings her a missing person's
case, she glimpses his partner's ID—and sees imminent
murder. And when her vision comes true, Ria becomes the
prime suspect. Carrick isn't convinced this beautiful woman
committed the crime...but does he believe she has the
special powers to solve it?